Titles by Robert Adrian

Destination Citadel

Target Citadel

Checkmate Citadel
(Coming soon)

The Sam Austin Chronicles

TARGET CITADEL

ROBERT ADRIAN

ISBN: 0990610411
ISBN 13: 9780990610410
Library of Congress Control Number: 2014917230
Cambrian Park LLC, San Jose, CA

To Un-hi,

Who never doubts whether I can do it

ACKNOWLEDGMENTS

I would like to acknowledge the gracious and insightful feedback on this book provided to me by Mark Baushke.

CONTENTS

INTRODUCTION

A ship was under way through an empty stretch of space, travelling well below the speed of light. Those aboard the ship noted an asteroid ahead and had slowed down to inspect it. Evidence of an ancient collision with another object was visible, and the ship's occupants studied the impact site with great interest. Although nothing else was visible to the naked eye, they learned enough about the site to know that the collision warranted further investigation. While they made a note of the path the asteroid had been following, the ship used its warp-field generator to travel along a different path. In spite of a complete lack of signposts, the vessel didn't appear to be lost, and presently materialized back into normal space.

The ship moved along a new path well below the speed of light, as if it were tracking something. After much travel, a signal reached the vessel. The ship paused long enough to analyze the signal. An instant later, it was as if it had never been there.

NEW BEGINNINGS

CHAPTER ONE

In some ways, life on Citadel felt back to normal a year after surviving the life-and-death conflict with an unknown race of aliens. No one would call it a victory, though. Certainly not Sam Austin, Citadel's leader. *Even though we finally destroyed the alien ship, we paid a pretty damned high price to do it,* he mused to himself.

Austin thought about that price as he listened to a report from his team on the status of their recovery from the attack. Melody Lambert, who was in charge of the communications infrastructure, stood before a large screen and manipulated images as she said, "The extensive damage to both the planet's infrastructure as well as to personal systems has been repaired." She pointed toward several images as she continued, "We've made a few improvements along the way, so we should be able to bounce messages all over the solar system, or next door, without any problems."

Curly Stephens, who was in charge of their space yard, brought up some familiar images of the yard along with more recent ones as she reported, "We all remember what a gut-wrenching combination of twisted metal and debris the yard was a year ago. You can see that it has been brought back to its original purpose as the construction and refurbishment facility for Citadel's space transports."

Stephens beamed with pride as she said, "Thanks to the new trade relationship between Citadel and the nations within Earth's solar system, farming, mining, manufacturing, and other commercial activities have been ramped up to well beyond where they'd been previously. Every bay in the yard is now busy as hell building the new transports that can handle this demand. For the first time, we have the beginnings of a fleet of transports that can reach Earth in just under three months, with passengers and cargo alike benefitting from an effective artificial gravity."

Austin nodded back at Stephens in admiration. "You and your people are truly miracle workers, Curly." His gaze shifted as Bret Yabuno, who was their overall technology expert, moved over to the screen and brought up several images.

Yabuno said, "Something else that's new is the enhanced security that's been placed throughout the system." He brought up an image of a heavily scarred ship as he continued. "Although the outer boundary of the solar system actually extends beyond the edge of the radiation field that surrounds everything, many people think of the radiation field as serving as the effective edge of their system, since there's no entry into the inner part of the system without passing through that field." Yabuno didn't need to gesture toward the image to make his point.

"The security now begins even before a ship can enter the radiation field," he said. "We've put in place a sophisticated array of sensors well back from the 'entrance' to the radiation field. Any ship wanting to gain access to the system has to pass within range of the sensors and wait for confirmation that permission for entry has been granted."

Extra lines furrowed themselves across Yabuno's brow as he added, "It's no longer feasible for a rogue ship to attempt to enter the system with a cargo that includes weapons or anything else that we don't want in our territory. Only after this process has been completed will a ship be given the updated safe path through the field."

Yabuno brought up additional images. "Various strategic locations within the system are now under the protection of weapons platforms. The planet Citadel itself is no longer helpless against intruders. We want to make any would-be invaders, including nonhuman ones, think twice before taking us on."

Earlier in the day, Austin had been talking with Curly Stephens at the space yard and noted a certain ship as it passed by after it had completed a maintenance cycle. Later that evening, he found himself reviewing his thoughts he'd entered into his private journal, his image on the display framed by the same room where he was sitting. "I always get a special feeling when I watch *Pathfinder*. In addition to her being our chief scout ship, she has the same proud name as the ship that helped us survive the attack from the aliens over a year ago."

Austin's voice took on a bittersweet tone. "Things didn't work out the way we intended. The original *Pathfinder*'s replacement was in the space yard, almost ready to take over so that her predecessor could be updated as well. She was so helpless in her bay that she couldn't even power up to use her speed to maneuver out of harm's way. It was the same for the transport that was in the other bay. That damned EMP weapon the aliens used trashed everything so completely that many of the structures just crumpled into grotesque impressions of their former shapes and functions. It was hard to look at the wreckage in places and tell where the bays ended and what remained of the ships began.

"At least the original *Pathfinder* had a far different fate," Austin said with satisfaction. "God, that was exciting; after our having been here for years without any prospect of making it a two-way trip, we were witnessing the trials for the first class of transports that could make the trip to and from Earth safely. We had the perfect spot aboard her, being positioned outside the solar system, awaiting the return of the *Keith Thomas* from what would have been one of her final trial runs." The bittersweet tone returned. "Everything changed when the alien ship showed up near the entrance to the radiation field."

"It seems strange now," Austin mused, "that that there wasn't anything at the entrance back then except for the array we set up to communicate with the Citadel system, as well as with Earth's system. It looked like we'd be OK, since their ship was way too large to follow the safe path into our system." An uneasy look appeared on his face. "It's still creepy to think about how the scout ship pulled itself apart from the *mother* ship like it was part of a living organism. Even though the scout ship was small enough to make it through the safe path, it dwarfed the *Keith Thomas*, and the *Keith Thomas* is a huge ship by human standards.

"We settled the Citadel system as a community of pioneers, rather than as a military outpost," he continued, "so there wasn't anything to prevent them from navigating quickly through the safe path and attacking the yard or heading toward Citadel." He shook his head at the senselessness of it all. "Those actions were unprovoked; we tried to communicate with them, only to be ignored as one might ignore an unwanted pest."

"*Pathfinder* had no way to get into the star system," he said, remembering his frustration. "She was blocked from the entrance to the safe path by the mother ship. We had little doubt what was in store for everyone once the aliens reached Citadel. The only option seemed to be to run away and abandon everyone we loved on Citadel to a certain death, which we couldn't do. All that was left was a desperate course of action that offered a *possibility* of survival for the people on Citadel. The price for that possibility was the lives of everyone who chose to stay aboard *Pathfinder* instead of trying to escape aboard life boats to the *Keith Thomas*.

"We knew that traveling straight through the radiation field toward the mining operations was a one-way ticket, even at extreme speed to minimize the time of exposure." Austin's eyes were moist as he said, "I asked for volunteers and ended up with everyone staying behind to help. I've never been so privileged to serve with such fine people.

"I don't really know how to describe seeing everyone failing physically as we reached the mining operations and retrofitted one of the asteroid projectors into a rail gun to launch asteroids at extreme speed. What we put together was crude and considered likely to fail, but it was our only option. By the time we'd finished with the retrofitting, most of the people were already gone. I was the only one to leave the cargo area alive, although I was in bad shape."

A melancholy look appeared on his face. "Gina Albretti, bless her, somehow managed to stay alive long enough to complete the programming needed to operate the rail gun from the bridge. She was already gone when I got there from the cargo area. As *Pathfinder* struggled in its race to reach Citadel, I could feel the silence and stillness of a tomb."

"I remember watching the alien ship as it approached Citadel. I knew that they'd get there first. Thanks to the broadcast from Citadel, I could actually see the first part of the attack, with that nightmarish EMP weapon. After that, many of the planet's systems failed, and I couldn't see much of anything."

"I knew that Citadel couldn't last very long from that attack," Austin said, "which meant I couldn't take the chance that we'd gotten it wrong with the rail gun. While they were being pounded by that weapon, I altered the course for *Pathfinder* so that even if the rail gun failed, I'd be able to destroy their ship by ramming it directly. Something in that course change must have caught their attention, and they shifted their weapon to bring it to bear on *Pathfinder*."

Austin's eyes were full of blue fire as he said, "That was fine with me! If they were concentrating on *Pathfinder*, they weren't pounding the hell out of Citadel. I was practically staring down their weapon when I was able to launch several asteroids on a collision course with them. As I nudged *Pathfinder* out of the way, I watched the asteroids collide with their ship at multiple points. The energy from the rocks transformed into a violently simple message for them."

Austin sighed. "I knew that was it for me. When I staggered into a life boat and launched it toward Citadel, my only objective was to find a final resting place on a planet instead of in the lonely eternity of space. I was damned lucky that the systems on board the life boat stayed intact long enough to touch down on the planet. I'm still amazed that they were even able to find me, considering how badly their systems had been trashed.

"It was tougher for Liz at that point, since I was unconscious. Even though they did everything possible for me, the doctor told her there was no way I'd survive. She kept telling me she wasn't giving up on me, even though I wasn't awake to hear her."

A wry look appeared on his face. "For someone who was supposed to be dead, I surprised everyone when I woke up several days later. Although I was in bad shape from the radiation poisoning, my body healed itself anyway." He grinned. "I'm not sure who was happier, Liz or me, that I'd walked on the Moon so long ago."

Austin thought back on the time, more than a century and a half in the past, when he'd been one of the *Apollo* astronauts. Back then, walking on the Moon was something new, as the Moon had been orbiting Earth for billions of years without any footsteps announcing the arrival of explorers.

In a twist of fate, his friend and partner had gone back to the lunar module to get some equipment they needed, leaving him by himself out on the lonely expanse of rock and dust, surrounded by jagged walls and small valleys. It was all framed by a brilliant black sky with Earth itself suspended as the main attraction.

"I could never say exactly when that cold blue light appeared," he said. "It seemed to invade and reflect through my suit and course through every cell in my body. Although there'd been no pain, the experience was so intense that I couldn't move, or perhaps I'd just forgotten how to do it for a moment. I wasn't aware of anything else until the light was gone and I heard Jack calling in a frantic voice over his suit's radio. The funny thing is that once I was able to sense things again, I felt *normal*. Jack didn't see anything unusual, and there was no evidence of the light's presence or of any impact on me."

"It just kind of sank in at some point that something had happened." Austin said. "I realized as the years passed that I didn't see any signs of aging when I looked in the mirror. I still had a full head of dark hair, with no streaks of gray. My face was practically unlined prior to my time as an astronaut, and no new lines showed up later. My strength and reflexes showed none of the deterioration that comes with age. I was never again sick from anything other than the extreme radiation exposure, and I've always healed fully from any injuries.

"I didn't make any secret of what had happened, although it wouldn't have made much difference over time, anyway. I tried to get answers from medical and scientific professionals, none of whom had any answers to give, only guesses. What people didn't know was that after many years had passed, I realized that my physical strength seemed to have increased gradually as well."

Austin frowned as he continued. "While that was nice for me, there was a huge potential downside to letting others know about it. We saw a terrible side of mankind when those people developed the New Plague, the horrific genetically engineered virus that exterminated over half Earth's population during the Bio War a hundred years ago. I decided against announcing these changes or cooperating further with experts in trying to determine the basis for my lack of aging."

The concern played across Austin's face as he continued, "I don't want to contribute to the destruction of the human race by helping to transform it into a race of ageless beings. It might even be worse if there were a group of ageless beings vying with the remainder of humanity for the soul of our race." The concern melted into relief as he said, "I'm glad that none of my children has shown any signs of inheriting my resistance to aging."

As Austin thought about the changes that had taken place over the past year within their system, he shook his head as he considered the things that hadn't changed much back on Earth. "Getting back to a more immediate concern, just as I had worried, once the crisis had passed, too many people in the other solar system assumed that they didn't have anything further to worry about where aliens were concerned. They haven't put the same effort into developing similar security features for their solar system as we've done throughout our system. While Earth, Mars, and the Moon have taken some steps to upgrade the defenses for their respective worlds, it still seems to be too passive of an approach. We already have plenty of evidence that a lot of mischief can take place that would be outside the range of those defenses."

Austin finished reviewing his journal, deciding that he'd dwelled in the past enough for now. He had plenty of reminders nearby that regardless of what had happened before, the future was indeed bright. One of those reminders was Liz, who appeared in the doorway. A familiar gleam in her eyes as she reached out to him and said, "The boys are down for the evening. Make sure the door is closed, because I want to take some time to show you how I feel about you." A few moments later she gasped, "Oh God! I guess you plan on taking some time showing me how *you* feel, too." The giggling took a long time to fade away.

CHAPTER TWO

Austin never failed to feel a sense of wonder as he looked around the lake nestled among the mountains that formed a part of his land. Since the water that supplied the lake was direct runoff from the snow that dusted the peaks and higher crevasses from those mountains, it was always refreshing to drink and cold as hell. After a long trip that splashed past clusters of jagged, cracked boulders that had little ground cover to protect them from the Citadel sun, the water coursed through areas crowded with shrubs and then trees and then other foliage that didn't quite match anything on Earth. Finally, the water reached Austin's productive acreage, some of which was diverted to irrigation for his fields and some of which flowed to his home.

Austin's sense of wonder continued as he looked upon his family. His two young sons, Matt and Luke, were a constant source of amazement, having high levels of energy and curiosity. They were both dark-haired, with deep blue eyes that missed nothing. Austin thought ruefully that that combination wasn't always a good thing, especially on a frontier world. While Matt had been born on Citadel, Luke had been born on Earth following their trip back to help protect humanity from the aliens.

Austin's eyes moved over to his wife, Liz, whose beautiful face was framed by clear blue eyes and dark hair. Giving birth to two children had in no way diminished the fact that she was a stunning beauty. Since virtually no one on Citadel bothered with swim suits, Austin had even more reason at the moment to appreciate what a beauty Liz was all over.

This was a day to share with friends. Their best friends, Bret and Donna Yabuno, were with them at the lake, along with their girl, Maddie. Donna was some eight months pregnant with their second child, so after an appearance in the shallower part of the lake, she spent most of her time stretched out on the ground a ways back from the shore, enjoying the warm sunshine. Donna too was beautiful, with brown eyes and brown hair. Her already ample breasts were even larger than normal at the moment. Maddie and Matt had taken quickly to swimming, so most of the attention was focused on Luke, to make sure he didn't get into any trouble with the water. The only thing anyone wore was a locator bracelet that kept track of everyone's movements and alerted the adults whenever anyone was moving away toward an unsafe area.

For now, Austin simply enjoyed the fact that they had a day where they could spend some time with friends and family. While keeping careful sets of eyes on their kids, Sam and Bret chatted about various matters of interest.

"I still can't believe that cheaters aren't anywhere near here, Sam," Yabuno said. "They're still thick as thieves near *our* land."

"Citadel *is* a frontier world, Bret," Austin said wryly. "We've had plenty of reminders that the place is in no way tame." He gestured toward the lake. "Although the water is safe enough, there's plenty of danger lurking elsewhere. At the top of that list is the most dangerous animal yet discovered on Citadel."

"They've certainly earned their nickname," Yabuno said ruefully. "It's funny that although they aren't Earth creatures, we've decided that they correspond roughly to the big cats on Earth. They're exceptionally deadly, opportunistic, and willing to wait with great patience for their prey before pouncing for the kill. I agree with the first scouts on Citadel who considered them to be especially sneaky in this regard. It seems appropriate that in view of the spots on their hides that resemble cheetahs on Earth, these animals would be called 'cheaters.'"

"Remember what it was like in the beginning?" Austin asked. "At first, cheaters were everywhere and everyone had to be on nearly constant guard against them. Even the Square, which is the closest thing to a central, *civilized* part of our settlement, had its problems with those critters."

Yabuno nodded. "It took a combination of enhanced security around the settlers' homes plus a willingness to be just as ruthless to the cheaters to persuade some, but not all of them, to move out of the area surrounding the Square." He chuckled. "Unfortunately for you, since you're far from the Square, without even any direct neighbors bordering your lands, many cheaters naturally relocated in your direction."

Austin grinned. "If Liz and I hadn't planned for this migration, we'd have been overwhelmed and unable to manage our lands. Instead, we've been able to carve an extensive perimeter fence out of the area around our house, which enabled us to build some things we needed, including additional living space."

"The Mill had a lot to do with it," Yabuno said. "I'm envious of what you built. It may have started out as a sawmill, but now it's a pretty damned well-equipped workshop!"

Austin nodded his appreciation. "Even after completing the enclosure, I worried about whether we'd ever be able to visit the lake on the mountain, in view of the dangers from the cheaters. After we returned from our trip back to Earth, I was motivated to do something so that Matt and Luke would grow up having learned to swim."

"You being you, it wasn't enough to have a simple wading pool within your enclosure," Yabuno said.

Donna heard him. "I know this is old news to Bret, but I still don't quite know everything you did." She laughed as Austin started to pull out his link. "Don't tell me to go online, Sam! Why don't you just tell me generally what you did?"

Austin put his link away. "To get the access to the lake we wanted, I went into the Mill and modified our ground transport so that neither it nor any passengers could be threatened by cheaters. Thanks to our mining operations, I developed a lightweight synthetic material that's even stronger than steel, and fashioned a reinforced canopy that still allows a good field of view within virtually every direction. I took a lesson from our encounters with the aliens," Austin said, "and installed a weapons platform on the transport for protection that can be operated remotely."

"You've also been able to use local materials to develop and install a road system that connects the key parts of your lands," Yabuno said. He waved back toward the transport. "As a result, you now have a means of travel that won't place you at the mercy of any predators." He chuckled. "Unlike Donna, I enjoyed reading all about it online."

Austin chuckled back. "Thank God we have an extensive barter system in place, with Liz as one of the leaders. She arranged for a number of cooperative work parties to help various settlers pool their labor to develop their own roads. She was also able, eventually, to obtain a second transport so that we can both be more productive around our lands.

"As far as cheaters are concerned, they're still thick as thieves near most places in our land. It just happens that most of the animals they like to eat rarely show up at this elevation. Cheaters are patient, but they aren't stupid. There's not much sense in waiting for prey that doesn't come around the neighborhood. Once I figured out that when visiting the lake, the main danger from the cheaters is on the trip up here, I just had to make sure that we could do it without becoming another meal for them."

Austin's face took on a predatory look of its own as he continued, "They're learning that there's no point in trying to hide when our transport shows up on a road. While they don't understand the tracking technology we use, they understand not wanting to be blasted to hell if they hang around."

Austin waved vaguely in the direction of his home. "One of these days, I'd like to set up an integrated system for keeping a watch on our roads so that we'll know when any cheaters are around the next bend. Maybe some of it will consist of imaging from satellites and some of it will come from sensors embedded in some portions of the roads."

Donna motioned toward the transport that was parked near where the shore began to transition into the forest. "You haven't finished listing everything you did there, have you?"

Austin nodded. "That's right. Even without anyone at the controls, that thing does a hell of a job scanning everything that's around and taking out anything that shouldn't be here." He gestured at his wrist. "These bracelets would let us walk deep into the woods and circle back here and that thing wouldn't even react, so long as we were wearing these things. They're also great for talking with anyone on the planet and receiving any feedback from the transport about any potential danger.

"They're also waterproof," Austin continued, "so they're fine even if we're swimming."

"Thanks for the update, Sam," Donna said. "Liz and I have other things to talk about now, so we'll leave the two of you alone." She and Liz laughed as they turned away from the men and resumed their conversation.

Yabuno looked around the group as he chuckled. "I'm glad to know that these bracelets don't take and post pictures online. You guys are family, so Donna doesn't mind your seeing her naked in what she calls her 'bloated whale' phase. Although we have pictures of her pregnancies to share with the kids as they get older, there'd be hell to pay if any pictures got out to the other settlers.

Funny thing is that especially on Citadel, most men and women don't worry about being seen without clothes while swimming or spending time at the shore. We all get that it's natural and comfortable. Donna certainly doesn't have a problem with it. It's a different thing when she's pregnant, however. She isn't really shy so much as feeling awkward."

Austin nodded. "Liz is much the same way."

"Things weren't like this when you were young."

Austin grinned. "People keep reminding me! Hell no, it *was* different back then, especially in the US. Although over time women looked for ways to show more and more skin, it was still pretty much bikinis until well into the twenty-first century. While I'm not sure if it was a good idea, at some point there'd been so much celebrity nudity in public that going topless seemed relatively tame around beaches and pools."

Austin chuckled as he continued. "When it came to taking off the bottoms, this was definitely an area where the men let the women take the lead. It wasn't until women got comfortable with full nudity that men followed suit. Now that we're well into the twenty-second century, most people, especially those under fifty, consider the earlier concerns to be pretty old-fashioned. And I'm the only one within many billions of miles of this spot who's over fifty, and I don't give a damn about it."

Austin stopped chuckling as he said, "The part that isn't funny is where some people view nude swimming as an opportunity to engage in voyeurism. Fortunately, it isn't much of a problem even on Earth anymore, and we've been careful to screen out the few people where it might be a problem here. While no system is perfect, we've managed to avoid any problems so far.

"Let's change the subject and talk about what's happening back in our old stomping grounds," Yabuno said. "When's the last time you heard from Her Majesty, Sam?"

Austin's eyes twinkled in amusement. "I see your opinion of the president of the United States hasn't changed."

Yabuno chuckled. "If you weren't the leader here on Citadel, I'd tell you to run for president again, just to get her the hell out of the way."

Austin laughed as he said emphatically, "You can put whatever word you want in front of *no* when it comes to whether I'd ever run for president again! Forty plus years was plenty. Jessie Branham, bless her, managed to talk me out of retirement once; I'm too busy with this 'retirement' to want to go back to all of the crap in DC." Austin took on a rueful look as he said, "It's been a while since Courtney and I last talked, and both of us should be working harder to stay in touch."

"What are your thoughts on the steps they've been taking to beef up their security to deal with any new alien threats?"

Austin sighed. "I wish they were doing a hell of a lot more than they've been doing. While it's a good sign that they've worked to improve their planetary and colony defenses, they need to set up better defenses throughout that system as we've been doing here. They're keeping all of their eggs in one basket and hoping that any further attack will be just like the last one. We have to assume that anyone smart enough to develop faster-than-light drive for ships as large as theirs is smart enough to adapt to what they've learned from humans and prepare something new."

Yabuno's tone was barbed. "They should have gotten over their problem with rail guns and upgraded their asteroid projectors, or developed separate ones for use as weapons."

Austin shook his head. "That one is tougher for them than for us. Rail guns have been nothing but a positive experience for us. The downgraded versions are invaluable for mining, and an upgraded rail gun saved our asses, period. That means we're good with the notion of a weaponized version that will pound the hell out of anyone who tries to invade our system again.

"Although the upgraded rail gun we brought to their system also saved their asses, upgraded rail guns nearly took out the Earth back when I was president. That pretty much cemented their reputations as something to be feared and restricted. Even though I was able to give the order to take out those guns before they could wipe out major real estate on Earth, no one wants to see a repeat where the order isn't given in time.

"To this day, there's significant opposition back there to building an upgraded rail gun. Where the hell do you place it and who controls it? Even if you think you've worked out the control issue, what happens if you were wrong and someone else gets control of it? The problems are only magnified if you have more than one rail gun. With multiple sites to worry about, Earth's or Mars's defenses might or might not be able to react in time to a launch. Whoever controls any rail guns has effective control of much of their solar system, perhaps even of the planets and major satellites.

"Although our population is increasing with every new group of settlers, plus the children that are born here, it's still at a relatively manageable size when it comes to keeping control over critical functions. Since the population here is based on a certain set of values, I trust the people here in a way that wouldn't make sense on Earth. I won't say that we've been 'lucky' with that trust, since we're careful in our screening process to avoid bringing over anyone who might try to take control of the place." Austin was quiet for a moment. "Of course, our screening process didn't stop a snake like Brittel from showing up and trying to sell us out."

Yabuno nodded. "That's true, Sam, but we tightened things up after we found out about him. Also, the memory of that snake hanging from the end of a rope after he was caught is still fresh in the minds of most people, and a good incentive by itself not to try to sell us out."

"I hope someone doesn't decide that Brittel's biggest mistake was getting caught, instead of committing the murder and treason itself. Who knows how it might have turned out if Brittel's fellow snakes from Earth had managed to get to Citadel with their weapons? With Brittel on the inside, he could have screwed us hugely before we would have found out about it. My biggest lesson from Brittel is never to take anything for granted."

"That sounds like a segue from human snakes to alien ones," Yabuno said.

Austin's face betrayed his worry. "I still wonder if I got it wrong somehow with the aliens. I've assumed that giving them a pounding in two different star systems would make them stay the hell away from both systems. Although we disagreed on some of it at the time, I thought it was the right thing to do, and I wouldn't do anything differently. The good news is that there's been no sign of them for over a year. What I don't know is whether that's really good news or whether they're just biding their time until they decide to come back and pound us some more."

There was a wry look on Yabuno's face as he answered. "While I'm not arrogant enough to piss upwind, we've taken the right steps to deal with them if they return. We've been working on hardening our ships further against their EMP weapon. Our systems on Citadel and in space are also tougher than before. Even more important, we've been working on our own EMP weapons to give us an offensive capability that we didn't have before."

A thoughtful look drifted across his face as he continued, "I've been working on something else that might take us to a completely different playing field, although I don't know if it'll ever be successful. Someday, if it works, we won't have to worry about their EMP weapon. We might not have to worry about *any* of their weapons."

"Until that happens, we'll just have to work on improving what we have. I just hope to God that we'll never have to rely on any of this for real again," Austin added quietly.

CHAPTER THREE

*S*ometimes *security and exploration can cooperate with each other instead of hinder,* Austin thought as he listened to Yabuno describe some upgrades to their defensive measures.

Yabuno stood before a large screen as he said, "Part of the upgrades include establishing a network of enhanced long-range sensors, to link up with what we've already set up within the Citadel system. Thanks to the work of Melody and her team, we've enhanced the series of communication beacons leading back to Earth so that we can now send messages over extraordinary distances within a fraction of the time it would take for even *Pathfinder* to travel the same distance."

He brought up a series of images as he continued. "These deep-space beacons will be linked via micro warp bubbles back to new arrays that work separately from the main array at the entrance to the system. Redundancy is built into this approach, so that taking out a key component won't cripple the whole system."

Yabuno brought up a familiar image as he continued. "*Pathfinder* has been given the responsibility for placing the beacons way the hell past where any of us has visited beyond our system." As he zoomed in on several areas of the ship, he said, "She's been outfitted with various sensors that are linked with the deep-space sensors she'll be setting up. Although the information will also be relayed to Citadel, *Pathfinder* will get the information in close to real time and be able to react to it quickly if needed."

"It's important to note just how tough the new *Pathfinder* is," Austin said with a hard look. "Although she's a scout ship, we've learned from the fact that she might not always encounter friendly races in space. She's been outfitted with a basic complement of weapons, which we hope will never need to be used."

Yabuno brought up an image of a man. "The new *Pathfinder* needs a captain who's an experienced space pilot. As it happens, Joe Albretti's background with the Space Command makes him a good fit for the assignment."

"Let's talk about him for a moment," Austin said.

Yabuno brought up an earlier image of Albretti as he continued. "Before joining the Citadel Group, Joe was a young officer in the US Space Command and held several field commands. He'd planned on making a career there until he married Julia. They wanted to settle down and build a life together, yet they had restless streaks that made living on Earth seem dull."

Austin shook his head. "It isn't easy to make a career with the Space Command and have a life out in space, especially if that life includes raising a family."

Yabuno nodded and then continued. "Although they didn't have military backgrounds, Joe's brother Mark and his wife, Gina, had similar natures and had joined the Citadel Group. Joe and Julia applied to become settlers as well. After extensive screening and evaluations, they were accepted in the first wave of settlers, along with Mark and Gina. They managed to arrange things so that they had adjacent lands."

Austin grinned. "As I recall, they were among the few settlers that had decided to wait a while before trying to have kids so they wouldn't have the distractions while clearing and adapting their lands for productive use. Mark and Gina waited awhile as well, although Gina had given birth to a girl some four months before the attack by the aliens."

Austin's grin was tinged with melancholy as he continued. "God, how I still miss Gina. She was full of life and not afraid to get in anyone's face if she thought it necessary. She told me to stuff it when I suggested that her baby needed her more than I did when we had to use the original *Pathfinder* against the alien scout ship. She was right, too. We wouldn't have succeeded if she hadn't adapted the systems so that one man could be on the bridge and control both the *Pathfinder* and the junk that we made into a rail gun. She died at her station, probably just minutes or even seconds after finishing the job." Austin looked back to the images on the screen. "That wasn't the only place where we had casualties, though."

"No," Yabuno replied quietly. "Although it would have been even worse if *Pathfinder* hadn't interrupted the aliens at a critical moment, we still had plenty of casualties on Citadel itself. Most of the casualties were treatable, although there were a few fatalities, as you know. Julia was among those unlucky few."

"I think everyone has been happy that Karen Thomas came into Mark's life," Austin said. "While we'll never forget Keith, her late first husband—after all, we named the Keith Thomas class of transports after him—with that mess with Brittel behind her, she was ready to move on with her life. She and Mark seem to be happy together, and Karen and little Angela have bonded well. Gina would be happy."

"Although Joe has been a devoted uncle to his niece, with the death of Julia, his heart hasn't been in working his land. Fortunately, because the Albretti lands are next to each other, Mark has been looking after things until Joe is ready to get back to the ground. Joe's made it clear that he's grateful for the change."

"Citadel will benefit from having Joe on *Pathfinder*," Austin said. "Let's hope that Joe's need to do something different works out for him as well."

CHAPTER FOUR

It was now more than three months since *Pathfinder* had begun her assignment, and they'd been able to cover a hell of a lot of territory. Albretti chuckled silently over the fact that there was so much more territory to visit that what they'd covered barely seemed like any start at all. The beacons worked well, and he was able to talk with Citadel with virtually no lag.

"We've found another distortion, Bret," Albretti said.

"What are the particulars this time, Joe?" Yabuno asked.

"At first we thought it must be a small asteroid, considering the size. We were lucky that one of the new beacons was scanning in that region, or we'd have missed the fact that a star 'blinked.' This thing must have passed in front of it and blocked the image of the star. We've been able to get more information that supports the notion that it is artificial. Something that's that large and artificial is something that wasn't built by humans."

Yabuno's expression turned serious. "How do we know that something like that isn't from the aliens that tried to erase us?"

"From this distance, there's no way to know for sure." Albretti shrugged. "It's probably even larger than anything we've seen before from our enemies. While we can't be certain, what's strange is that it doesn't seem to be doing anything other than drifting. Infrared doesn't show any heat signature that would be consistent with propulsion."

"What do we know about where it must have originated?"

Albretti brought up some images on a large screen. "First of all, although we found it because of a star 'blink,' it isn't anywhere near a star; we were just lucky that it happened to be in line with a star and our sensors at the right time. As far as the path is concerned, it doesn't make sense; there's no way it could have originated in that location, which suggests that it was on a different course originally."

Yabuno's face brightened. "Interesting, considering that there isn't any propulsion. I wonder if gravity is responsible or if there was some kind of collision with something else. Is it really as close to our system as it seems?"

"Yes," Albretti replied, bringing up an image for comparison. "We all know how much easier it is in some ways to spot something at an extreme distance, because of the objects out there than can give us some clues. This thing is so close to our own system that nothing lights it enough for us to see it directly from Citadel."

"At its present speed, how long before it reaches our system?"

"It'll reach the outer boundary of our system in about six months. Albretti looked at Yabuno wryly."I'm guessing that we might want to check it out before it gets here."

"You're damned right!" Yabuno said excitedly. "We'd better find out everything we can about this object in case there're any nasty surprises. Get *Pathfinder* back here right away. You're going to take a bunch of nosy people out there as soon as we can get the team together."

CHAPTER FIVE

Choi, a retired four-star U.S. general, always enjoyed hearing from his favorite granddaughter. He appreciated the effort she made to stay in touch, often with full audio-visual messages like the one he was watching. He understood all too well the time limitations she faced due to her being posted in space on assignments with the Citadel Group.

"It seems like yesterday that I was placed in command of *KT-2*," Sara Choi said. "She was brand new, Grandfather, without even a scratch on the paint job! Everyone marveled, rightly, at what a hell of a ship the original *Keith Thomas* is, especially since it was built near Citadel by the original designers. With *KT-2*, we had the chance to show that we could build the next one just as well in the Citadel Group's yard."

Sara's face darkened. "I sure didn't expect what happened next. We'd been putting the new transport through her final testing when all hell broke loose within our system. I can still hardly believe the first message I received, telling me about the arrival of an alien ship that looked like the stuff of nightmares, and seemed to be determined to wipe out humanity from everywhere in our system.

A frustrated look flashed across her face. "It was a reminder that as remarkable as the technology in *KT-2* was, we had no ability to defend ourselves against the alien ship. That's why my instructions were to hide and try to reach Citadel if everything was a lost cause in Earth's system. At least we were still able to monitor what was happening after we moved toward the asteroid belt. I've never heard such grim news like what came in from Mars, with reports of widespread damage. Some of the damage was of the kind that would lead to slow deaths for most of the population. There were also plenty of reports of deaths that hadn't waited while the systems broke down.

"As if that wasn't enough, we had to watch as the aliens then headed toward Earth to do the same thing to them," Sara noted with some anger. The anger dissolved into relief. "What a moment that was, when we learned that *Keith Thomas* showed up in our system, and with Sam Austin in command!" There was a look of sly admiration on her face. "Leave it to Sam to have a role for us to play when we'd been feeling pretty damned useless up until that point. It felt great to serve as a decoy for those bastards and then help give them a taste of their own medicine with the weapon we got from the *Keith Thomas*."

Sara practically beamed as she thought about Austin's comments to her after the crisis had passed. "Sam gave me just about the highest praise possible when he said my grandfather would be proud. I know how much he respects you. While it isn't in your nature to remind people, everyone knows how, many years ago, you were the top general in the US Space Command. You were there at the time of the crisis with the rogue elements on Mars that tried to destroy Earth with targeted asteroids. As the US president at the time, Sam decorated you and your people for your roles in saving the planet." Sara's gaze was full of love as she continued. "It would be just like Sam to know how much you mean to me, just as my grandfather."

She brought her conversation to the present day. "You know I've long been fascinated by the Citadel project and the planet itself." She gave off a resigned laugh." As you've reminded me plenty of times, I'm not married. I know this means I won't be accepted as a settler, but that isn't the only way to get there now, at least for a visit. Since the transports are needed to make trips between Earth and Citadel on a regular basis, it is natural that I was selected to stay in command of my ship."

She gave off a relieved chuckle. "I'm glad that the original one-year voyage has been reduced to three months, and might even be reduced further in the near future. While I know that I won't be there as a tourist, and will be expected to take my ship back to Earth once it is loaded with its cargo, I understand that I'll have time to stretch my legs before I head back. The ship will have to be reconfigured from being primarily a passenger ship to being primarily a cargo ship and undergo inspections before it will be recertified for the trip to Earth and loaded with cargo.

"Citadel is still a settlement world, so there won't be anything like a hotel where I can stay. People either stay with someone they already know or stay aboard their transports. I hope that I won't have to stay aboard my transport the whole time."

Sara ended the message with a reminder of her love and a promise to send a message from Citadel if she had the chance.

Sara had been in luck when she arrived at Citadel, as *Pathfinder* was setting up a long-range sensor array. She and the captain found that they had some mutual acquaintances, and he agreed to let her come along and watch what they did.

She felt sad for him when she'd learned about his having lost his wife and sister-in-law in the attack. She didn't know whether to feel guilty over the fact that that wasn't the only thing she felt about him. She was attracted to him in a way that left her tingly in some interesting places. He hadn't said anything, but she felt a similar vibe coming from him. Although she knew it had been over a year since his wife's death, he probably felt guilty over whether he should even be thinking about another woman. Sara knew that regardless of how much time she had before she'd need to head back to Earth, she needed to let things progress at whatever pace was comfortable for him.

There was an unused cabin on *Pathfinder*, which Joe let Sara take over. She appreciated that he was always a gentleman. Even though he had duties to carry out as the captain, he managed to find time to show her around *Pathfinder* and even let her see their operations with the long-range sensors. During one of their tours, she noticed a plaque on a bulkhead and asked about it. Joe grew quiet as he paused, just looking at it for a moment. Finally, he spoke. "It's in memory of the people who died on board during the attack." Joe pointed to a spot. "Gina's name is there."

Sara touched him on the arm gently. "I'm sorry, Joe. Tell me about her."

A small smile hesitated on his face. "Gina was the best thing that ever happened to my brother, Mark. She was like a breath of fresh air. You always knew where you stood with her. If she thought you were full of shit, she'd tell you. If she thought you were a good person, she'd tell you." Joe's smile became a grin as he said, "If she thought you were a good person who was full of shit, she'd tell you."

Sara laughed. "I've heard that she was the same way even around Sam."

Joe laughed back. "That's the only way Sam would have it. When he told them what he was going to do after the yard had been destroyed, she was the first one to join him in Engineering. He told her that her baby needed her more. She told him that she was doing it for her baby and to shut up and tell her what she could do!"

The laughter faded. "Mark and I knew what was happening to Gina and the others, of course, since we tracked their approach to Citadel and knew they were passing through the radiation field. At least Mark and Gina had a chance to say their good-byes. Julia was blasted from some electronics that couldn't handle the effects from the weapon." Joe looked away. "She never regained consciousness, so we couldn't say any proper good-byes."

"I'm sorry I asked you about it, Joe."

He looked back at her. "Don't be sorry. It's been more than a year since it happened, and I can talk about it now. Mark and Karen have been amazing with their support. Karen was a widow before she met Mark, so she understood what each of us has gone through. Angela is pretty damned lucky to have a new mommy."

Joe's face brightened. "That reminds me. Mark and Karen called me a short while ago to invite us to have dinner with them tonight."

Sara's face also brightened. "I'd love to join you for dinner with them, Joe."

Several days later, they were aboard *Pathfinder* as they learned about the object that the sensors had detected. After Joe made his report, he found Sara in her cabin. She'd kicked off her boots and socks, getting comfortable as she finished her review of a report from her own ship. He told her about his orders to return to Citadel to take on a team to check out the object.

Joe seemed a bit hesitant as he added, "I'm not quite sure how to put this, but we're going to have a bunch of people on board for this trip."

"Sounds like things will be pretty exciting," she said with interest.

"I'm sure they will, but that's not the only reason to mention it."

Sara's brow furrowed with concern. "What's wrong, Joe?"

Joe seemed to fumble with the edge of his link as he said, "Space will be at a premium for this trip. We're going to need this cabin."

Sara looked sad as she said, "I understand, Joe. You need to kick me out."

Joe still looked uneasy. "Well, yes and no. I need to kick you out of this cabin, but I don't want you to leave. I was hoping that you wanted to share *my* cabin."

The concern was pushed aside by delight. She walked up to him and pointed. "Pull on this zipper, Joe."

"This is your jumpsuit zipper."

A new look came into Sara's eyes as she rolled them. "Of course it is, silly! Pull!"

As Joe pulled on the zipper, he expected to see some underwear and a T-shirt or a bra. As the zipper went down, he saw plenty of skin, and nothing else. As the zipper went down past her navel, he saw her breasts revealed completely. With a brief shrug of her shoulders, her arms were free from the sleeves and the jumpsuit was barely around her hips. There was no underwear to be seen. Joe found her brief move to free her hips from the jumpsuit incredibly sexy. In an instant, she was standing in front of him, nude. Although her eyes had never left his, she giggled and said, "It's OK to look at me, Joe. I *want* you to look!"

Joe took a deep breath. "You're beautiful everywhere, Sara!" He chuckled as he asked, "How the hell did you know I was coming here to ask you to my cabin?"

Sara giggled. "I *didn't* know, Joe. I've been wearing nothing under this jumpsuit for two days now, waiting for you to ask me! I've never been as glad for anything as I am for that object to show up and force the issue!" The teasing look came back into her eyes as she walked up to him. "I guess we need to be clear on what you have in mind. Are you asking me to your cabin to make love to me and to share your bed?"

The same look came into Joe's eyes. "Hell, yes, Sara. I've been trying to figure out how to ask you for the last few days as well!"

As Sara reached out and pulled on the zipper to Joe's jumpsuit, she said, "I hope you don't think I'm going to get dressed right now just so we can go to your cabin. These jumpsuits aren't coming back on until you finish with your love making, which won't be for quite some time if I have anything to say about it!"

Sara gasped. "You're making it pretty damned distracting for me to get this suit off you when your hands are doing those things." She giggled. "That doesn't mean I want you to stop; I've thought about you for some time, and this is part of what I've thought about."

Joe quickly kicked off his own boots and socks. As the other jumpsuit fell to the floor, Sara found she could hardly talk anymore with Joe kissing her as he carried her over to the bed.

CHAPTER SIX

As *Pathfinder* edged cautiously toward the object, everyone's gaze was glued to the main screen. Even before they'd tried to do anything about the dim light, it was clear that this was more than just an artificial object; it was a ship. Spotlights had been placed around the object to give them a good look. Although not dark, the surface seemed to soak up most of the light.

Yabuno said, "Even with all of the wizardry we can throw at this thing, from special filters on the optics to computer-enhanced images, it's still difficult to get a truly sharp image of it. It's doing its best to remain an enigma. At least we think we've found a hatch."

"How large is the hatch?" Austin asked.

"It's hard to be sure, but it appears to be about the same size as the hatches we use for people to enter our space ships," Yabuno replied. As a probe was launched toward the ship, transmitting images back to *Pathfinder*, Yabuno continued. "Since the probe we launched is small enough to get through one of our hatches, we should be able to get this one inside the derelict, if we can find the key."

Even as the ship came further into view, it was diffi-cult to tell whether its color was blue, gray, or even some-thing else. The computer seemed to be having the same difficulty; with each moment the color shifted subtly, as if a little more of the ship's true self was revealed.

The ship was so large that in rapid order it filled the entire screen. At that point everyone lost any reference points to judge the distance to the hatch. Finally, the computer and the probe seemed to reach some sort of agreement. The computer settled upon a medium blue-gray, and the probe came to a stop.

The probe was given its instructions, and an arm snaked out toward the hatch. If it was a hatch, however, it didn't seem to have any projections or buttons to press. While they were waiting for something to happen, the computer changed its mind again, and Yabuno saw it first. A small circle appeared that seemed to have been painted onto the surface of the ship just to the right of the hatch. It looked just a little darker than the rest of the ship. The probe was instructed to make contact. There was no reaction of any kind, and Austin wondered whether the circle had any other significance.

"Why not have the probe shine a light onto the circle directly?" Austin asked. "It may be some kind of photoreceptor."

"That may be true," Yabuno replied, "but what if there's a special code we have to crack just to get inside?"

"Nothing ventured, Bret," Austin answered wryly. "Give it a try. The probe is expendable."

Yabuno gave the command to the probe. As the light flashed across the circle, there seemed to be a faint reflection back. It seemed more imagined than seen, but if so, several people had the same imagination.

"What was that?" Austin asked. "It looked like the circle reflected the light back to the probe."

Yabuno said, "That would be unusual, since the rest of the ship hardly reflects any light at all and the circle is a little darker than the rest of the ship."

"Try it again, Bret," Austin said.

Yabuno repeated the instruction, but the results were anything but the same. Hardly a moment after the light flashed across the circle, a different light streaked out from it, enveloping the probe within a blue light. The light wasn't dazzling, but it was the coldest blue Austin had ever seen. It was even colder than anything they'd seen from the alien ship or what had enveloped Austin on the Moon so long ago. It was as if the entire ship was bathed in the cold light, with portions splashing over to the probe. The probe's optical sensors no longer seemed to be able to lock onto the hatch. In fact, the image from the probe was fading altogether.

The screen went dark, and people started looking at each other in puzzlement and alarm. A buzz went around the room as Yabuno sent several commands to the probe and muttered, "Damn it, she won't respond to my signals anymore."

For the first time since the probe had launched, Yabuno turned away from his control console and said to Austin, "This thing has gone dead on me, Sam. Someone or something's going to have to retrieve it if we want a closer look at what that light did. I don't mind admitting that something about that light gives me the creeps. We need to figure out if it's a good idea to send out another probe to retrieve the first one. We also need to decide if we want it in a lab a good distance away in case we start something we can't stop."

All eyes were on Austin as he said, "Send out another probe to retrieve the first one. For safety, let's set up a remote lab to do some analysis and then review the findings."

CHAPTER SEVEN

Austin looked at the crowd of humanity seated around the table. "I know that plenty of people have been involved with the analyses, but I want to keep the conversation focused. Bret, why don't you take the lead in presenting the findings? Others can jump in at any time with their thoughts."

Yabuno rose and approached the large screen, bringing up an image of the derelict as he began. "Sure, Sam. We started off by doing a review of the physical condition of the probe. We did an extensive series of tests on the outer surface of it and couldn't find anything unusual. We began to disassemble it to trace down the cause of the malfunction. All of the components appeared to be in good working order, although we couldn't get the probe to function.

"After a lot of trial and error, we decided to concentrate on the controller chips and the visual sensors themselves." Yabuno pointed to some new images as he continued. "Somehow, the information in the main controller chip has been altered. We don't know what the altered information means."

Austin looked at the images intently. "Any guesses?"

Yabuno brought up a series of symbols for everyone to see. "They may represent mathematical equations, but in a language we don't understand."

"What about the visual sensors?"

"We did the same thing with the visual sensors." Yabuno shrugged. "There doesn't seem to be anything wrong with them, even though information isn't traveling to the rest of the probe. We decided to scan the visuals under different wavelengths of light. When we used infrared light, we finally found something unusual." With a movement of his hand, a new set of symbols appeared. "We found millions of pieces of information etched onto the surfaces of the visuals that had been directed toward the circle next to the hatch. We don't know how it was done, since the probe shows no sign of having been exposed to any radiation, light, heat, or magnetic fields."

Austin frowned in confusion. "What is this information?"

"We don't know," Yabuno replied. "Although there isn't much to use for a starting point, our analysis tells us that there is a relatively low degree of similarity between the information in the sensors and the information in the chip. If that's correct, then there are different messages intended. If it is a series of mathematical equations, we haven't yet found a common reference point that would be the key to a translation. We should also keep in mind that some or all of the concepts in this information may have no equivalent within our knowledge. If that's the case, then even a Rosetta Stone, if there is one for this stuff, might not help much."

Austin finally looked away from the images as he asked, "That brings us back to the question of why the light was directed at the probe at all. Regardless of the message itself, some form of intelligent life has attempted to make contact with us."

Yabuno shook his head. "Yes and no, Sam. While there isn't much hard evidence available, I have a theory about the ship."

"Let's hear it," Austin said, his gaze full of interest.

Yabuno looked back at the image of the derelict as he began. "This is all speculation, of course. I don't think anyone is alive within that ship. From what we've been able to see of its exterior, it appears to be very old, perhaps even thousands of years old. Either the systems have been failing gradually over time or something happened to it, or both, but I don't think it is functioning fully. I think some of the ship's sensors are still functioning and sensed the contact from the probe and reacted to it. Perhaps the ship has been approached by probes in the past. Perhaps the ship's creators used probes. Who knows," Yabuno said with a shrug.

He continued. "Anyway, I think your guess about the circle being a photoreceptor is right. I believe that the right message from the probe would open the hatch. The light it emitted was a reaction to the failure of the probe to send the right signal to the ship. The symbols etched in the visuals may be intended in part to tell us how to open the hatch."

"What about the symbols in the chip?" Austin asked. "If they aren't the same as what's in the visuals, what do they mean? For that matter, couldn't the symbols in the visuals be a warning to stay the hell away, or else?"

"They could be a warning, but it would be easier to send that message by just destroying the probe."

Austin's face showed skepticism. "As you said, the ship might not be functioning on all cylinders right now. Any weapons might be offline or inoperable."

Yabuno looked rueful. "I *told* you this was speculation. I could be full of shit and that ship might be getting ready to blast us so all that's left is a few carbon stains. The reason I don't think it's a warning is that there wouldn't be any need to have different pieces of information in different places. My best guess is that the information in the visuals may help us to get inside the ship and the information in the chip might help us do something else. It might even be a repair manual, or perhaps operating instructions."

Austin frowned as a disturbing thought came to mind. "While we're working on that puzzle, we need to consider another, nastier question. What are the chances that this ship belongs to the aliens that tried to wipe us out?"

A different voice spoke up. Several heads turned toward Sara Choi. "I don't think this ship was built by those aliens, Sam."

The frown vanished from Austin's face. "For anyone who doesn't know her, this is Sara Choi. She's the captain of *KT-2*, the first sister ship to the *Keith Thomas*, and helped us to take out the alien ship that pounded the hell out of Earth and Mars. Some of the people in this room, including me, probably wouldn't be here without

Sara and her crew doing their part. Recently, she took on an assignment as captain of *KT-2* for a cargo run to Citadel and arrived not long ago. She got a good look at the alien ship that day." Austin looked back at her directly. "Tell us why you think they don't hold the deed to this ship, Sara."

Sara nodded her thanks to Austin and walked up to the giant screen. "First, since both ships are alien ships, I guess we should make a distinction between them. Maybe we can call the one that attacked us the invader ship and this one the derelict.

"I don't think anyone who saw the invader ship could ever forget what a crazy approach it took regarding form and function. While it may have made sense as far as its internal workings were concerned, it led to an approach that was anything but streamlined. It was also like an organic creation; some of those external structures were there in part to accommodate the invader ship being able to pull itself apart into a mother ship and a scout ship. While I didn't see the scout ship, I find the process believable in view of the mother ship's appearance." One could see the discomfort in her face as she moved her hands near the image. "There were also plenty of surfaces that appeared to be quite rough, or at least were crisscrossed with lines or grooves."

As she gestured toward the derelict, her movements became smoother. "The derelict, on the other hand, is the epitome of streamlining. The structures on the surface are probably there because they're truly necessary, and not because of cultural conventions. The structure itself doesn't look organic. If there is a scout ship in there somewhere, there is probably a more conventional means of launching it than what looks like a form of cell division."

"Both ships use color schemes that make it hard to get precise readings on things such as dimensions," Yabuno noted. "Doesn't that suggest a common connection?"

Sara brought up close-ups of both ships' surfaces. "The color scheme for the invader ship is quite different from the one on the derelict. The invader ship tended more toward browns and blacks, and the derelict tends more toward blues and grays and sometimes blacks. It's more than that, though. It feels like the browns and blacks were used in a different way to affect the information we can get than the blues and grays and blacks were. In each case, I think the color scheme is a fundamental part of how each species thinks about itself.

"One other thought is that technology usually becomes more advanced over time, barring natural or artificial disasters." She pointed at both images. "It's hard to think of the derelict as being less advanced than the invader ship, which is what you'd expect if it were really thousands of years older and part of the same civilization."

Yabuno nodded. "Those are all good points, Sara, and are pretty persuasive as far as I'm concerned." He looked over at Austin. "Any thoughts, Sam?"

Austin had a worried look on his face. "Sara's comments are persuasive for me as well, but I can't help wonder if the aliens behind the invader ship know about the derelict, or at least about the technology or race behind it."

Yabuno replied, "There isn't any way to know for sure, Sam."

Sara spoke. "It might explain why the invader ship was here in the first place, though. They might have been trying to track down the derelict with faulty, or at least incomplete, information. If finding the derelict was their objective, they were only off from the correct location by around two years, give or take. Depending on how long the derelict has been drifting, that might be a pretty close estimate. If the timing had worked out differently, they'd probably have found the ship. There wouldn't have been anything we could have done about it, either."

"I'm not sure what we can do about it even now," Austin said. "If we can't translate the information the derelict provided, we might not really have much more than a huge piece of modern art."

"We might have something more than that, once Earth finds out about it," Yabuno said.

Austin sighed. "Yeah, I know. While I'd like to keep things cordial, Courtney may not be so accommodating. She may demand that we agree to a joint form of sovereignty over the derelict, or at least that we agree to share everything we learn about it."

Yabuno sprang to his feet. "She's full of it if she thinks we'll agree to hand it over."

"Agreed," Austin replied with a nod. "An obvious initial issue is the fact that the derelict can't be taken to Earth with our technology, so it'll stay in our neck of the woods for now. There are risks as well as rewards associated with proximity to that thing, so how to deal with it has to be our call. However, I'm not opposed to an open approach when it comes to sharing scientific information. I'd want to draw the line at any information that might be dangerous if misused, however. There's no way that someone, somewhere within that system, would be able to resist the temptations relating to that type of information, given the opportunity."

Austin's expression grew colder as he continued. "The other area is information that could be used against Citadel. I'll be damned if, for example, I'll agree to turn over to them a more advanced version of faster-than-light drive just because it sits within a derelict, when they haven't been able to match what we've developed on our own. While we've been careful to enhance our security since the attempted alien invasion, we'll always need to be careful about snakes like Captain Card and his group, who tried to take over part of our planet even before the aliens arrived. I'm not about to turn over game-changing technology that could encourage another collection of snakes to try to create more mischief. There are still too many people within that system who expect to get a free ride from the efforts of the people who are taking the risks."

Yabuno grinned. "Sounds like you're going to have a wonderful conversation with Her Majesty!"

Austin merely rolled his eyes in response.

CHAPTER EIGHT

Sara and Joe spent every moment together they could manage in the short time remaining before she had to rejoin her ship for the trip back to Earth's system. This wasn't as easy as it might seem, because each of them had a ship to oversee. Sara's ship had finally been loaded for the trip to Earth, and everything was ready for departure. She had invited Joe to watch as the conversion to primarily cargo storage was underway.

Joe pointed to the huge hatches that had been opened to allow for the living-space modules to be removed. "I never appreciated just how many people you can carry in one of these ships until I saw all of those modules. I know you don't just keep them pulled out for the trip, because you'll need them again for the return trip."

She nodded. "That's right. We bring them out into space to get some elbow room to reconfigure them, and then we flatten everything and put everything back inside while keeping it out of the way of the cargo we'll take on. When we have a moment, I'll take you inside the cargo holds so you can see how much room we have."

She chuckled. "You'll want to be careful not to get dizzy from all the space! It feels as large as inside the old dirigible hangers back on Earth. The one at Moffett Field in California is so large they can set up multiple hot air balloons inside and still have plenty of room left over!"

The night before her departure, they were in bed together in Joe's quarters. Joe marveled again at her striking beauty, as well as the curves of her body that he enjoyed caressing. With a languid motion, she smiled as she guided his hand to her breasts. "My mom had quite a rack in her day. She still does, in fact. We're the same size there, so I guess I got that from her."

Joe grinned. "You're the first woman to tell me she got her superb, full breasts from her mother! What else did you get from her?"

"She's Italian Roman Catholic, so I was raised the same. She has a funny quirk. Whenever someone is trying to pull a fast one, she always calls it a 'witches' brew.' I don't know where she got the term, but I always know how she really feels about something when she says it."

She smiled again as she said, "I adore my Korean side of the family as well. In fact, after my mother I'm probably closest to my grandfather on my dad's side. Both my grandfather and dad married later in life, which is how I have a grandfather who's over one hundred years old, even though he doesn't seem that way to me."

Joe touched her face gently as he said, "It's like you have the best parts from both sides."

Sara grinned as she touched his hand. "It's a good thing I got my ass from my dad, or there might not be enough room in this bed for both of us!" Her expression softened. "Seriously, while I might not have my mom's hips, there's still room for making babies."

Joe's expression softened as well. "The best way to make babies is with your husband."

"That's how I want to make them, Joe."

"Will you marry me, Sara?"

"Yes." With a mischievous tone, she said, "I hope this means your batteries are recharged, because I want to do some celebrating!"

The celebrations lasted far into the night. Early the following morning, Sara and Joe were speaking to Austin via the screen in Joe's cabin. From the looks on their faces, it wasn't hard for Austin to guess why they wanted to talk with him.

"This is terrific news!" he said warmly. "Congratulations to you both. I'm so happy for you." With a more practical look, he continued. "I'm guessing that there's more that you want to discuss than your engagement, though. Why don't you tell me what's on your minds?"

Joe said, "As you know, Sam, Mark and Karen have been looking after my place while I've been in charge of *Pathfinder*. It's been a great way for me to work through what happened over a year ago. I've found my time as *Pathfinder's* captain to be more rewarding than I'd expected originally. Now that Sara and I want to get married, I'm torn between wanting to go back to my lands and staying on as *Pathfinder's* captain."

"You already know that it isn't quite that simple to go back to your lands if you get married, though," Austin said with understanding.

Joe nodded. "Yes, I know. Sara's never gone through the screening needed to be considered as a settler. I know Citadel doesn't grant automatic settlement rights to someone who marries a settler."

"That's right, Joe." Austin's gaze shifted slightly toward Sara, and there was a kind tone to his voice that helped to soften his comments. "Sara, I think the world of you. You're bright, have great courage, and aren't afraid of challenges. Humanity owes you a huge debt for what you did. Your grandfather is one of the finest people I've known, and there's a lot of him in you. I told him so when I sent him a note congratulating him on reaching the century mark.

"That being said, as Joe has noted, you haven't gone through any of the screening that's required for any potential settler on Citadel. While there is a significant waiting list for settlers, we've always had a policy that members of the Citadel Group are entitled to be considered for settlement ahead of others. All that means is that if you qualify, you won't have to wait at the end of the list. The screening includes medical and psychological histories, as well as confirming support for certain values that are considered key to Citadel. Even if you qualify, there's plenty of training that you'd need to undergo before being cleared to be a settler."

Austin shifted his gaze back to include Joe as he continued, "Most couples that apply don't qualify. What are your plans in case Sara doesn't qualify?"

Joe and Sara gazed at each other for a moment before turning back to Austin. Joe said, "No matter what happens, we're going to get married. If it doesn't work out for us to be settlers on Citadel, then we'll take it from there. For now, I can remain as the captain for *Pathfinder* and Sara can remain as the captain for her ship. If Citadel doesn't want us, then we'll find a place somewhere else where we can start our lives together."

Joe took Sara's hand in his and said, "That life starts now. We'd be honored if you'd perform the ceremony before Sara has to leave for Earth in a few hours. While we'd like it to be in person, we'll have to do it via this link in order to save time."

Austin beamed. "It would be an honor to perform the ceremony!"

After the ceremony was concluded, Sara looked at Austin almost shyly. "Please forgive us for signing off so quickly, but now that we're married, there's something we need to do before I have to leave for Earth." With a giggle, she said, "Joe and Sara Albretti are now signing off from their bedroom!"

CHAPTER NINE

Not for the first time, US President Courtney Harrington was pissed at Sam Austin. She fumed to her chief of staff, saying, "Austin made me look like a fool following the alien attack. After I'd stated in no uncertain terms my strong opposition to his ridiculous declaration that Citadel was now a sovereign state, he went behind my back to convince the rest of the diplomatic community to recognize Citadel anyway."

Her eyes flashed with anger. "The other nations should have taken their cue from me, and that would have been the end of it! Instead, even Congress had the nerve to ignore my wishes and pass a Constitutional amendment recognizing Citadel. The states didn't waste any time in ratifying that abomination and tying my hands. It was a sorry day when I had to recognize Austin as a fellow head of state."

Harrington poked her finger at her hapless listener. "A lot of this mess with Citadel is the handiwork of that sly fox J. W. Preacher III. He's a master at manipulating events, and somehow got himself named Citadel's ambassador to the community of nations. He's managed to acquire a rather stately residence in Georgetown, on Embassy Row, no less! He didn't waste any time in calling it their embassy or in engaging in diplomatic activities with real ambassadors. He's even claimed diplomatic status for the Citadel Group, which I'll be damned if I have to accept! He's also had the nerve to negotiate trade agreements with plenty of nations, to supply materials, produce, and medical supplies that are only available on Citadel.

"To rub it in," Harrington complained, "Preacher has made it clear that while the United States is welcome to enter into a trade agreement with Citadel, the US won't receive any special terms that aren't available to others. We won't even be able to impose our own requirements on Citadel! Whoever heard of the US having to accept that kind of deal?" Harrington frowned. "I told him that his terms were unacceptable, but Congress went around me again by forcing me to accept their terms. I'm getting tired of having my vetoes overridden!"

The chief of staff replied, "They have us over a barrel, Madame President. Citadel builds and controls the ships that are used to transport the goods between the two star systems, because they're the only ones with a reliable technology for the faster-than-light travel that makes journeying between the stars even possible."

Harrington's frown was practically a scowl. "I have other issues with Austin as well, including the question of security for Earth's solar system. Austin seems to think that we need to overreact to the last attack and go overboard in militarizing practically every square inch of this star system. He doesn't even live here or appreciate that as the US president, I have the preeminent role in seeing to the protection of Earth from space-based threats. I'm satisfied that we've seen the last of the aliens as a result of the destruction of their ship."

The chief of staff said, "Unfortunately, Madame President, Austin's views carry a lot of weight, and there's been a lot of chatter from the other nations and the space community over whether we're doing enough to provide for their protection."

Harrington dismissed the comments with a shake of her head. "Personally, I detest destructive weapons and have sought to discourage their use whenever and wherever possible. Instead, I've instructed our people to focus on developing a means of communicating with the aliens so that we can avoid any further unpleasantness in the future."

While the chief of staff thought that what they'd experienced was something far more dangerous than *unpleasantness*, he didn't say so out loud. He also didn't comment on the fact that their efforts hadn't gotten anywhere.

He had hoped to escape, but Harrington wasn't quite finished. Her eyes rolled as she said, "As if everything wasn't bad enough, now I have to deal with Austin over a new issue." In response to his confused look, she continued, "I'm talking about the derelict space ship that's been discovered outside the Citadel system. The reports I've received have indicated that the ship is even bigger than the one that attacked us. God only knows whether that ship was created by the same race that invaded our system, or by someone else.

"I demanded that the derelict be turned over to the Space Command for further study, but Austin rebuffed me out of hand. I then proposed what I consider to be a reasonable compromise, which was that the US and Citadel share sovereignty over the ship and any information or technology gleaned from it. Austin had the nerve to tell me that the US didn't have an automatic entitlement to everything in space! In spite of his attitude, I then suggested that the international community be placed in charge of the ship. Austin hasn't even responded to that suggestion."

Harrington continued to fume about Austin after she finally dismissed her chief of staff. She'd been determined to show that she still mattered by demanding that that Citadel at least agree to share with Earth's system any technology gleaned from the derelict. Harrington reviewed an updated combination of audio/visual back-and-forth responses that were the closest they could come to a direct conversation in real time.

"There's no way that I will agree to a blanket obligation to share with other nations anything that we learn from studying the derelict, Courtney," Austin was saying. "History already has shown what can happen when people get their hands on knowledge that can be dangerous if misused. Inevitably, that knowledge will get out and be misused.

"Further, I won't agree to release any technology that could be used against Citadel. We've already seen a willingness on the part of some people to try to get a free ride from the resources and lives we risked to get to

Citadel. Some people have even tried to force their way into our system and take what wasn't theirs to take."

"No one on Earth condoned those actions," Harrington replied.

Austin wasn't about to be dismissed. "No one on Earth did anything when they learned about it, either. We gave you plenty of information that we gleaned from their files, showing the ringleaders behind Card's voyage. The silence has been deafening."

"Citadel wasn't yet recognized as a nation then, Sam. While regrettable, what happened was akin to corporate espionage, rather than hostile acts against a nation. Besides, aren't you being selfish? Think of the potential benefits to mankind from that technology."

Austin shook his head. "I don't have the luxury of that approach. I'm the leader of a nation, and I need to look after the well-being and security of these people. Besides, we've already provided materials and information that have been of significant benefit to mankind, in the form of better vaccines and medicines, for example."

It was Harrington's turn to shake her head as she replied, "That's been in the form of trade goods, from which you've benefited as well."

Austin pushed back. "We've made contributions to science outside of trade goods, with no strings attached. The bottom line is we won't provide information that hasn't been vetted against the dangers of potential misuse."

"I suppose you expect to do the vetting, Sam," Harrington replied with a skeptical look.

Austin returned the look easily. "Of course we will, Courtney. If we included people from Earth, that information would end up there, regardless of any promises made relating to confidentiality." Austin practically scowled as he added, "I know something about those promises and the fact that they aren't reliable. Innocent people tend to pay the price for those promises when they aren't kept, and the people making those promises rarely seem to be held accountable when they break their word.

"At least on Citadel, we can keep any such information contained. As you've been fond of pointing out, Citadel's population is vastly smaller than that of most other nations on Earth. Much more importantly, because of the vetting and screening that we do regarding would-be settlers, our population is far more likely to be trustworthy when it comes to evaluating and safeguarding game-changing information."

Harrington took malicious pleasure in driving in the knife as she said, "That vetting didn't protect you from the actions of Greg Brittel. He was one of your key people, and look how that turned out." She was disappointed to note that Austin didn't flinch.

"That's true, but another Brittel hasn't risen to take his place, either. On Earth, there would have been hundreds, perhaps thousands, of people who would be ready to do what Brittel did. While I won't claim that this approach is perfect, it's the best one that we have."

Harrington felt the conversation wasn't getting to where she wanted it. "I can't support that approach, Sam. Earth *must* have a role. What if it turns out that the derelict belongs to the aliens that attacked us? Aren't we entitled to use their technology to protect us?"

"*We* were attacked too, Courtney," Austin countered with energy. "Besides, we're pretty sure that the derelict doesn't belong to the invaders. For want of a better term, it looks more sophisticated than the invaders' ship. Frankly, if the derelict had belonged to the invaders, then things probably would have turned out quite differently in both of our solar systems."

"I'm still not prepared to sign off on this approach, Sam."

The look from Austin managed to cross over from wry to insulting. "You still have trouble understanding that the ship has sailed on whether your sign-off is required, Courtney. This conversation is a courtesy between friendly nations. Once again, *we're* the ones who are taking the risks in checking this ship out. That gives us the final say over what happens next."

Harrington closed the file with an impatient slam of her hand on her desk. She hated the fact that the presence of the derelict so far away, with no way to bring it to Earth, meant that she had no real leverage over Austin or Citadel. She was feeling a lot of stress these days. Like most presidents, a key objective was to be reelected. The polls showed an increasing lack of confidence in her leadership, which was translating into a widening lead for her likely opponent. She resented the fact that many people wouldn't give her the respect she felt she deserved as president and defer to her judgment on most matters.

She hadn't gotten it that her judgment sucked on too many matters.

She had trouble understanding that these issues had begun to show up shortly after she had been elected. By the time of the attack by the invaders, those concerns were having a major impact on her reelection prospects. It hadn't helped that there was more support for Austin than her, even though Austin wasn't a candidate.

The appearance of the derelict reminded people that she didn't seem to be in charge of events. If she didn't do something about it and soon, she'd be a one-term president, which she had no intention of letting happen. She needed an audacious plan. Her eyes widened as something came to mind.

NEW ADVERSARIES

CHAPTER TEN

Harrington had assembled her political brain trust in the Oval Office to discuss the plan she'd devised to ensure her reelection. The team included her campaign manager, chief of staff, attorney general, vice president, secretary of state, secretary of defense, and national security director. Although it was expected that her campaign manager, chief of staff, and vice president did everything with a partisan objective, even the others were loyal partisans first and public servants second. Performing the business of the people was important only to the extent that it enabled Harrington to be reelected.

Harrington looked around the room and began, "Good morning, people. Let's start by telling me where I stand on getting reelected."

All eyes shifted to Henry Dormer, who was Harrington's campaign manager and a cynical weasel who believed that the truth was something to be avoided unless it happened to help his client. "Courtney, the latest polls have continued to trend downward. If anything, they've become worse since that new alien ship was discovered near Citadel. Your opponent has continued to hammer us on whether the security measures taken in this solar system have been sufficient. People are wondering, again, whether they will be safe in the event of another attack."

Harrington frowned. "More people should get it through their thick heads that the aliens aren't coming back. We kicked their asses, so there won't be any reason for them to run the risk of it happening again."

"With respect, the people see the ass-kicking as having been delivered by Austin and Citadel. Everyone in this system was caught off guard by the attack. The way the people see it, if the Citadel ships hadn't gotten here when they did, we wouldn't be here having this conversation, because we'd all be dead."

"I'm sick to death of hearing about Austin and Citadel." Harrington turned to her secretary of state. "Ned, what can we do to undermine them as to their ridiculous claim of being a separate nation?"

Secretary Chambers replied, "We have a special issue as far as recognition is concerned, Madame President. Because the states have ratified a Constitutional amendment that confirms diplomatic recognition of Citadel, we don't have the same flexibility to withdraw recognition. We would need a solid legal or diplomatic basis for it, which we lack at this time. They have the same rights as a nation as does Britain or France."

"What would serve as that basis?"

Chambers was slightly unsettled by the question. "We're on much stronger ground if we seek to withdraw recognition based on a serious change to the status quo, such as hostile acts, than where no real change has taken place. The most obvious example of a serious act would be an act of war. Another would be committing something that shocks all nations, such as crimes against humanity. The usual disputes between nations probably wouldn't be sufficient."

"What about the fact that they haven't yet established a formal government?" Harrington demanded. "All they have in place so far are the organizing documents that set up the Citadel settlements as a kind of business venture. Austin told me that he planned on getting it done, but I haven't seen any evidence of it yet."

"We'd be on very shaky ground at best," Chambers replied, "since recognition was already granted without that formal government in place and without being made conditional on the formation of a formal government within a certain time. There would need to be a significant change to that government, such as it is, in order for us to withdraw recognition after the fact."

Harrington pushed the issue, saying, "There must be something we can do about Citadel!"

Chambers's face was more troubled as he answered, "There is no basis for action against Citadel, Madame President. In view of other issues around the world, I'm concerned that focusing on Citadel would be a distraction that we don't need at this time."

Harrington's campaign manager said, "Courtney, it's no secret that you don't like Austin. If we don't have the right political cover, trying to withdraw recognition could blow up in our faces and hand the election to the other side."

Harrington had a vaguely feral look. "I think the appearance of the derelict outside of Citadel is a great opportunity for us. If we use it correctly, we can create an issue that gets people terrified and has the added benefit of sticking it to Austin."

The others in the room were puzzled and said so.

Harrington explained, "I've been going back and forth with Austin over how the derelict will be controlled. I've demanded a role for Earth, but Austin has basically told me to pound sand. He said he doesn't trust people on Earth to do the right thing with any information that is learned from the derelict, and reserves for himself the right to decide what gets passed on to Earth. He's claimed, without offering any proof, that the derelict isn't something that belongs to the alien invaders. He won't even agree to share technology with us if it will help us to defend ourselves against another attack."

The campaign weasel spoke up. "I see where you're going, Courtney. This is an opportunity to shift the focus from the opposition's claims that you haven't been strong enough on security to a focus on Austin as the bad guy who's placing our security in jeopardy. You've been demanding answers from Austin but haven't received any satisfaction. We can stretch this out and build up the pressure, which should also build up our poll numbers. The problem is we'll need to do something dramatic to seal the deal with the public—we all know that people to tend to rally around the flag in a crisis."

Harrington replied, "During this time, we should be building our case against Citadel. At the right moment, we should move against them."

Chambers said, "I don't follow you, Madame President. We've been discussing the fact that Citadel is a sovereign nation. What do you have in mind?"

Harrington looked around the room coolly. "I want to take over their Earth-bound operations and all of their transports in this solar system. I want to send those transports back to Citadel to take control of the derelict. As part of this effort, I want to break Citadel's hold on critical technology once and for all. I want to extract from them everything about their faster-than-light drive, their artificial gravity, and their faster-than-light communications. I also want to know everything there is to know about their security measures and what it takes to get through their radiation field. I want them to be at our mercy and know who's calling the shots."

Walker, the attorney general, was aghast. "Courtney, the president can't just take over parts of another country she doesn't like or simply steal private property! Even putting aside the diplomatic issues, the courts won't just step aside and give us permission to do whatever we want."

Chambers said, "Those 'diplomatic issues' aren't minor, either. What you are describing is an act of war. There hasn't been any declaration of war by Congress, and they're likely to want to know what's happening."

Harrington looked at her vice president, a woman with the unfortunate name of Rhoda Molder. Although Molder was ambitious, she lacked the skills needed to get the top job on her own. She was also something of a weasel herself and not above undermining anyone she felt stood in the way of her advancement. Fortunately for

Harrington, Molder saw Harrington as being able to contribute toward Molder's eventual advancement. Molder
said, "Although Ned is right about declaring acts of war,
if we work it right, we should be able to put off Congress,
provided we can come up with another way to frame the
issue."

The secretary of defense, a man named Rainey, said,
"We know damned well that Citadel wouldn't be stupid
enough to commit an act of war against us. That means
we'd have to be the ones to move against them. People
don't like bullies, and they don't like to see the good guy
throw the first punch. How the hell are we going to deal
with those facts of life?"

Harrington looked at her national security director, a man by the name of Bering, and waited. He said,
"One area where courts don't question the government
is where we make a claim that we need to take some
action because of national security. We don't even have
to explain the basis for the claim. That also has the benefit of helping us with the act of war issue."

Walker wasn't convinced. "You might be able to get
away with a bogus national security claim against most
people, but we're talking about Sam Austin, who's still a
hero in the minds of most people. He's also a former US
president. You'd damned well better have a story that will
pass muster with a judge, let alone the court of public
opinion."

Bering didn't even bother to soften the look on his
face as he said, "*Everyone* has something to hide, Walker.
We'll either find something that Austin or Citadel has
been hiding, or we'll come up with something on our

own. Austin guards his privacy too much. People who do that *always* have something to hide. Once we figure out what it is, we'll also prevail in the court of public opinion. Even though Citadel has been recognized as a nation, people still tend to think of it as Austin's creation. Topple Austin, and people won't worry much about the rest."

Walker snorted. "Everyone who's tried to invade Austin's privacy before has had it blow up in his face. That includes government employees. I should know, since one of my predecessors prosecuted some of them many decades ago."

Harrington spoke up. "No one who's tried it before has had the support of the president. Let's be clear about what's at stake, people. The objective is to get me reelected. If that happens, then we can simply refuse to cooperate with any calls for information. It's been done before, and with the help of the people in this room, it can be done again."

"What if you aren't reelected, Courtney?" Rainey asked.

Harrington surveyed the room with hard eyes. "If I'm not reelected, then you'll all be out of a job. Which situation do you prefer?"

The silence in the room was Harrington's answer. She'd picked her people well.

Walker spoke. "It's late in the conversation to mention it, but one thing we need to be careful about is whether it is right to use the Oval Office for campaign activities."

As the others in the room avoided eye contact, Harrington responded. "We've been discussing a major issue of state as it relates to Citadel, which we should be free to discuss wherever I damned well want to discuss it." She continued with her original point. "I expect you to work together to do what needs to be done. I don't give a damn about the impact on anyone that gets in the way of this operation. Wars have collateral damage, and make no mistake, we're at war."

Harrington stood up as a signal that the meeting was ended and the war had begun.

CHAPTER ELEVEN

Austin was reviewing the latest dispatches from Earth. Among them were messages from J. W. Preacher III and the Citadel Group. As usual, Citadel's ambassador was an astute judge of people and events.

"The trade arrangements that we've negotiated with our fellow nations are working out well for everyone," he said with a pleased look on his face that showed a bit of personal satisfaction with his efforts. "It hasn't hurt that our first trade agreement was signed with Mars. Mars in particular continues to be a solid trading partner, no doubt in part due to our history of helping them out when they needed it, without asking anything in return. It was also a good idea to release to the public some of the medical knowledge that you've developed in your neck of the woods. The word I've been hearing is that it is having some positive impacts on treating some difficult diseases."

The pleased look on Preacher's face changed to one of concern as he continued. "The news is rarely only positive, of course. I'm been receiving reports that all is not well within the Harrington administration as it relates to Citadel. We know that Harrington wants to be reelected, Lord help us. We also know that she's behind in the polls against her opponent. She seems to be using a new tactic, which is to try to distract people from her own failings on the security front by painting Citadel as the new bogeyman. She's been doing everything she can to make Citadel's refusal to share with Earth any information from that derelict seem like some kind of nefarious plan to do harm to Earth, to Citadel's advantage. She's also been suggesting that the derelict belongs to the invaders, and Earth should have that technology to be able to defend itself.

"You need to know this so that you can gauge what sort of response you want to provide, depending on what you learn from the derelict. Harrington is hammering Citadel and you over the fact that you've claimed not to have really learned anything yet. She's been suggesting that you've either not been honest about your progress, or you need to call in experts from Earth to help with the analysis. The surrogates she has enlisted to serve as these 'experts' are all solidly dependable supporters of hers and will say whatever she wants them to say." A wry look appeared in his face as he continued. "We must assume that any information that is provided to them will go straight to Harrington.

"While I can't say that this approach will get her reelected, the polls have been tightening in her favor as she keeps making these points and there isn't any response from Citadel. Our policy of not getting involved in domestic politics on Earth has been a sound one;

however, there is a downside to it in this case, which Harrington has been able to exploit."

Austin noted the worried look on Preacher's face as he continued. "Although this type of nonsense isn't unusual for Washington politics, I've also been hearing some disturbing murmurs to the effect that Harrington has something dramatic in mind to cap this off, although no one seems to know what she might be planning. I'd feel less concerned about this issue if she had true statesmen in key positions. Unfortunately, she has a high degree of contempt for her political opponents and she has a series of hack loyalists in key positions to help her deal with those opponents. I'm not sure how outrageous her demands might have to be before one or more of them refuses to carry them out. This makes me especially glad that the issue of Citadel's recognition as a nation has already been settled. Harrington has been doing her best to poison the well that we might not have been able to get it done if we'd had to wait until now."

The worry in Preacher's face turned into something harder as he added, "Don't make any mistake about whether she has you in her sights and will strike at you if she can; she does, and she will!"

Austin finished reviewing the rest of the dispatch and then reviewed the dispatch from Astrid Henkel of the Citadel Group. After finishing the report that covered the Group's activities, she continued with a frown that was soon matched by Austin.

"Now that I've finished with my report on our technological activities, Sam, I need to express some concerns," Henkel said. "Although we've long been aware that we are being monitored by the US government, we believe that those efforts have been stepped up dramatically over the last several months. We have detected efforts to intercept our communications and monitor our activities and our people. We have traced these efforts back to various US intelligence and espionage agencies.

"While we've maintained our usual countermeasures, we are becoming concerned that more-intrusive efforts may be underway to gain access to sensitive information, including our core technologies. We have avoided moving the remainder of our people out of the US for now, in order not to tip off the US government that we are aware of their activities. Fortunately, since we have long used full encryption for all communications and have updated our other security measures regularly, taking additional precautions along those lines would not be considered remarkable.

"In some ways, our ability to maintain security with respect to our information is compromised by our public activities, including selecting prospective pioneers. In fact, we have rejected an increasing number of candidates whose backgrounds led us to believe they were part of attempts to plant spies within our community." Henkel brought up several images to make her point. "While we haven't concluded that all of the attempted 'plants' were from the US intelligence community, we have a high degree of certainty about a number of them. All of this adds up to increased pressure on our operations at a time in which there should be less pressure due to our having been recognized as a nation.

"While the endgame of the current administration is unclear, there's little question that one objective is to weaken Citadel. Citadel would be in a much weaker situation if its core technologies were to be compromised. Citadel would also be in a weaker position if people could be planted among prospective settlers in order to compromise its operations, technology or both.

"One plus in this situation is the fact that the extreme distance between the two solar systems requires that the US operates against Citadel remotely, primarily against the Citadel Group's operations in Earth's solar system. So long as the US is limited to remote operations, we are in a better position to deal with those operations than if the US were ever able to reach Citadel directly."

Austin set aside the dispatches and pondered his next moves. He decided to check with the rest of the team to share with them the contents of the dispatches and get an update on the derelict.

CHAPTER TWELVE

From an early age, Alan Turner had been one of those people who seemed destined to pursue a career in mathematics. Even though he was still a young man, he had already established a reputation as someone who would be among the leading lights of his generation. A funny thing then happened. Turner looked into his future and saw that it consisted of a life mostly devoted to theory. He surprised himself when he realized that he wanted to live a life that was focused much less on theory than on practice. He surprised himself and his wife further when he expressed an interest in settling on Citadel. His wife surprised him even more when she embraced the idea with great enthusiasm. She saw it as a way to be much more his partner than she ever would if he stayed with theory.

It turned out that Turner and his wife were quite handy with tools and equipment and were well suited for settlement life. The part that sealed the deal for Turner and the Citadel Group was the fact that he wanted to be able to continue with his theoretical work on some level, even though he didn't want to be defined by it. The Citadel Group was looking for such people in order to establish a knowledge base that would expand over time and enable Citadel to maintain its technological edge over Earth.

Turner had been delighted by the challenge of the alien equations and taken the lead in attempting to master them. Several months later, he wasn't sure he'd still use the word "delighted" to describe his feelings.

Turner listened as Yabuno continued with their conversation with Austin. "Damn it, Sam, we're still trying to work out what the equations mean," Yabuno said, pacing the room in a sign of frustration. He gestured to Turner. "You know Alan knows more about mathematics than practically anyone alive, and even he's reaching dead end after dead end. Although he's been able to spread the work out among our people back at the Citadel Group, no one had has any kind of breakthrough. If these people can't do it, I don't know who can."

"Harrington is pounding us over our supposed lack of good faith when it comes to the derelict," Austin said. "I'm trying to figure out if it's worth it to send these images to people on Earth who are outside the Citadel Group, to show everyone that Harrington is mistaken."

Yabuno had a sour look on his face. "Why do we give a damn what Harrington thinks about anything?"

"We give a damn because she's still the leader of the most powerful nation on Earth," Austin replied pointedly. "She has enormous resources available, to be used for positive or negative purposes. What I've been hearing indicates that she's using some of those resources for negative purposes relating to Citadel. I have to decide whether she can be persuaded to focus on positive purposes instead."

"Why wouldn't she do both?" Yabuno scoffed. "She could put up a pretense of cooperation while still trying to undermine us. If the unthinkable happens and she's reelected, then she'd just work that much harder to screw us without having to worry about what the public thinks. It wouldn't be the first time that a president has done it."

"I've thought of those points," Austin replied with a nod. "In view of her hostility toward us, I don't want her around for another term, either. I'm trying to figure out if there is some form of cooperation that will get us there." Austin turned to Turner and asked, "Alan, where do you stand on whether it makes any sense to share these equations with anyone outside Citadel?"

Turner snorted. "Once the genie is out of the bottle, Sam, it can't be put back in again. The moment anyone else figures out to how to get access to the derelict, we have to assume that they'd distill that knowledge into a form that would let a visitor get access, possibly even without our knowledge. Even though I can't understand these equations, I know at an emotional level that they are sophisticated in ways we may never be able to understand fully. I don't know if I'd ever feel comfortable knowing that someone has a spare key to that knowledge."

"It would be one thing if that spare key stayed on Earth," Yabuno added, "but we have to assume that someone from Earth will get access to the derelict at some point. That means the spare key will be used."

Turner continued, "Even if we can decipher these equations, we'd have to figure out how to use what we learn in a way that won't cause harm to this solar system. So long as the derelict remains here, the consequences from using that knowledge would fall on us, for good or bad. If the consequences are bad, I'd rather that they happen because of *our* actions than because of the actions of people who are safe and secure in another solar system."

Austin was silent for a full minute before he spoke. "I see your point. I'll postpone at least for a while any decision to share these equations with anyone else."

CHAPTER THIRTEEN

President Harrington's staff continued to try to make the campaign all about Citadel's refusal to share information gleaned from the derelict. Although Harrington herself was careful not to come right out and say so, the rest of her team was happy to call Austin a liar and accuse him of being willing to place in jeopardy the security of Earth's solar system. While the smear campaign was having some impact, the polls still showed that Harrington's opponent was ahead. Harrington's team met again in the Oval Office.

Bering continued with his briefing on his findings. "So far, we've been unable to penetrate the Citadel Group's security to get direct access to their technology. They've adopted encryption protocols that we haven't been able to break. Although we've been able to place an operative on one of their transports, the operative hasn't been able to gain access to secure files on the inner workings of those vessels."

Bering brought up additional images on the screen. "We've had more success in monitoring the activities of

Citadel Group personnel. Although most of them are located outside the US, there are still some located here that we can intercept if needed."

"What do you mean by 'intercept'?" Walker asked.

"Let's not be naïve," Bering said with a slightly dismissive look. "We may need to restrain and interrogate these people in order to obtain the information we want."

"On what basis?" Walker demanded.

"On the basis of national security implications relating to potential know-how Citadel may be planning to use against us."

"What is this potential know-how?"

"This is know-how that Citadel has obtained from the derelict."

With a skeptical voice, Walker asked, "How did you arrive at the conclusion that there is information that Citadel may be planning to use against us?"

"We have anonymous sources that can't be named for national security reasons."

Walker looked at Chambers. "Do you really expect to be able to appear before the Allied Nations and make these claims with a straight face?"

Harrington cut off Chambers's response. "Ned isn't going to appear before the AN or anyone else until after the crisis has passed. All communications will be run out of this office. We can claim that we're evaluating their findings on the derelict and will be implementing whatever security features we uncover. Once I've been reelected, it won't matter whether there's anything to be had, because the aliens aren't coming back anyway.

"In fact, it probably makes sense to plan on destroying the derelict at some point. We can't bring it back here anyway, and it will give us cover for our actions and make it impossible for Citadel to claim that there wasn't anything lethal on board. We can claim that in the interests of protecting humanity, we destroyed our information and will still keep Citadel hanging over claims that it hasn't been forthcoming with what it has learned." There was no humor on her face as she said, "A nice bonus is that Citadel will never get to benefit from any information from the derelict."

"What do we do if someone is able to make credible allegations relating to these activities and the press gets a hold of them?"

Harrington's tone was dismissive. "It won't really matter. The press can squawk all it wants. We're not going to investigate ourselves, and our national security claims will keep Congress at bay for now. After the election, we can always say the intelligence was faulty if necessary."

She was enjoying listing her objectives. "In the meantime, we'll be able to weaken Citadel fatally once we have their core technology. With that technology, we can build our own ships and send them to Citadel and ignore theirs altogether. We can add insult to injury by using their facilities to build our ships. We can probably even get away with planting new colonies on Citadel that will answer to us and overwhelm the settlements that are there already. Once there is a dispute over control, we can play the peacemaker and offer to negotiate a solution that puts Austin where we want him. Austin wouldn't

like it, but he wouldn't have much choice but to agree."
Harrington was practically beaming at the thought.

Chambers asked, "How do you propose that we
obtain control over their transports?"

Bering replied, "We've identified key people within
the Citadel Group that we will need to neutralize in order
to take control of the transports."

Rainey asked, "What do you mean by 'neutralize'?"

Bering's face took on a sardonic look. "Nothing as
dramatic as you might think from reading the crap that
passes for most fiction novels, Rainey. We mean that we
would capture them and take them to secure areas where
we can keep them from alerting their comrades before
we take over their transports. Where feasible, we would
also capture the captains of the transports and hold them
in order to persuade their crews to accommodate us."

"Why don't you just replace everyone with your own
people?" Rainey asked sarcastically.

Bering sighed. "With more time, that's precisely what
we'd do. However, we have a deadline that prevents us
from taking that approach."

Harrington's eyes narrowed. "What deadline?"

Bering replied, "The derelict continues to drift
toward the Citadel solar system, Madame President. It
is now just over three months away from reaching their
system. The only way this works is if we get control of it.
Once it is inside their system, our leverage is gone and
it will look like we tried to destroy another nation. If we
move quickly enough, the transports can get to Citadel
just in time for us to intercept the derelict, although the
timing will be close."

"Tell me more about the transports, Bering," Harrington said.

Bering brought up several images on the screen. "We know that there are ten transports in our solar system now. Thanks to some good fortune, there are only three transports in their solar system. While a fourth is scheduled to arrive there within the next two weeks, one of the three that are there currently will depart in around three weeks. While the one that will be leaving soon from their solar system won't get here in time to be of help, there is another transport that is scheduled to arrive at our solar system in around a week."

Harrington looked at the transports with a proprietary expression. "We can't allow them to alert Citadel to what we're doing."

Bering made a weak attempt at warmth. "We've already thought about that, Madame President. As we speak, a ship is approaching the communications beacon at the entrance to our solar system. With your approval, we will disable that beacon. There have been other communications problems over the years, so a blackout shouldn't cause undue alarm. We can take control of these other ships once they arrive."

"Take out that beacon and make preparations to capture those transports," Harrington responded. The look on her face as she scanned the room was unpleasant to behold. "I expect all of you to be fully on board. There had better not be any leaks over what we're doing, because if I go down, I will make certain each of you does as well."

CHAPTER FOURTEEN

Although Choi was over one hundred years old, he was sharp mentally and remarkably spry. Even extreme old age couldn't change his ramrod-straight posture that was the result of decades of military service. Although he'd been retired for many years, he still kept in touch with his friends throughout the Space Command and elsewhere. He'd been pleased and a little surprised to hear from an old friend out of the blue.

Nearly forty years earlier, Tim Buck had been a lieutenant in the Space Command. Choi was a four-star general and scheduled to retire in a few years but kept receiving extensions due to his great value as a leader and strategic thinker. With the blessing of President Austin, the latest extension had sailed through Congress easily. One of Choi's great strengths as a leader was his ability to find and develop new leaders. He had watched with interest as Buck carried out his early assignments and decided to offer to become a mentor to the young officer.

Buck was unsure whether he really had what Choi saw in him, but he accepted the offer gratefully. Buck's own career advanced rapidly, and Choi had been proud to be present when Buck received his first star. Buck was now a four-star general and regarded as being the same kind of essential asset that required extensions to his tours.

After warm greetings had been exchanged and Buck had been invited into Choi's home, Choi could sense that the visit wasn't social in nature. "Tell me why you look so serious, Tim," Choi said without smiling.

Buck was silent for a moment before answering. "A matter has come up that troubles me greatly, General, both because of what it means for our country and what it means for you personally."

Choi was confused. "I'm an old man and have seen many things, so it's hard to think of anything that would affect me personally. In fact, I've received good news recently about my granddaughter Sara, who just got married to a fine young man on Citadel."

"Let's set aside for the moment the impact of the matter on you personally, General. We've talked before about your opinion of people who don't respect the proper chain of command. I share that opinion, which is why this is such a difficult conversation. I've been sworn to secrecy, yet I believe that this matter is something that goes beyond regulations and theories of command. The matter is so serious that I could be imprisoned or even face execution if it were to become known that I discussed it, even with you. Things might not go so well for you, either."

Choi looked back at Buck. "You know me too well to ask for absolution, Tim. However, I have a great deal of faith in your judgment." A small sign of warmth appeared on Choi's face as he continued. "How could I not, when I helped nurture that part of you? If you feel that you must share this matter with me, do so because of concern for our country, instead of any concern for me personally."

With a nod, Buck began. "It's no secret that President Harrington's reelection campaign is in trouble politically. It's also been no secret that her approach has been to attempt to smear Sam Austin in order to create a climate of unease and even hysteria."

"I would tell you that these political considerations are not for active-duty military professionals to concern themselves about, but you already know it, so I assume that more is at stake. Please continue."

Buck fidgeted in his chair. "I have learned that the president intends to act against Citadel and the Citadel Group by taking control of all Citadel Group assets. This includes everything in the US as well as overseas and elsewhere in this solar system. The US intends to capture and interrogate key Citadel Group people to learn as much as possible about Citadel's core technologies. Some of these people are entitled to diplomatic immunity. Harrington intends to send the captured transports to Citadel to take control of the derelict spacecraft before it enters Citadel's system. They've already disabled the communications array with Citadel to make sure no one alerts them to what's happening. Under our own Constitution and laws, Citadel is a sovereign nation, and these actions constitute acts of war."

Buck's expression grew even more troubled. "Sara has been targeted specifically for capture, as they will need her to take her transport back to Citadel as part of their surprise attack."

Choi did not respond to the concern about Sara. Instead, he asked, "What is the basis for these actions, Tim? No one would be crass enough to do these things for political gain. There has to be more to it."

"Bering has been claiming to have intelligence to the effect that Austin has uncovered vital technology from the derelict that could be used to help us defend ourselves against another attack by the alien invaders."

"You don't believe him," Choi said. It was a statement instead of a question.

Buck frowned. "I could say that I believe Bering to be a political tool instead of an intelligence professional. I could say that I believe that he has gotten away with lying under oath to Congress when making statements relating to activities in space, where people I know and respect claim to have information directly contradicting those statements. I could even say that there are people who won't work with him because of the type of man he is. However, these things can be argued to be merely political disputes that shouldn't concern active-duty military professionals."

Buck didn't bother to hide his anguish. "The strongest reason I don't believe Bering is that the man he claims is doing these things is Sam Austin. I don't believe for a minute that Sam Austin would ever do anything to place the security of the United States in jeopardy. This is the man who put his own life on the line, against the wishes of his own people on Citadel, to come here and fight to the death against the alien invaders. He could have stayed on Citadel to help them lick their wounds, but didn't."

Buck stood up as he asked, "*This* is the man who now wants to harm us?" He began to pace. "Bering hasn't released any actual intelligence to support his claims, so we are being asked to take his word for his claims. Once I came to the conclusion that Bering was lying, the entire house of cards came tumbling down as far as justification for doing anything against Citadel is concerned. In fact, it becomes much worse. It isn't just a series of unlawful orders that any officer is duty-bound to disobey; it's a series of crimes against humanity!"

Choi was silent for a time. "Have you discussed these concerns with anyone higher up in your chain of command?"

"I've pushed back on the basis for taking these actions, as have a number of my colleagues. However, we keep being given the same answer, which is that the decision to act is for the civilian authorities to make and for us to carry out. We've also been ordered to stay away from the press and have been reminded that treason charges may be brought against anyone who disobeys these orders."

Choi's face was impassive. "Why have you come to me, Tim?"

"Some of these actions are being carried out even as we speak," Buck said with disgust. "The Space Command has had to soil itself by taking over the Citadel transports in our solar system. The transports were on peaceful status, so there wasn't much resistance. The communications array with Citadel has been disabled, so the only way to get a message to their solar system is on a ship. I want you to know so that you can alert Sara if possible to the danger. Her ship will arrive at any time now."

There was no emotion in Choi's voice as he asked, "What do you intend to do?"

"I won't carry out unlawful orders or be a party to committing crimes against humanity, even if it means I may have to face severe consequences."

"You could go to the press and explain the situation," Choi pointed out.

Buck nodded. "I've decided to do it, although I can be prosecuted for disobeying direct orders. Even if the rest of the house of cards tumbles, disobeying direct orders about going to the press is still a court-martial offense." Buck looked at Choi with resolve. "I'm prepared to accept the consequences."

"There is another approach, Tim."

Buck was confused. "What do you mean, General?"

Choi stood up, looking every inch the general he'd been for much of his life. "*I* could go to the press. What the hell could they do to me? I'm old, retired, and have every right to criticize the government. Threatening me with prosecution if I talk about the government's unlawful actions is meaningless."

"They might try to slime up your reputation, General."

Choi snorted. "My reputation was established before most of these people were out of diapers. Besides, the people whose opinions I value know me. It makes more sense for me to talk about this matter publicly than for you to do it. Although the new information you've brought to me is crucial, I've observed and been disturbed about President Harrington's actions and motives for some time."

"If you talk about it publicly, you might not be able to help Sara," Buck warned.

Choi's face was filled with love for his granddaughter as he said, "If I failed to do the right thing because of Sara, she'd be the first one to be disappointed in me, and rightly so. I'll try to do the right thing for both our country and for Sara, if I can." A determined look appeared on his face. "There's someone I need to see. Please leave, Tim. It's better if people don't see you meeting with me."

Ambassador Preacher was at home in the Citadel embassy on Embassy Row in Georgetown. He was waiting by an inner threshold to greet his old friend after the security scans had been completed.

"General, it's been far too long since we've seen each other." Choi greeted Preacher just as warmly as Preacher escorted Choi into Preacher's private study, which was outfitted with several extremely comfortable chairs.

"Every time I'm of a mind to complain about the disadvantages that come with getting old, I think about you and hope I can be so fortunate when I'm your age," Preacher said. After a shrewd assessment of Choi's face, he said, "However, we've known each other too long for me to believe this is just a social call. Tell me what's on your mind."

Choi's face finally betrayed his great worry as he began, "J. W., I've just learned from a highly credible source that Citadel is in great danger from the Harrington administration."

Preacher was far too experienced to jump up dramatically and interrupt Choi's statement, so he stayed quiet while Choi continued. "We've all been aware of the campaign by President Harrington to engage in lie after lie to confuse people into ignoring her own failures relating to providing security for our solar system. Her lies are intended to make people focus on a supposed plot by Sam Austin to withhold vital know-how from Earth that would help us to defend ourselves against another attack by the alien invaders.

"She has been able to get away with this nonsense in part because Austin refuses to be drawn into a political campaign taking place light years away in another solar system. While the polls show the race to have tightened, she hasn't yet managed to turn the race around to ensure her reelection. Her campaign has been leading up to something dramatic, a major crisis that would encourage people to stand behind the flag and support the president.

"Unfortunately, the dramatic action would have a direct impact on Citadel. Harrington is ready to claim that vital information can no longer be allowed to be withheld from Earth by Citadel, and that doing so when our security is at stake is tantamount to an act of war. The director of national security has operatives who will kidnap various key Citadel Group members and interrogate them to gain access to Citadel's core technologies and operations. I've learned that the Space Command has been ordered to take control of all of Citadel's transports and other space assets in this solar system. These transports will then go to Citadel and take control of the derelict before it drifts into Citadel's solar system."

Preacher's face was impassive. "I assume that some action will be taken against the communications array to Citadel, to prevent anyone here from notifying Citadel about what's happening?"

"It's already happened, J. W." Choi's face had a look of anguish that was startling because it had never been seen in public. "If I'd been told that the Space Command would be called upon to play its part in this nightmare, I'd have told that person he was full of it. I've since sent out some subtle feelers and confirmed that everything that I've been told is actually happening. I just wish there were some way to contact Citadel."

Preacher's impassive face softened into a sly look as he walked over to his desk. "We may have some options after all." He pressed several keys on his keypad as he continued, "I've just sent an emergency message to the Citadel Group that will shut down all access to Citadel's technology files. No matter what happens to the people, access to the files will be denied. Only Sam Austin can override this command, and he isn't likely to do so under the circumstances. Even Bret Yabuno, as smart as he is, probably couldn't break the encryption. The only other person that might be an exception is the man who developed the encryption, Alan Turner, and he's on Citadel with Sam and Bret."

Choi was puzzled. "How can the Citadel Group function if everything is shut down?"

"Everything *isn't* shut down," Preacher replied with a small chuckle. "However, all development activities are frozen, as well as manufacturing of any transports, for example, since access to technology is required to do those things. There are certain other things for which access is no longer available, but I won't describe them."

A sly twinkle appeared in Preacher's eye. "Sam and I have never trusted Harrington fully, so we set the wheels in motion the last time he was here. Bret, Alan, and a few others were with him, so the key people were together to put in place some special measures."

"Will your special command alert the Citadel Group people to the dangers?" Choi asked.

"The command includes a first-priority message that tells people that we are in a grave situation that has led to the need for the use of the encryption I've described. There are emergency protocols that people are to follow to protect themselves, but if the intelligence operatives are already moving against our people, the protocols may not be effective."

Preacher added wryly, "One thing that the protocols will do is make it a hell of a lot more difficult to try to study Citadel's transports to learn about the underlying technology. If Harrington's people want to take our hijacked transports to Citadel, they'll need to leave within a few days at most, or the derelict will be out of reach within the Citadel solar system by the time they arrive there."

Choi shook his head. "You understand these matters better than I do. But wouldn't that just make it easier for Harrington to keep up the pressure on Citadel until the election?"

Preacher chuckled at Choi's comment. "You're every bit the crafty fox people make me out to be, General.

Harrington has to show that she actually has control of the derelict, or else Austin will just make her look like a fool again. If she doesn't have control of the derelict, no one will believe her claim to have discovered the critical technology that Austin has supposedly been holding back. Presumably, after she's won reelection, she'd put out some story about discovering that the technology has a flaw in it that would make it unusable. They'd claim that Austin didn't know about the flaw and was planning on using the technology against Earth, and Earth had no choice but to act against Citadel.

"Once the derelict is safely within the Citadel solar system, all Austin has to do to defuse the situation is to invite some neutral scientists to look at the information that they've been able to come up with and get their confirmation that everyone is still at square one as far as getting into the derelict or understanding its technology is concerned. Once that happens, the pretext for war is gone, and so is Harrington's career. While it is a tradeoff that will result in the information making its way to Earth, it would be worth it to deal with her."

The warmth left Preacher's face as he continued. "If that happens, Harrington will be facing impeachment. Depending on how far she tries to take things, she might even face charges of crimes against humanity for initiating an aggressive war against a nonbelligerent nation."

Preacher walked back to his desk. "Fortunately, we have another trick up our sleeve. Although the communications beacon has been disabled, we have access to an alternate beacon. It won't become active until it is launched, so I'll need to bring it online and direct that it be launched."

Choi allowed a brief flash of admiration to cross his
face. "You are much more than you seem, J. W."

A different voice spoke from the doorway. "Not as
much as you might think, Ambassador."

Preacher and Choi whirled to find armed men
standing in the doorway. One of the men walked over
to Preacher's desk to pick up the keyboard and toss it
to another man standing by the doorway. The first man
turned back to Preacher and said, "Ambassador Preacher,
my name is Major Wolfe, and I work for the National
Security Authority of the United States government. For
your own safety, the United States government is taking
you into custody while the United States defends itself
against Citadel."

Preacher snapped at the man, "Have you lost your
mind? Your presence in this embassy is in violation of
the laws of nations and is an act of war. Get out of here
before you make matters any worse than they already
are. The United States government has recognized the
Citadel government and accepted my credentials as its
ambassador. As such, I claim diplomatic immunity from
your actions. There is no lawful basis for you to take any
actions against me personally under any circumstances
and none against Citadel itself without a declaration of
war from Congress. After you get out of here, I'm making
a formal protest to your government and to the AN. I'm
also making a formal protest over the other actions that
I've been informed that the United States has initiated
against Citadel."

Wolfe replied, "I'm afraid you won't be making any
protests for now, Ambassador. In view of the concerns

that the United States has about Citadel's activities, we are searching this embassy for any further information about Citadel's hostilities toward Earth. Any communications with anyone other than approved United States personnel will require the permission of the president."

Preacher the genial ambassador had vanished to be replaced by a much more formidable opponent. With a dangerous look, he said, "I know my rights. I'm entitled to legal counsel, and I demand that I be permitted to speak with him immediately."

Wolfe dismissed Preacher's comments. "You lost your right to counsel once your country engaged in hostilities against the United States, Ambassador. The matter isn't open for discussion."

Choi turned to the man and said, "I happened to be visiting Ambassador Preacher, but I'm not associated with Citadel. I assume that I am free to leave."

Wolfe shook his head. "I'm afraid not, General Choi. We know about your visit with General Buck and the reason behind your visit with Ambassador Preacher. I have orders to detain you for reasons of national security."

Choi's voice never rose above normal volume but Wolfe flinched as Choi said, "Major, I'm a retired US general with far more familiarity with what constitutes a national security issue than you will ever have, God willing. I am also an American citizen and I demand my rights under the United States Constitution be respected immediately, or *you* will be the one facing charges. It is not an excuse to say you are just following orders, Major. Who issued those orders, and under what authority?"

Such was the respect that Choi commanded that even Wolfe could not refuse to answer. "The orders were issued by the director of national security pursuant to a national security directive signed by President Harrington, sir. The directive declares that there is a national security emergency and suspends certain Constitutional provisions pending the conclusion of the emergency."

Many senior officers had withered under the glare that Choi directed at Wolfe. "You're telling me that the president issued her own blanket arrest warrant that gives the director of national security the authority to arrest anyone he wants, so long as he claims that the arrest relates somehow to national security? Do you have any idea how many provisions of the Constitution or various statutes that directive violates?"

Wolfe stood his ground. "Nevertheless, General, I have my orders, and you will be taken into custody immediately."

"Very well, Major. You've just failed the most important exam you will ever face as a United States officer. I've warned you about the consequences."

CHAPTER FIFTEEN

The head of the Citadel Group's space yard, Dan Bacas, had plenty of work on his plate. A sane man might say there was too much work on that plate, but Bacas sometimes embraced a little craziness. He never let the craziness replace the need for discipline or hard work, however, which is why his operations were the envy of much of the solar system. Every one of his bays had some kind of craft under construction, including several of the Keith Thomas class of transports that would be added to their fleet to travel out and back beyond the stars.

Although Bacas knew the he couldn't afford to burrow down into the weeds too far, he prided himself on getting away from his desk practically every day and taking a look at how things were going with each project. Bacas didn't believe in bureaucratic crap and made sure that red tape didn't screw up his operations. He knew plenty about the actual building of these space jalopies, including where things could go wrong, so he also insisted on safety in everything they did. No one could get away with bullshitting Bacas, so no one tried. Instead, each conversation was simply an honest assessment of how things were going and where any help was needed. His link ensured that anything that was needed was handled before he ever got back to his desk.

He'd just finished a tour of the yard when a message came through. Normally, Bacas might have been tempted to set aside the message until he'd had a chance to get through other stuff that he knew needed attention immediately, but his eyes widened as he noticed the name of the person sending the message and the urgency behind it.

"This is a surprise," he began. "I don't usually hear from you."

"Please don't use any names, Dan," said the caller. "If any monitoring is going on, we need to keep my name out of it for now. You know this isn't a social call. I don't have much time, as all hell is breaking loose and Citadel is on the receiving end. If you don't do your part, there won't be a Citadel soon."

"You have my attention. What's happening, and what do I need to do?"

"The United States has declared war on Citadel," the voice declared grimly. "While the US is using some other fancy language instead of saying 'war,' what's happening is war. They've taken over Citadel's embassy and are going after all of our assets and locking up some of our people. One of the things that the US wants is Citadel's core technology. With that technology in hand, everything that makes Citadel unique will be within the control of a hostile country. An emergency lockdown of all core technology has therefore been initiated."

"I assume that the lockdown has been extended to the yard."

"Yes, it's already gone into effect. You just might not have noticed it yet."

Bacas wanted to ask what else was coming, but he already knew the answer.

"You know what else needs to happen, Dan," the caller said.

With a heavy heart, Bacas asked, "Are you absolutely sure this is necessary?"

"Yes, I'm sure. While I can't claim that it will be even remotely as painful to me as it will be to you, I can sympathize. I know that even thinking about it is probably killing you right now."

"If we do this, they'll already have won."

"If we do this, they'll have hurt us hugely. If we *don't* do it, they'll have won. Which would you prefer?"

Bacas practically snarled as he said, "You know I don't want those bastards to have the satisfaction of getting anything from me that might help them beat us." He paused for a moment in thought. "Why can't we send some of these ships to Mars? I'd bet they'd help us out."

"The US has already violated international law by taking over our embassy without any formal declaration of war. Do you really think we can take the chance that they'd respect Mars's sovereignty at this point and not try to capture any Citadel ships there? The Keith Thomas transports can't land, so they'd be a tempting target in orbit. While a small number of ships might be safe there, there are too many of them in the yard for the Space Command to ignore if they were sitting in orbit around Mars."

Bacas's shoulders sagged with frustration and sadness as he stared at the answer. Finally, he said, "No, I guess we can't take any chances."

"There's one more thing you have to do, Dan. You have to make absolutely certain there's no way to recover the information that has been locked down. There can't be any back doors or alternate paths to any core technology from the yard. One reason you must be certain is because we have to assume that you will be taken into custody and interrogated. Don't be under any illusions about whether your being a US citizen will protect you, because it we already know it won't. No matter what happens, if you know that the information can't be recovered, then they'll know it as well and move on.

"The Space Command has been tasked to carry out the dirty work, although at this point you should be suspicious of anyone from the US, regardless of the agency. If you can do everything you need to do at the yard before the Space Command arrives, then take your people and try to get to Mars and seek political asylum. Once you get to the ground, you'll probably be safe. While the US is willing to invade Citadel, it probably isn't willing to invade Mars on the ground. You need to start, and I need to sign off. Good luck and Godspeed."

"The same to you," Bacas muttered as he took a moment to absorb what had happened.

Bacas received word that Space Command was en route to the yard, although there was no official reason given for the visit. With time slipping away, he took a last look at the list showing the status on each of the ships coming to life in his bays and thought of the incredibly complex information contained within those files. He gave off a sigh that reflected many months, sometimes years, of hard work and experience and then entered a few brief commands. In an instant, every bit of the yard's useful information relating to Citadel's core technologies that hadn't already been locked down had entered into a realm where it couldn't be recovered.

Among the equipment in use at the yard was a device that could be converted quickly into a portable EMP generator. Bacas sent a priority message to everyone at the yard to stop work and listen to an emergency announcement.

He said, "I've just received word that the United States has declared an unofficial war on Citadel. Even as I'm making this announcement, US personnel are moving against various assets of Citadel. In fact, they've already moved against the Citadel embassy itself. We have therefore been instructed to take extraordinary measures to protect core Citadel technology from falling within the control of the US. Toward that end, all of the yard's technology files have been placed into an encrypted status that can't be broken by anyone here."

There were tears in his eyes as he continued. "That's not all we need to do, however. There are six ships in this yard that have warp-field generators, artificial gravity, or other sensitive Citadel technology. We need to take all of these to a place where the US can't take them apart and learn about them. While I'd rather destroy them here, with the amount of time available, there's no way that we can be sure to do a thorough enough job trying to wreck them while they're sitting in this yard.

"We can't head anywhere toward the interior of this solar system, so the closest place available at this point is Jupiter. We'll need to attach remote thrusters to every one of those ships and take them there immediately. We have to make sure that every ship is sent straight down to the surface of the planet. At least they'll have a proper grave there.

"Once the ships are all lined up for the trip to Jupiter, I will pilot the ship that will escort them, to ensure that they get where they must go. I need only a small crew of volunteers. The rest of you should haul ass straight for Mars and seek asylum. Get to the surface as fast as you can; I wouldn't trust the US forces to respect any ship that's in orbit. Several Space Command ships are already closing on the yard, so we need to hurry. That's all, people."

As Bacas moved toward the first ship in line to oversee getting it ready for its escape, his second in command, Gus Kramer, practically ran into him.

Bacas could guess at the subject. "What is it, Gus?"

"Dan, you have to get your ass out of here *now*," Kramer said. "You know too much about our technology to take a chance on your being captured."

"The yard files have been encrypted, Gus," Bacas replied sadly. "Honest to God, I don't have the key to unlock them, so there isn't much anyone can do without them."

Kramer snorted. "That's bullshit, Dan, and you know it. I know *I'd* be screwed if I had to work without those files. Guys like you and Curly Stephens back at Citadel can reconstruct information that the rest of us couldn't, just because you know so much about how everything goes together."

Bacas's voice took on a harder tone. "If I don't get these ships to Jupiter, there'll be something a hell of a lot better for them to use than whatever might be bouncing around inside my head. The bastards would like nothing better than to get their hands on some nice, shiny new ship systems just waiting to be taken apart and analyzed."

Kramer's tone hardened as well. "Agreed, Dan, which is why you need to let *me* be the one to take them to Jupiter." He laughed without humor. "I think I know how to take ships somewhere under remote control, and I can hardly miss a place as large as Jupiter. At that point, who gives a damn whether our friends with the Space Command are pissed off and get their hands on me? After the ships become part of the Great Red Spot, there isn't much they can get out of me that they couldn't figure out for themselves. In the meantime, while they're worrying about me, you'll be on Mars, where you can be ready to get things going again once the madness has stopped."

A streak of frustration flashed across Bacas's face. "Damn it, Gus, these ships are *my* responsibility! That means there are times where I have to be ready to accept the blame if something goes wrong. I can't really do that if I'm sitting on my ass, safe and sound on Mars, while the prizes didn't get protected."

"*You're* a prize too, Dan, although right now you're being more of a pain in the ass." Kramer's voice softened.

"Come on, Dan, you know I'm right. We'll need you more than ever soon enough." Kramer's hand reached out to Bacas's for closure, which Bacas wasn't ready to accept.

He shrugged it away. "We're wasting time arguing, Gus."

"I already have the crews attaching the remote thrusters to the ships," Kramer countered, "so the only time that's being wasted is getting you into a ship to Mars. Besides, you haven't considered how the crew will react. They know just as well as I do what it would mean if you were captured. If you insist on taking the ships to Jupiter, they'll *all* follow instead of heading for Mars." Kramer waved in their direction as he added, "If you don't give a damn about yourself, how about giving a damn about them?"

Bacas was silent for a moment as he placed his face in his hands. *I've never shirked my responsibilities in my life,* he thought. *No matter what I do, I'll be shirking at least some of them.* He looked at Kramer. "OK, Gus, I'll make a deal with you. I'll head out to Mars the moment I see you head out with the ships toward Jupiter. I have to be able to say that I didn't bug out without even knowing if you guys had the thrusters facing the right way!"

Kramer grinned. "Fair enough, Dan, although if they're facing the wrong way, that's only because you taught us to do it like that!" He reached out to Bacas again. This time Bacas accepted the gesture, reluctantly, and they shook hands. He handed the EMP device to Kramer, and their eyes met. Kramer nodded silently toward the device in his hands and left.

Bacas was aboard his transport, waiting with increasing anxiety at each passing minute. Five of the ships had been fitted with remote thrusters and were already lined up just outside the yard, ready to depart. The final adjustments had just been made to the thrusters for the last ship. As the ship was being towed into the line, Bacas could see from the panel that Space Command was closing on their location. As the line departed for Jupiter, Kramer contacted Bacas and said, "We're heading out, Dan, so it's time for you to get going too. Make sure they don't catch you."

Bacas pointed to a display. "I've already disabled the location beacon for my ship, so they can't track me that way. The Space Command isn't yet in visual range, and it isn't easy to track what they can't see. Besides, if they have to choose between people heading who knows where and ships with core technology, they'll go after the core technology. His expression tightened. "There's no way they won't be able to see *you*, lined up like a fashion show, so get up to speed as fast as possible. I hope you don't have to use the EMP device I gave you, but if you can't get to Jupiter in time, destroy as much of the key systems as you can." Bacas headed out, with the display showing Space Command ships closing in rapidly.

CHAPTER SIXTEEN

As the lead Space Command vessel closed on the Citadel Group yard, an officer stood on the bridge, keenly interested in the ships that were departing from their destination at high speed. He turned to the officer standing nearby and swore in frustration. "Damn it, we're supposed to capture those ships so we can see how they work, instead of watching them get away. I want those ships under our control, now! I also want to know who the hell tipped them off about us in the first place."

Captain Len Murphy looked at the officer coolly. "As far as who tipped them off, Major, that's not my problem. As far as going after those ships is concerned, whether we catch them depends on how good their remote thrusters are."

"It also depends on how good you and your men are, Captain."

Murphy stared at the major for a full ten seconds before saying, "Major Roetter, even though you aren't in the Space Command, I've been given orders to help you with your mission. I'm a good soldier, and I follow orders.

Don't forget, however, that you're still a guest on my ship. While you might still surprise me, so far you haven't shown that you know jack shit about how these ships operate." Murphy's eyes narrowed. "I don't need someone like you trying to tell me my business in running my ship. I sure as hell don't need any suggestions from you on whether my people are good enough to go after those ships. If they can be captured, we'll do it. If they can't, it won't be because we're a bunch of screw-ups."

There was more than a hint of menace in Roetter's face as he said, "I know enough to know that those ships are heading for Jupiter. I also know that if we don't capture those ships, I'll make sure that my superiors know it was because you let them outrun you."

Murphy hadn't become a ship captain by being easily intimidated. "You make whatever reports you want, Major. For now, I suggest that you and your people stay the hell out of the way of my crew." Murphy left without another word.

As he entered engineering, he found his chief engineer gripping a rail to hold himself in place as he watched some panels. He turned to greet Murphy.

"Captain, I see we're chasing after some of the ships from the Citadel Group's yard."

Murphy nodded toward a display as he replied, "Can we catch them, Chief?"

The chief shrugged. "It depends on what tricks Dan Bacas has up his sleeve. He's something of a legend as far as his engineering know-how is concerned. Ships that come out of his yard seem to work better than ships that come out of any other yard around here."

"We're not chasing his yard, Chief; we're chasing some remote thrusters."

The chief motioned toward the display as he replied, "He has the advantage of using every thruster available in his yard and setting them all to full throttle without giving a damn whether they'll be burned out at the end of the journey, Captain. If he's really heading to Jupiter to ditch those ships, and he probably is, then he doesn't even need to worry about deceleration. Those ships will just head straight down to the surface, and we'll never see them again."

"Still, they're just thrusters. We should be able to overtake them."

I'd love to have those thrusters, the chief thought. His grip on the rail tightened, and he couldn't keep the envy out of his voice "They have a head start on us, Captain. Also, Citadel's been using some pretty powerful thrusters, instead of the gutless ones our yards use. He's probably also done something to them to increase the power further. It doesn't have to be pretty; it just has to last long enough for a one-way trip. On the other hand, *we* don't have that luxury. You know as well as I do how dangerous it is to stress our engines beyond their maximum-rated safe speed. We'll also have to worry about decelerating or changing course at some point as we approach Jupiter, if we don't want to follow those ships straight down."

Murphy pressed, "Can we get close enough to disable them somehow? What about interfering with the signals so that the thrusters either cut out entirely or start to veer off in another direction?"

The chief replied, "While we have a chance of overtaking them before they reach Jupiter, we won't be in

range much before then to even try something like that."
There was a hint of admiration in his voice as he continued. "Their course appears to be a straight shot, relatively speaking, taking into account the gravity fields the
ships will encounter on the way. That means that once
their thrusters have gotten them to their maximum acceleration, they may be able to avoid having to use them
continuously. They might need the thrusters for minor
course corrections or to maintain speed if gravity from
somewhere along the way starts to slow them down. Since
they're heading for Jupiter anyway, that shouldn't be
much of a problem for them. Unless you want to push
our engines beyond their maximum-rated safe speed,
we'll have to wait a few hours to know whether we can
catch them, Captain."

Murphy shook his head. "Stay at maximum safe
speed, Chief, and keep an eye on her. There isn't any
reason to endanger the crew or the ship."

The chief and Murphy had known each other for a long
time and usually were able to work well together without
needing to ask a lot of questions. *This isn't one of those times,*
the chief thought. He paused for a moment before asking,
"With respect, Captain, why are we chasing them at all? I
haven't seen anything stating that war has been declared. It
doesn't seem right to treat someone like Bacas as an enemy.
I got to know him a year ago and he's a good man, which
is more than I can say about some of the 'soldiers' we've
taken on board. They aren't from Space Command, and
they don't always know when to stay the hell out of the way.
Some of them even seem to think they can give orders to my
men. There'll be hell to pay if they don't back off."

We're following them because something is screwed up some-where big time, Murphy thought. *That asshole Roetter is as twisted as they come, but I can't say any of that directly to the chief.* Murphy wasn't able to hide the look of displeasure on his face, though. "I'll tell you what I told Major Roetter, Chief. I'm a good soldier and I follow orders. My orders say that if Roetter wants to chase and capture those ships, we are to help him chase and capture those ships."

Murphy shrugged as he continued. "I don't have any more use for them than you do, but my orders don't say I have to like it, and neither do yours. I haven't been able to figure out just where they're from. I know that they don't give a damn about why people like you and me joined Space Command. The way I see it, the sooner we help them complete their mission, the sooner we get them the hell off our ships."

The giant planet had filled up their forward screens for hours now, with the Great Red Spot beckoning them like the biggest bulls-eye of all. Gus Kramer was still feel-ing the pressure, as the Space Command ships had been closing the distance slowly on them. He took another look at the thrusters. *That's not a good sign*, he thought. *Most of them aren't firing anymore.*

Kramer, at least, was at the front of the line. At the rear was another ship from the yard. He figured his assistant was feeling the pressure even more, since the Space Command ships would look even larger in her aft screens. He contacted her. "Denise, how're things look-ing at the end of the line?"

Denise Vickers had looked at the same thrusters and was even more worried. "I don't have to tell you how close the Space Command ships are to us, Gus. Our ships are doing well so far, but it wouldn't take much to shift them into an orbit around Jupiter instead of straight down. It would really suck if we've taken them this far only to have to leave them where they could be collected at the Space Command's leisure for analysis."

"How are the thrusters holding out?"

Vickers shook her head as she motioned to a split screen. "You have the same data I do, and the visual exam from this end of the line doesn't show anything different. While a few of them are still functioning, most of them are pretty much burned out at this point. It's a good thing the course was fairly straightforward, because there isn't much left in the thrusters to handle a major course change."

Kramer motioned at the same images. "I'm worried that the Space Command might be able to adjust the course of our last ship by sending a signal to some of the thrusters. Are they close enough to try?"

"Just about there now," Vickers replied. "We didn't have time to fully shield the thrusters from all outside signals, so they might be able to cause some mischief. We'll have to be ready to cut the thrusters loose and rely on forward momentum."

Kramer frowned. "That's just inviting trouble. They might be able to send a signal to screw with the thrusters if we leave them running. Let's shut those thrusters down now and make them think of something else to stop us."

"OK, Gus." She looked away for a moment before saying, "The thrusters are shutting down. Anything else?"

"With six ships to guard and only two ships for escort, I can't keep my ship ready to back you up. I have three ships in front to worry about, so you're on your own, Denise. Good luck."

The view from the forward screen of the lead Space Command vessel was spectacular. A Keith Thomas class transport loomed directly ahead, with everything framed by Jupiter itself. They were close enough that neither the dark background of space nor any of the distant stars from that background was visible. Major Roetter and Captain Murphy were both on the bridge. Roetter turned for a moment toward Murphy as he said, "I hope to God that we're finally close enough to get our hands on those ships, Captain. Your career depends on it."

Murphy didn't bother looking at Roetter as he spoke through his link. "Are we in range, Chief?"

The chief replied, "We're just barely in range, Captain. We probably don't have more than ten minutes left to make this work. As you can see from the image, they've shut down their thrusters and are relying on existing momentum to take them to Jupiter. I think we can startle the hell out of them and wake up some of their thrusters. We're ready to send a signal to the last transport's thrusters to begin a shift in course. With luck, we'll get it into orbit instead of a crash landing."

Roetter's face was red with anger. "Damn it, Captain, I want *all* of those ships captured, not just the easiest one to reach! We'd have made it here sooner if you'd had the courage to push the speed of your ships."

Murphy's face reflected extreme cold rather than the heat that was on Roetter's face as he turned back to the man. "Major, the last ship isn't the *easiest* one to reach; it's the *only* one we can reach. We've stayed at maximum safe speed the entire time to catch up to them, which is dangerous as hell. Pushing the ships beyond their maximum safe speed over a sustained stretch is a good way to ensure that *none* of those ships will be captured." Murphy turned away from Roetter as he said to the chief, "Go ahead, Chief; nudge that last ship into orbit."

On board Vickers's ship, she began to curse as she saw the last ship in line start to veer off course. Kramer answered her call immediately. "We have a problem, Gus. The Space Command sent a command to the thrusters for the last ship, which is now veering off course."

"Can you get it back onto the correct path?"

Vickers gave the order to the thrusters only to see that nothing happened. "We're screwed, Gus. The thrusters aren't responding."

Kramer scowled, not at Vickers but at himself as he said, "Shit! I should have had us disable the thrusters when we shut them down so this couldn't happen."

Vickers was upset as well. "This is on both of us, Gus, because I should have seen it too. Shutting them down *should* have been enough, because they're pretty much burned out at this point and shouldn't even be able to come back online after being shut down. Our friends back there happened to find a few that can still function."

"I don't think there's anything the Space Command can do with the other ships now," Kramer said. "If they could, they would have done it to screw us up even more. They're far enough ahead to be out of range of any attempts to take them over, and the forward momentum should be enough at this point anyway. Where do we stand with the thrusters for the last ship?"

Vickers's voice was tight as she answered. "The damage is done. We need them to get the transport back on its path, but they won't respond to instructions to make course corrections. I've taken them offline and disabled them so that they can't be used by our friends again." Vickers's face and voice showed her agitation as she continued, "Damn it, Gus, we were so close to making it! If we ever see him again, how the hell can we look Bacas in the eye and tell him we let him down?"

Kramer chuckled with grim humor. "We have one last option, although it guarantees that we'll be guests of the Space Command if we survive. Care to try it?"

As Vickers realized what Kramer had in mind, she chuckled with the same grim humor. "Hell, yes, Gus. At least we can help Citadel avoid a shutout!"

Something other than a frown finally appeared on Major Roetter's face as the last ship began to veer from its path to destruction. Murphy wasn't sure the change was an improvement. Roetter said, "Finally, something has gone right around here, Captain Murphy. It's a good thing for you that the last ship is a Keith Thomas class transport. It has pretty much everything we need. We can take the time to check it out while we head to Citadel with the other transports."

"Why won't *any* Keith Thomas transport do?" Murphy asked.

"We've already captured a number of ships of that class, and we expect to capture a final one shortly. However, we need every one of those ships to make the trip to Citadel, to make sure we can capture the derelict and keep Austin away from it with a large show of strength. This one wouldn't work for that trip because it hasn't finished its testing for deep-space operations and doesn't have a crew assigned. We don't know enough about the operation of these ships to try to run them ourselves, so this ship isn't going anywhere except back to Earth under tow."

Instead of responding to Roetter and showing his contempt for the man, Murphy turned away, keeping his thoughts to himself. *You guys are idiots for wanting to take even one of these ships to Citadel, let alone a bunch of them, when you don't know how they work.*

The chief spoke. "Sorry to interrupt, Major, Captain, but that ship may not be going back to Earth, either. Take a look."

Roetter was shocked at what he saw. "What the hell are they doing?"

The two escort ships were no longer running parallel to the line, but had maneuvered into direct contact with the last ship. They watched as portions of the two ships crumpled from the stress of the contact. The ships' own engines were overloaded in a desperate gambit to send the transport to its doom.

The chief replied, "It's just like it looks—they're moved their own two ships over to the transport and are trying to push it back onto the original path. Doing it is pounding the hell out of their ships, though. We'll probably have to pick them up." *God, what balls they have,* he thought with more than a little admiration.

Roetter's voice was icy. "I want you to destroy those two ships."

Murphy was aghast. "You can't be serious, Major! We're not at war with them, and they aren't committing any aggressive acts against this ship."

"Your orders are to obey my orders, Captain. I order you to destroy those ships immediately."

"My orders are to assist you in the capture of those ships, Major. They don't include killing civilians that don't represent any threat to this ship."

"They represent a threat to our attempts to capture those ships."

Murphy stared hard at Roetter as he said, "I won't do it, Major."

"You'll do it or face a court martial, Captain."

"Speaking of a court martial, I'd face one for certain if I did what you want. Attacking unarmed civilians in these circumstances would be a war crime. In the Space Command, we don't commit war crimes."

A sneer crept into Roetter's voice. "If you're looking for a way to cover your ass, you can always say you were following orders. My orders mean it wouldn't be a war crime."

Murphy stared at Roetter with a different kind of coldness. "It's been settled since long before my grandfather was born that no one can give an order to commit a war crime. Nobody is going to commit one on this ship while I'm in command of it, Major. If you thought otherwise, you sure as hell don't understand what it means to be an officer in the Space Command."

There was a tense silence as the two men stared at each other, which was broken by the chief. "Captain, as we figured, they pretty much destroyed their two ships."

"Where is the transport headed, Chief?"

"They got it back on course, Captain. It's headed straight for planet side on Jupiter. There's nothing we can do to stop it now."

"Where are the people from their yard?"

"They're in a couple of escape pods."

Roetter spoke. "Those people are *my* prisoners, Captain. Bring them to me once you have them aboard."

Murphy didn't bother to respond to Roetter. "Let's pick them up, Chief. After we've checked them out and dealt with any injuries, bring them to Major Roetter."

Roetter was disappointed to learn that Bacas wasn't among the prisoners. Still, the man in front of him was the yard's second in command, so his technical knowledge would be useful to them. Kramer was standing before Roetter, with one of Roetter's men nearby with a rifle held in a lazy position that could be trained on the prisoner in an instant if necessary. "Where is Dan Bacas, Mr. Kramer?" he asked.

Kramer replied, "Not anywhere near you, Roetter."

Roetter slapped Kramer hard as he said, "You will call me 'Major Roetter' or 'sir,' Mr. Kramer. If I'm not in a good mood because of your attitude, then it will go harder for Ms. Vickers when I speak with her."

Kramer managed a half smile. "Did you practice that dialogue in front of a mirror, Roetter, or does it come naturally? Knowing that a piece of shit like you is pissed off will really make my day."

An instant later, Kramer's head snapped back from an even harder slap. This time, Kramer lunged for Roetter's throat but ended up on his knees, stars dancing around his vision as the guard brought his rifle down on Kramer's head with practiced brutality. Roetter paused for a moment, as there was some noise from outside the compartment. Murphy entered the compartment accompanied by three armed soldiers. He gave a quick nod to one of his soldiers, who moved toward Kramer and brought him back to his feet with much more care than the force that had slammed him to the deck. One of the other soldiers moved toward Roetter's guard and removed the rifle from the guard's hands in a quick jerk. The third soldier had already pointed his own weapon at the guard, so there was no trouble.

Murphy faced Kramer and said, "Please forgive my tardiness and the treatment you received, Mr. Kramer. I had planned on being present, but Major Roetter started without me."

Roetter was furious. "What are you doing here, Captain? This man is my prisoner and I haven't finished interrogating him."

Murphy looked at Roetter the way he might look at some shit on the bottom of his boot. "Your interrogation is over, Major. I told you already that there are certain things that don't happen on a Space Command ship. Mistreatment of prisoners is one of those things."

"You are being insubordinate, Captain!"

"I don't think so, Major. In spite of all your talk about your orders, I haven't seen any orders giving you the right to mistreat prisoners or attack civilian targets. If you think you have that authority, then I'll need to see it in writing from my chain of command. Until then, your authority on this ship is at an end. The reason for my delay in arriving here is that I have new orders to deliver you and your people to a Citadel Group transport that has just been captured. It looks like you were right about your taking a long journey out of this solar system to Citadel. While that's probably not good for Citadel, I can't say that I'm sorry to see you leave."

Roetter's face darkened. "I will hold you responsible for letting those ships get away and interfering with my interrogation, Captain. You can kiss your career good-bye."

Murphy was dismissive of the threat. "I don't know how or where you received your commission, Major, but *I* will be recommending charges against *you*. If you want to avoid a court martial of your own, I suggest you not come back to this solar system. In the meantime, stay away from the Citadel Group people on this ship, and from my people." Murphy thought, *You'd better not get too close to any airlocks, either, asshole!*

CHAPTER SEVENTEEN

S ara Albretti found herself tied to a chair, with her arms bound behind her. She was still trying to take in everything that had happened. She'd been looking forward to arriving back in Earth's solar system. She had a lot to share with her family, particularly her mother and her grandfather.

Her ship had appeared just outside Earth's solar system as they'd taken their warp-field generators offline and collapsed their warp bubble. They'd been puzzled by the apparent silence on the communications beacon, although they weren't alarmed. It had taken a lot of effort to get it working in the first place, and another glitch might have happened to take it back offline. She didn't worry about it, as another transport was in the area and approaching. They'd confirmed that the beacon was in need of repair and that communications to Earth's solar system had been affected as well. They'd asked to come aboard, and Sara hadn't seen any reason to say no.

Before they knew what was happening, armed men and women had swarmed out of the shuttle and taken over the transport. As she turned to try to get word about the danger to any of her crew, she'd been stunned with something and found everything around her fading to an unthinking darkness.

She had no idea how long she'd been out. Her head reacted as a series of staccato sounds echoing off the deck brought her mind back into focus. Someone walked into the room. Bright lights surged against her face, practically blinding her. A moment later, the lights went down to a normal level, and Sara could see an unfamiliar face looking back at her.

"Who the hell are you?" she asked.

"My name is Major Roetter. I work for the United States National Security Authority. As of now, I am in charge of this vessel."

"Since when does the US government engage in piracy, Roetter?" A moment later, Sara's head was reeling from a hard slap across her face. Roetter was pleased. *Damn, it's good to be able to do this without any Space Command idiots watching over my shoulder. Now, I can do what I need to do.*

Roetter's face showed little emotion as he said, "That was necessary to ensure that we don't get off to the wrong start. When you talk to me, you will call me 'Major', 'Major Roetter', or 'sir.'"

"As far as I'm concerned, you're just a pirate until you've explained yourself."

Roetter thought for a moment and said, "Very well, Captain Albretti." He noticed her reaction. "Yes, we know about your recent marriage to Joe Albretti. We know quite a lot about you. We can save that conversation for another time, however.

"Pursuant to authority granted by the president of the United States, the United States has taken control of this vessel."

Sara was confused. "Why would the US be interested in this vessel?"

"The United States is actually interested in all of Citadel's vessels, including this one. The US has determined that certain actions must be taken against Citadel in order to ensure the security of this solar system."

"What actions?"

"You don't need to know all of them, but as of this time, the US has taken control of all of the Citadel Group's operations on Earth and elsewhere within this solar system."

She was aghast. "I don't believe you! Those are acts of war! There's no reason for the US to go to war with Citadel. Citadel has never done anything even remotely hostile toward this solar system. In fact, if it weren't for Citadel, you probably wouldn't even be here right now. I should know, because I was in command of the other ship that worked with Sam Austin to take out the alien invaders. For all I know, you're just a rogue operative trying to sell an insane scheme for God knows what reason."

"I won't try to justify the actions of my government to you," Roetter replied, still showing little emotion. "I'm satisfied when I've been informed that the United States has intelligence to the effect that Citadel is withholding from this solar system important technology that Citadel has obtained from studying the derelict craft that is just outside its solar system."

"That's news to me," she said with a puzzled look. "I was there when they first started looking at the derelict. They couldn't even figure out how to get inside the thing, let alone learn anything else about it. Unless something has changed since I was there, your intelligence is full of it."

With a little more emotion, Roetter said, "It doesn't really matter whether you believe me, so long as you cooperate with your part of my mission. We have been ordered to take this ship and the other Citadel transports to Citadel and take control of the derelict."

"Good luck," Sara challenged. "You don't know anything about running something as complex as this ship, and I'm not going to help you."

Roetter didn't show any worries over her words. "While you are correct that we can't run this ship by ourselves, you are wrong about your not helping us. We are at war and I have my orders, so I will do whatever it takes to carry out those orders." Roetter made a quick motion toward the hatch. One of his men brought in a maintenance engineer and forced the man down to his knees. His hands had been tied behind his back. From the waves of pain rippling across his face, it was clear that they hadn't been gentle in subduing him.

Roetter didn't bother looking at the man. "This man is one of your maintenance engineers. Although that title sounds ordinary, I believe that means he is responsible for helping to maintain the proper functioning of your warp-field generators. You have several other people who perform a similar function, which means I don't need this man." Roetter's man reacted to a slight nod from his superior by pulling out his pistol and aiming it at the engineer's head.

Roetter continued. "You have ten seconds to decide whether to help us take this ship to Citadel. If you refuse, my colleague will shoot this man. I will then select someone else and bring him here. He too will die if you continue to refuse to cooperate with us." Roetter checked his watch. "Time's up." There was no response from her, so Roetter nodded toward his colleague. A brief moment later, the engineer was slumped over with a bullet hole in his head.

Sara's bonds left her unable to wipe away the shocked tears that streamed down her face at the loss of a fine man. Roetter said to his colleague, "Bring in the next person."

"Wait!" she cried out. "Don't kill anyone else."

"Will you help us take this ship to Citadel?"

"Yes."

Roetter waited a full ten seconds before asking, "Yes, what?"

His captive shed angry tears this time as she said, "Yes, Major."

A satisfied look crossed his face as he said, "Thank you, Captain Albretti. You will inform your crew about the change in circumstances. We are bringing supplies out to this ship from the one that brought us here. Your ship was the last one we needed, so once the supplies have been loaded, we will head out. You can do the math, so there's no point in denying that we'll be under a tight timeframe. We need to get to the Citadel solar system in time to take control of the derelict before it drifts into the Citadel system.

"While you might think this presents you with an opportunity to interfere with our plans, we won't tolerate any interference or insubordination from anyone during this trip," Roetter warned.

At some point during her capture, restraint, and face slap, the front of her jumpsuit had been torn open. Although the view was nothing like what she'd provided to Joe, it was still enough to make her uncomfortable in the wrong company, and Roetter was anything but the right company. He made a point of gazing down at her partially exposed breasts with a brazen look. "This ends the lesson. Don't make it necessary for me to provide you with another one. If you do, don't count on your husband being interested in what would be left of you."

At a nod from Roetter, someone stepped behind her and removed her bonds. As the sound of her captors' footsteps faded, she fell to the deck, in desperate need of a shower.

Later, while Sara was in her cabin, still unsettled from the murder, Roetter called her to the ship's bridge. He demanded that she provide a list of the weapons carried by the transport and access to the weapons and the core technology files. She refused, explaining, "First of all, the technology files are encrypted, and none of us has the encryption key."

Roetter was skeptical. "Do you expect me to believe that you can't get access to the technology files for your own ship?"

Her gaze at Roetter was steady as she answered. "I don't care what you believe, Major. Somehow our security protocols were activated while your people were taking over our operations. Once our ship reached the communications beacon, the protocols encrypted our files automatically. I didn't even know about it until you brought it to my attention."

"Who has the encryption key?" Roetter demanded.

"Sam Austin is the only one with it," she was glad to say. "It's a security feature to prevent our ships from being misused."

Roetter's skepticism increased. "I suppose you're going to tell me that the ship's weapons are locked out as well?"

Sara's gaze turned cool. "That's exactly what I'm telling you, Major. It's part of the security protocols. This ship can't be used for offensive purposes unless we say so."

"I want your engineers to uninstall the ship's weapons and separate them from the firing mechanism so that we can use them manually," Roetter ordered. "For an analogy, think of the way a car's ignition key used to be able to be bypassed so that the car could be started."

"That analogy doesn't work very well, Major," she replied. "As you may know, modern transports can't be bypassed like that; everything is integrated. The same is true for this ship and things like its weapons. Separating the weapons from the launch mechanism will just end up destroying critical components. This isn't a warship, and we don't have backup weapon systems."

She waved vaguely astern. "The only place where it might be possible to do what you suggest is a space yard. You've probably noticed that we don't have one en route. Besides, even if we could do what you want, you'd have to dismantle part of the ship to do it. We can't do it while we're in this warp-field bubble, and you've already pointed out that time is of the essence."

She reeled from the hard slap to the face as her captor said, "I don't like your tone, Captain. I think you're playing games with me and have more options than you'd like to admit." Roetter looked around the bridge. "I'm going to find out with one of your people on this bridge. If you don't tell me the truth, you'll have another death on your conscience."

The coolness faded from her face as she cried, "Damn it, I *am* telling the truth!"

The assistant chief engineer happened to be on the bridge. Roetter had him brought close to Sara and pointed a pistol at the man's head. Roetter said to the man, "What about it, Assistant Chief Engineer? Is the captain telling me the truth, or are there other options to get access to any of your weapons?"

The man looked at Roetter without flinching. "The captain is telling the truth, Major. The weapons can't be brought back online until the encryption key unlocks everything. The key isn't located anywhere but Citadel."

Roetter looked around the bridge. "Anyone else interested in saving his life?" There was a terrible silence. Roetter shrugged and squeezed the trigger. In an instant, the man was on the deck, dead from a single shot to the head. With a lack of emotion, Roetter said, "I guess you were telling the truth after all." As he looked around the bridge, no one other than Sara would meet his gaze. "I have another question, and I expect it to be answered promptly."

Roetter looked back at Sara. "Can the other systems still be used, such as towlines, remote probes, thrust generators, et cetera, to shift the derelict away from the Citadel solar system?"

She considered the cost of not answering the question to be too high and answered, "Yes, Major, those systems can be used as you've suggested."

"I'm glad you didn't have to waste another life this time, Captain. We're heading out within the hour."

A look of disgust appeared on Roetter's face as he added, "Gather some of your people and get your former colleague's body off the bridge. He's left behind a mess. Clean it up."

CHAPTER EIGHTEEN

Captain Hank McKinney had been in command of Citadel transport *KT-5* for over seven months, and he had a major problem. The problem wasn't a new one, as men and women had been dealing with it for centuries. His problem related to the fact that *KT-5* had spent three months on a cargo run from Earth to Citadel. After a short layover, they had spent the last three months on a cargo run from Citadel back to Earth. McKinney hadn't seen his wife in all that time, and a lot of his thoughts of her were of the clothing optional variety. Most of the rest of the crew felt the same way about their loved ones.

It didn't help that they were carrying cargo instead of people, since new people on board often kept things lively. McKinney was glad that they were about to arrive home, as there were plenty of people on board who were becoming increasingly distracted by unrequited lust. McKinney had become aware of hints from some of the women who considered him a more than satisfactory means of dealing with their own lust. A rueful thought flashed through his mind. *Some of them have been looking pretty good to me too. It's been getting harder and harder to stay focused on the job lately. I'm damned glad I'm due for some leave when we get back, because I'd rather spend it in bed with my wife instead of being exiled to a lumpy couch or worse.*

He frowned as he thought about a couple of people who he suspected would have some explaining to do to their spouses when they got back to Earth. As long as what they did during their private time didn't hurt their performance or the performance of the rest of the crew, he didn't concern himself.

His frown dissolved as he thought about a few of his crew members who were the envy of the rest of the crew. Those few were married to each other and didn't have to worry about putting their sex lives on hold for the duration. While McKinney knew that that could create some issues for the rest of the crew, he was clear that everyone else would have to deal with it or look for an assignment on another ship.

McKinney arrived on the bridge and looked over to his navigator for an update. She nodded as she saw him. She'd been among the women on the ship that had hinted at being interested in a different kind of navigation in her quarters. She knew their arrival back in Earth's solar system meant that nothing was going to happen, but she wasn't a bad sport about it. She knew he'd been tempted, but respected his decision to avoid problems with his wife. They'd be able to remain friends and colleagues and work together. "Good day, Captain," she said.

"Good day, Amy," he replied. "Are we ready to return to the real world?"

Amy Soren replied, "All stations show we're ready, Captain."

"Tell the chief to bring us out of the warp bubble."

They watched as the image on the large main monitor changed from unremarkable darkness to a familiar image of stars and dust framed by endless swathes of black.

Soren frowned as she noticed something that wasn't a normal part of the picture. There were three ships heading toward them at high speed in what could only be described as an intercept formation. "Captain, we have company, and it's coming in fast. They look like they want to be sure we stick around for a talk."

McKinney was puzzled. "Why would anyone give a damn about our arrival? Check out the chatter from the solar system and find out what's been happening while we've been away. Can you identify the ships?"

"They aren't any of our ships, Captain. Judging by the size, best guess is that they're some of the larger patrol ships that the Space Command uses to throw its weight around."

"Why the hell would they want to do that?" McKinney wondered. "We're not at war." McKinney's face took on an alarmed look. "I hope there isn't a new problem with aliens!"

Soren's had an odd expression as she said, "I can't raise any chatter from around the solar system, which is strange. I'd swear someone was trying to jam the signals, although I don't know who would do that." Her face went pale as she listened to something. "I think you'd better listen to this message, Captain. It's from the Citadel Group."

"Pipe it in so everyone on the bridge can hear it."

They began to feel ill as they listened to the words.

"To Citadel Transport *KT-5*, this is Ambassador Preacher. There isn't any time for greetings, so listen carefully. You are most probably being approached right now by multiple ships from the US Space Command. Under no circumstances must you allow them to board your ship. The president of the United States has launched what has amounted to an unofficial war against Citadel. If you are boarded, Space Command soldiers will attempt to place you under arrest and seize control of your ship. This has already happened with other Citadel transports, so this is a fact, not an idle speculation. The crews of the other Citadel transports have been forced to take the transports, along with Space Command soldiers, back to Citadel, with the objective of taking control of the derelict and taking other actions against the local authorities as the situation permits. Your ship would be taken back to Earth and dismantled and studied to enable the US to understand Citadel's core technologies.

"You may have already noted that you are unable to make contact with anyone within Earth's solar system. This is because the US has disabled the Citadel beacon nearby and has been jamming all communications originating from the solar system. You may wonder why you are able to receive this message. The reason is straightforward—we built capabilities into the beacon that were not publicized. While the beacon cannot send messages to Citadel at present, it can transmit encrypted messages to key Citadel locations in this solar system. Your transport's communications system has an automatic link to the specialized frequencies used by the beacon.

"You may be thinking about your options. The first thing to note is that all of your transport's core technologies have been placed into an encrypted status and your ship's weapons have been taken offline. This is a protective measure that was intended to limit the value of capturing the transports, but it didn't take into account the current situation. While you may be able to rig up alternative weapons to defend yourselves against the Space Command ships, using them in this instance would make the phony war a real one, which we want to avoid at all costs.

"Your best option at this point is to set course for Mars, if you have an open path available. Mars will offer sanctuary to Citadel's people and ships. However, if you are unable to get to Mars, then there may not be another location within this solar system that is safe for you. Your next best option may be to return to Citadel, although you might find yourselves outnumbered by the ships that have already been captured. You will have to make the best decision you can based on your assessment of the situation. Whatever you do, don't allow the US to capture the knowledge that would enable it to destroy the grand experiment that has been Citadel. Good luck and Godspeed."

McKinney broke the silence by asking Soren, "How long before the Space Command ships are within range, Amy?"

"We're already in range of their weapons, Captain. The way they've bracketed us, we can't get around them to get into the solar system without something nasty happening. They're hailing us."

"Let's hear it."

A courteous voice said, "Welcome back, *KT-5*. We hope all is well. We have an urgent situation that we need to discuss immediately. We request permission to come aboard your ship to discuss it."

McKinney replied, "What is the nature of your situation?"

"We can't really talk about it over communications that might be monitored, Captain McKinney. The conversation needs to be face-to-face. We're sending over our shuttles now."

"Hold up, Space Command. I haven't given you permission to come aboard, and I won't do it until I know what this is about. Why are your ships circling us like we're a target?"

"We're doing this for your protection, Captain. We insist that you let our people on board. Everything will be cleared up the moment we get aboard and talk with you."

"It doesn't take multiple shuttles to have a conversation, Space Command. Send over a two-person escape pod, and we can talk. You can understand my position; I don't want to expose my people to whatever is the situation until I know what it is."

The courtesy drained from the speaker's voice. "We're going to have to insist on doing it our way, Captain McKinney. You can't go anywhere; you are surrounded. Our shuttles will be there in just over a minute. You will let them in when they arrive. We can make it a lot harder for you if you make it harder for us." The transmission ended.

McKinney looked around the bridge and then back to Soren. His face was dark with anger. "Amy, is there any direction still available to us?"

Soren glanced over her shoulder. "We can still head back the way we came, Captain. We'd need to make a one-hundred-eighty degree turn, but they can't get their shuttles out of the way of their weapons before we can complete the turn."

McKinney chuckled without humor. "Do it now, Amy, and tell the chief to get ready to get us the hell out of here!"

As the ship began to rotate, a message came in from Space Command: "*KT-5*, what are you doing? You are ordered to stand down and permit our shuttles to board your ship."

McKinney nodded to Soren as he responded. "Sorry, Space Command, but there's been a slight delay. I just realized that I left the water running back on Citadel. You know how it is—I have to get back there before the entire planet is flooded!"

Before Space Command could respond, *KT-5* vanished, with a slight spatial distortion being the only evidence she had just been there.

The large monitor once again showed nothing but the same darkness they had seen for the last three months. No one was watching it as McKinney held a war conference on the bridge. They struggled to deal with the fact that their entire world had just been turned upside down. Soren asked, "Are we really going back to Citadel, Captain?"

McKinney replied, "We have to weigh the benefits against the consequences, Amy. On the one hand, I doubt they'd expect us to show up, which means we'd have the element of surprise on our side. We might be able to help even the odds a bit."

"We wouldn't have any weapons."

"Neither would they, if the encryption protocols apply to all of Citadel's ships."

"They may be able to talk their way into getting control of their weapons reinstated. Besides, they'd still outnumber us, Captain. Since they're military, we have to assume that they also have the training for this situation. Although we've had some training as well, it might not be enough to keep them from putting us out of commission permanently. Also, we're still three months away from Citadel. It's hard to see how showing up three months late is going to help."

The chief spoke. "One other reason not to head back to Citadel is that we haven't had an opportunity to do an inspection of the warp-field generators. They've been hard at work for three months, and we brought them offline and then did an emergency restart, which is even harder on them. We might do fine, or we might be buying ourselves some major trouble if we just head back to Citadel for another solid three months. If we have a breakdown out in the middle of nowhere, we might not see any roadside assistance for a long time!"

McKinney nodded reluctantly. "I see your point, Chief. The inspection needs to take place in a yard, doesn't it?"

"Yes, Captain. While we could try to check things out by ourselves, that's a half-assed approach compared to what we would be doing in a yard. However, if we don't plan on taking any trips where we need to sustain a warp-field bubble for an extended period, I think we'll be fine."

Soren had a calculating look. "The chief's comments are a reminder that one of our strongest advantages is our warp-field capability, and we should make full use of it. While it might look like we've gone back to Citadel, they can't afford to make that assumption. There's nothing that says we have to try to enter this solar system from the same place as everyone else. The problem for them is the solar system is far too large to cover everywhere, especially near the edges. Their best bet is to deploy back toward certain strategic locations and hope they can intercept us before we can reach Mars."

The other faces in the room showed keen interest as McKinney said, "What do you have in mind, Amy?"

"Right now, Earth and Mars are pretty damned far apart from each other in their orbits. There's no way the Space Command can simply set up a blockade around Mars, as that would be an act of war. Therefore, the Space Command has to respect the territorial integrity of Mars and keep to a proper distance. We could enter the solar system and make our way over to Jupiter and Saturn. As it happens, they're near enough to each other right now that we can use them as shields as we sneak into the asteroid belt. We can make our way through it quietly and do a fast run to Mars once we're close enough."

McKinney was still interested, but nervous. "There are long-range sensors in the solar system, Amy. They're there to detect aliens, but they'd do just as well in detecting us."

Soren shook her head. "First of all, they couldn't place long-range sensors *everywhere*. As far as the outer planets are concerned, they set their long-range sensors to look for ships as big as the one that invaded this solar system. Our ship is far smaller than an alien ship and might be able to slip under the radar. We have the benefit of knowing where the sensors are located, which should help.

"Even better, there are a lot fewer long-range sensors in the asteroid belt itself; the alien ships are too big to get through without worrying about collisions. It's a lot easier to bypass the asteroid belt altogether, which is what they did when they invaded. As big as this ship is, I should be able to work out an approach that avoids any collisions and stays away from the long-range sensors that are in the outer portion of the solar system. The tricky part will be avoiding the sensors in the asteroid belt. While there are plenty of areas where there aren't many asteroids, those are the places where many of the sensors are located."

"What about the mining operations?" the chief asked. "If they've been occupied by the Space Command, they could alert the patrol ships in time to intercept us before we can reach Mars."

Soren's expression faded to a somber look. "The only mining operations that might have been occupied are Citadel Group operations. It'll be a pain in the ass to work it out, but while we might not be able to keep out of sight of our mining operations entirely, I believe we can at least keep our exposure to a minimum."

The chief's face was equally somber as he said, "We might have to keep our fingers crossed that other mining operations won't report our presence to the Space Command."

McKinney had a hard look on his face. "That'll be *my* job. Let's hope that we aren't the only ones that don't like to be bullied."

McKinney was staring at the scrambled assortment of asteroids displayed on the monitor as he thought about the hours following their return. *So far, we've managed to get back into the solar system undetected, we hope. Thank God we could hide behind Jupiter and Saturn like Amy said. The sprint to the asteroid belt was interesting; it felt like our ship was an elephant trying to run through a field of grass, hoping no one noticed.* McKinney was pulled from his thoughts by Soren.

"We have another mining operation coming up, Captain," she called out.

"Which one?" McKinney asked.

"The Solomon Mines."

"Another one that's operated by an outfit located on Mars," he said with relief. "That should be a good sign. Still, I'd like to avoid being seen by them. Can we do it?"

Soren shook her head. "Not likely, Captain. There's not enough cover for us. This will be the first one that we can't get past without their cooperation. How do you want to play it?"

"Let's keep our distance. If they want to pretend they never saw us, they'll stay silent. If they want to talk to us, we'll respond and see how it goes."

Soren's eyes grew wider. "I guess it'll be the latter. They're giving us a call."

McKinney had to work to change the grimace on his face to a neutral expression as he told Soren to accept the call. He faced the main monitor as an image of a woman appeared. She was in her fifties, with a pair of eyes that were equally neutral but full of intelligence. She began the conversation. "My name is Gwen Somers, and I'm the superintendent of this mine. What brings you here, Captain McKinney?"

McKinney couldn't keep the look of surprise from his face as he replied, "The fact that you know who we are tells me that you also know why we are here, Superintendent."

The woman's tone was one of wry humor. "That sounds way too formal. Why don't you call me Gwen?"

McKinney matched her tone. "In that case, why don't you call me Hank?"

"Hank, tell me why you are here."

"Since you know who we are, you must know that we're trying to avoid the Space Command. They tried to arrest us just as we returned to this solar system, even though we haven't done anything wrong. What the hell's been happening since we've been gone?"

The humor left Somers's face. "A lot of people have concluded that President Harrington isn't very good at her job. She wants to be reelected anyway. She's decided to manufacture a crisis involving Citadel that she hopes will make enough people mad at Citadel instead of her so that she can get reelected. She has the Space Command out trying to round up every Citadel ship with any advanced technology that is in this solar system. Rumor has it that she's sent a bunch of those ships back to Citadel to stick it to them. For all we know, she may have already taken some of Citadel's ships apart to understand the technology. Your ship might be on the list as well."

McKinney was puzzled. "How do you know all this?"

Somers gave a humorless snort. "It's been clear for some time to the people who don't live on Earth what she's doing. The question that still needs to be answered is why no one on Earth has the balls to stop her from doing it."

McKinney shook his head, both at the news and at the hard question that needed to be asked. "Gwen, where do you stand on the Space Command's efforts to find us?"

A trace of anger passed across Somers's face, although it wasn't directed toward McKinney. "I remember what it was like when the aliens pounded the hell out of us on Mars, Hank. I was on leave back there with my husband. I happened to be in a relatively well-protected area below the surface. My husband wasn't so lucky; he was on the surface when his compartment was hit. While he had his spacesuit on, everything was such a mess that he was trapped. There was no way anyone could get to him before his environmental support systems would fail." A small tear appeared. "While I was preparing to deal with my husband's death, we received word that Sam Austin had ordered a diversion to Mars of the two transports that Citadel had at the time. They were able to rescue a lot of people that were trapped, including my husband. Sam even had additional supplies transported from Earth to keep us alive until we could complete our repairs."

She made a small gesture with her hands as she asked, "How do you thank someone who did what Sam Austin and the people of Citadel did for us? One way is to return the gesture if you can." Her tears were gone now as she looked fiercely at McKinney's. "As far as I'm concerned, you were never here. Everyone in this operation is from Mars and has stories that are similar to mine. It isn't hard to figure out where you're heading; I hope you reach Mars safely. From what I've heard, some of your people have already received sanctuary there; I'm sure you'd be welcomed too. You'd better not wait too long in any place until you are safe, so you should leave now. Go with our best wishes, Hank." A wry look crept back into her face as she added, "Don't bother trying to thank us; we already owe such a huge debt that it feels better to try to repay even a little of that debt without any thanks back to us."

The image of their unexpected friend vanished abruptly from the monitor. McKinney looked around at the faces of the people on the bridge and knew there was nothing more to say. He told Soren to continue on their path.

As they continued in their quest to reach Mars without detection, Soren shrugged her shoulders as if wrestling with a problem. McKinney noticed and asked her about it.

"Something that Somers said has me worried, Captain. She didn't have any trouble figuring out that we were trying to reach Mars. I'm wondering how big a stretch it would be for the Space Command to figure out what we're doing."

Now it was McKinney's turn to shrug his shoulders. "I don't know, Amy. Thanks to your navigating skills, we got into the solar system as carefully as possible, but someone might have gotten lucky and spotted us somehow. Even if we weren't spotted while trying to tiptoe around some awkward places, it isn't out of the question to work out in general terms where we'd have to emerge from the asteroid belt if we wanted to make a run for Mars. That still covers a lot of territory." McKinney raised an eyebrow. "Do you think we should have just hidden out of the solar system for a few months and hoped that everything blew over?"

Soren shook her head. "No, I don't think that would have worked. First, we don't have any idea what would happen after everything 'blows over'; it might even be worse than it is now. Second, I don't like just sitting around and not trying to help the Citadel Group somehow. There isn't much we can do to help from where we were, but maybe there's something we can do from Mars. I think it's worth the risk. I just hope we can get there OK."

McKinney straightened up, as if he'd figured out the answer to something important. As he left the bridge, he said, "Let me know when we're coming up on the next mining operation. I want to run something by the chief."

McKinney was already back on the bridge when Soren let him know about the mining operation that was up ahead. He asked, "Whose operation is it, Amy?"

The look on Soren's face told him the answer before she replied. "It's a Citadel Group operation, Captain. What's more, there doesn't seem to be as much chatter going on there as I'd expect."

McKinney gazed away toward the main monitor. "What are our chances of avoiding being seen by them?" he asked.

"The only way to do it would be to head past the cluster of asteroids over to the right." The dark patches under Soren's eyes reflected the strain of having to worry about navigational issues for hours. "They might have figured it out as well, which means someone could be on the other side of those asteroids, and we wouldn't see them until they had a chance to try to box us in. What do you want to do?"

"We don't have much choice. We're right on the edge of a cluster of Citadel Group mines, so we have to make a run for it now instead of later when they can get at us from multiple sites. If they're waiting for us, they have to stay hidden until we show up, or they'll lose the advantage from being able to choose where to spring the trap. They still have a lot of space to cover, so they can't afford to place a fleet nearby." McKinney voiced a grim thought. "Besides, it might not be such a bad idea to try to settle things while we're still among a bunch of asteroids. Take us past those asteroids on the right as you suggested, Amy."

As the ship edged toward the asteroids, McKinney turned toward Soren and spoke quietly. "When I give the word, I want you to make sure you know the exact course to get us the hell out of there. You need to assume that your visuals will be compromised and unreliable."

Soren's face showed puzzlement as well as an increase in energy as she asked, "What's going on, Captain?"

"The chief has put together something that should keep the odds from sucking so much. You'll need to plan on doing one or more double backs on our course so that the surprise will achieve its full effect. The moves will have to be quick, and you'll need to do this while our rear cargo hatches are open. Don't worry; the alarms will be disabled."

"Why would the cargo hatches be open?"

McKinney answered her wryly. "That's a question they'll probably want to ask at some point!"

KT-5 crept along the asteroid cluster, staying out of sight of the Citadel operation. All of the transport's exterior displays had been switched off in the hopes of making her as invisible as possible. Not surprisingly, the asteroids were rich with minerals, some of which were interfering with their ability to get clear readings on their surroundings. As they maneuvered around an impressive specimen, they found themselves practically surrounded by several much larger ones, any of which could crush them into unrecognizable debris. The monitors had been reconfigured to provide a complete view around them, including rear, above, and below. What dim light was available often faded into virtual blackness from the extensive shadows cast by the asteroids.

The same shadows that helped to conceal them could do the same for others. In an almost casual movement, a Space Command ship made an entrance from between two asteroids behind them, cutting off any chance of retracing their path. A few moments later, Space Command ships had emerged from the darkness on either side of them, hemming them in further. They were being guided past the only opening that could lead beyond the asteroids, and toward a dark outline in front that was taking on the appearance of another Space Command ship. The visuals from the monitors showed nothing but scenes of massive chunks of rock above and below them, moving slowly. The ship behind them was ready to close the distance rapidly if *KT-5* made any attempt to back up. They were boxed in.

McKinney didn't bother with any messages to the Space Command ships. He turned to Soren and said, "It's time to go back the way we came, Amy. Give us a hard one-hundred-eighty-degree turn and haul ass back to that opening." McKinney then spoke into his link. "OK, Chief, once we're done with the turn, let's send our surprise to our nearest three targets."

"You got it, Captain."

As *KT-5* carried out the turn, all four Space Command ships moved toward the Citadel ship. In their haste, they hadn't noticed that the rear and side hatches of their quarry were open, spilling out something that was practically invisible in the darkness. The ships that had been ahead or to the sides of *KT-5* became coated with the substance. McKinney spoke again to the chief. "Light up the place for these assholes, Chief. Amy, don't stop until we're right in front of the rear ship."

A moment later, there was a massive flare-up of light near the three ships that had been pursuing them. The Citadel ship's instruments could no longer get precise readings on much of anything in that direction. As expected, the original pursuit ship had reached the escape path and blocked it. Soren knew her stuff and brought *KT-5* practically bow to bow before backing off slightly and doing another one-hundred-eighty-degree turn. The pursuit ship didn't follow *KT-5*, knowing that none of its clever tactics would mean a thing in the long run if the escape path remained blocked.

Unfortunately for the people aboard the pursuit ship, they hadn't appreciated the entire purpose of the turn by *KT-5*. Once again, something spilled out of the open rear hatch, floating toward and coating the ship. A moment later, as *KT-5* pulled away, McKinney sent another message to his chief, and a massive flare of light erupted in front of and around the pursuit ship, blinding it as effectively as the other three ships. It was now just as difficult to get any readings on the vessel as it was on the other ships.

McKinney ordered several remote thrusters deployed toward the pursuit ship. Their sensors were useless, so they relied on old-fashioned visuals to attach the thrusters to the vessel. It would have been impossible to handle the extreme brightness without the heavy filters they used. There was no way to get a signal past the high interference, so they'd preprogrammed the thrusters to commence operations once they'd attached themselves to the ship. With an almost delicate touch from the devices, the ship began to move away from the opening. To make certain that the ship wouldn't be able to calculate its own escape through that path or back the way it had come, the thrusters had been instructed to apply a gentle spin to the ship as they moved it. Since the ship was blind, it would be madness to try to maneuver at all. The place was still a trap, but now it was the pursuers who were trapped.

As directed by McKinney, Soren had kept note of the escape path. *KT-5* practically inched its way along the path until at last there was only the blackness of the sky populated with stars instead of asteroids. As they headed along what was now an open path to Mars, Soren asked McKinney, "Just what the hell was that stuff, anyway?"

McKinney's temporary feeling of relief was visible in his grin as he said, "That stuff was a new ore that we've been mining. We happened to have a load aboard to have the Citadel Group take a look at. As we saw, it has some interesting properties!"

"Why would we carry something that dangerous on our ship?" Soren asked with alarm. "If anything got out of control, we'd be just as blind as the Space Command's ships."

The chief joined them and said, "I can answer that one. The stuff is pretty safe by itself. In fact, it just looks like some harmless dark powder. It requires some fairly intense agitation to make it do what it did. In our case, we had some distress flares that we rigged to go off after we dumped the stuff out the hatches. We have a pressure system to do emergency venting of the cargo holds, so we just adapted it to spray this stuff out toward their ships.

It was so dark out there they never saw the stuff or even knew our hatches were open. The first three ships were considerate enough to pass right through the powder."

The chief made a dramatic gesture with his hands. "Once the flares went off, the particles reacted and lit the hell out of everything." He grinned as he nodded toward Soren. "You did a great job of getting us nose to nose with the fourth ship. Once we were turned around, we sprayed them with some more of the stuff, with the same result."

Soren shook her head slightly in confusion. "It wasn't just bright lighting that was happening out there, Chief; I couldn't get any readings on their ships once the fireworks started. It was as if they were in the middle of a storm of interference."

McKinney nodded. "That's exactly what it was. The whole point was to screw up anything they could use to maneuver or locate us. Eventually, the bright lights will fade, but the interference will continue for quite a while. Even if they can stick their heads out their windows to watch where they're going, they won't dare travel at any kind of speed. It's way too dark outside to gamble on whether they can see anything ahead of them in time to avoid it. While we're pretty much clear of the asteroid belt, it'd be pretty stupid to assume that there aren't any stray rocks around."

"Can't they send a message to the mining operation asking for help?" Soren asked.

The chief snorted. "Hell no! So long as that interference continues, they can't send out any kind of signal. For now, the most they can do once the bright lights fade is to crawl back to the mining operations, and I mean *crawl*. One wrong move, and they're asteroid dust. Once they're back at the mining operations, they can send a message to Earth letting them know that their trap didn't work."

"Why don't we have the same problem?"

"We didn't get the stuff on our ship," the chief said with a satisfied chuckle. "I made damned sure we sprayed it out far enough that it wasn't going to be anywhere near us. Also, we never sprayed it until you had us facing the other way. By the time the flares went off, we were somewhere else in their 'trap.'"

"What kind of long-term damage will their ships have?"

The warmth faded from the chief's face as he said, "In view of what they've already done to the Citadel Group, it wouldn't bother me if their ships were toast without any access to a yard from this far out, but the interference is temporary. In fact, virtually all of the stuff will vaporize, so they might not even be sure what happened. It was too dark for them to see much of anything, and we haven't yet announced anything about the ore."

Hours had passed without incident, and they were finally closing on Mars and safety. McKinney spoke with the port officials: "This is Citadel Group transport *KT-5*, requesting asylum and permission to enter into Mars orbit."

The port responded, "Citadel Group transport *KT-5*, your request for asylum and permission to enter into Mars orbit is under consideration."

McKinney nodded at Soren as he replied, "Thanks, Mars; we'd appreciate a decision pretty quickly."

Soren frowned. "I hope they hurry things up in making that decision, Captain. It looks like we have three Space Command ships after us on an intercept course, and they're moving at high speed." She gave off a sarcastic sigh as she asked, "Don't these guys have something better to do?"

"Can we get to Mars before they catch us?"

Soren shook her head. "No. We'd have to do a hell of a dance to get around three ships this time. Let's hope they aren't in a 'shoot first, ask questions later' mode. If they are, it could get ugly." She looked at McKinney hopefully. "I don't suppose we could try another trick with that ore?"

McKinney shook his head. "No such luck, Amy. We already dumped most of what we had, and they'd probably see it coming this time and just move out of the way."

Soren tensed as she noted a new development. "Mars has just launched five ships on an intercept course. This is just what they'd do if they have decided to keep us the hell away so they don't have to take on any part of the fight with the US." Her face showed despair. "I'm sorry I can't promise you any fancy moves to save our asses this time, Captain. We can't take on three ships, let alone eight."

McKinney kept a hard gaze on the main monitor as he said, "Stay on course for Mars, Amy. If they really want to stay out of this fight, they'll have to get dirty to do it."

The bridge was unusually quiet as the eight ships grew rapidly in size on the monitors, along with Mars itself. "Which group will reach us first?" McKinney asked, an underlying tension plain in his voice.

"It'll be pretty close, although the ones from Mars probably have around a twenty-second advantage." Soren looked down at her panel. "I guess this is it, Captain. We're getting a message from the ships from Mars. If they were going to help us out, they'd be sending a message from the port. They're probably calling to tell us to stay the hell away."

"Let's hear it."

A calm voice filled the bridge. "Citadel Group transport *KT-5*, this is Mars defense patrol, instructing you to alter your course immediately."

McKinney replied, "Mars patrol, you realize what will happen to us if we comply?"

The voice remained calm. "Complying will be in your best interests, *KT-5*."

McKinney had trouble keeping the bitterness from his voice as he said, "I can see that it would be in your best interests, assuming that doing the right thing for a friend doesn't seem to be your intention."

The voice took on a laconic tone. "I thought that might be what you're thinking. If you folks would just shift slightly to your starboard, it would make it easier for my ship to slip past you so we can block your admirers from pursuing the chase."

McKinney was dumbstruck. "You're not ordering us away from Mars?" he blurted.

"Hell no, *KT-5*! We're happy to grant your request for asylum. While you're shifting a bit as instructed, it would be a good idea for you to keep your foot hard on the accelerator so you don't waste any time getting to Mars. As far as the Space Command is concerned, we're not fond of bullies, and we're not going to let them enter our space and throw around some bullshit threats. However, if we're going to do this, we need to do it *now*!"

McKinney nodded to Soren as he said, "We will comply with your instructions immediately, Mars patrol. Thanks a million!"

"Our pleasure, *KT-5*."

True to their word, the Mars patrol ships moved past the Citadel ship and took up protective positions. Three of the ships faced the three Space Command ships, and the other two stayed on either side of *KT-5* as she made her way to Mars. The commander of the Mars ships called back, "*KT-5*, you are welcome to stay on the line and listen to what we say to bullies."

The commander contacted the Space Command vessels and said, "Space Command, this is Mars defense patrol. Please state your reason for entering Mars space."

The commander of the Space Command ships replied, "Mars defense patrol, we are in pursuit of the Citadel Group transport that has just passed your ships. They have already engaged in unlawful efforts to avoid capture and are wanted for interfering with the operation of four Space Command ships."

"What's unlawful about not wanting to be boarded by the Space Command?"

"The Space Command is carrying out the orders of the United States in defending itself against hostile actions taken by Citadel."

"So you're saying that the US is at war with Citadel?"

"We aren't here to discuss whether there has been a formal declaration of war. Hostile actions have taken place that give us the authority to act to defend ourselves."

"I guess we have a problem, Space Command. As far as we can tell, the only ones that have been engaging in hostile actions are you folks. What would you do with the ship and her crew?"

"That isn't for us to discuss, Mars. By treaty, the Space Command has jurisdiction for patrolling the space lanes and maintaining security. You are obliged to assist us in capturing the Citadel transport."

"You don't need to tell us about our treaty obligations, Space Command. One of the things our treaties make clear is that your jurisdiction doesn't extend to Mars space. Also, your charter applies to efforts to maintain security on behalf of *everyone* in this solar system. While you may think that the interests of the United States and everyone else are the same, we sure as hell don't see it that way. If you can provide us with a resolution from the AN Security Council approving this action, we'll be glad to take it up for consideration. Until then, be advised that Citadel transport *KT-5* has requested and been granted asylum from Mars."

The commander's voice took on a more menacing tone as he continued. "That means you are to stay out of Mars space. Make sure you pass the word to the rest of the Space Command, because we would view any effort by Space Command to recover either the crew or the ship to be a hostile act against Mars."

While the ships from Mars weren't warships, they were capable of defensive actions. Every ship listening to the call took note of sensor readings that unmistakably indicated signs of weapons being brought online. This happened so rarely that all vessels understood that Mars wasn't backing down.

It was different with the Space Command ships, which had counted on being able to get what they wanted by bluffing. With their bluff called, they had little choice but to turn back the way they had come. As the images of those vessels faded from view within *KT-5*'s aft monitors, the image of Mars itself grew even more massive as they made their final approach into orbit. A shuttle was waiting to take them to the surface. The first person on the shuttle to greet them was a familiar face. Dan Bacas greeted McKinney with a bittersweet look. "It's been too long since we last saw each other, Hank."

McKinney said, "Has everything gone to hell, Dan? You need to bring me up to speed on what's been happening."

As Bacas put his arm around his old friend and led him into the shuttle, he replied sadly, "Everything *has* gone to hell, Hank. I feel like crying whenever I think about it, and you will too after we talk." The shuttle's journey down to the surface felt to McKinney like it took forever.

CHAPTER NINETEEN

These were unsettled times at Citadel. The derelict would arrive at the Citadel system in a few days. In spite of months of effort, they'd remained unable to decipher the symbols provided by the vessel. They'd tried to duplicate the response from the derelict by having another probe do what the first probe had done, but there was no reaction from the alien ship.

Yabuno frowned in frustration as he summarized everyone's feelings. "It's as if we've been given one chance to figure out what to do. If we're too stupid to figure out the equations, then we don't have any business aboard the derelict anyway. Damn that ship for being so stubborn!"

Austin turned to Alan Turner. "I know I've asked plenty of times and you're probably sick of hearing from me, but how do things look at this point, Alan?"

Turner's gaze back at Austin showed the effects of months of unsuccessful efforts. With a gesture that spoke more of frustration than enthusiasm, he brought up the images on a large screen. "I wish I had some more positive news, Sam, but we still don't know what these equations represent. The only thing I can add is that there is something about them that is tugging ever so slightly at my mind, although I can't tell you why. There's nothing specific, and it may be something that isn't mathematical at all. For all I know, the equations may simply remind me of some artwork I've seen somewhere. That's all I have to report."

"Let's talk about where we stand on what it would mean for the derelict to pass through the radiation field," Austin said. "Bret, you and your team have been chewing on this one for a while."

"This has been another tough one for us, Sam," Yabuno replied. He brought up an image of the derelict and a Keith Thomas class transport as he continued. "We've been thinking for a long time about whether there's any practical way to shield that thing from the radiation. The short answer is that it just can't be done. We have a hard enough time providing shielding for our transports, which only provides a limited amount of safety in the event of exposure to the field. We already know that anyone in a transport that stays too long in the field would be toast. Strictly speaking, we should be talking about the ship itself instead of preserving life inside, since we've assumed that there isn't anyone alive inside. However, even the systems on our transports can tolerate only a limited exposure within the field before they begin to degrade."

Yabuno brought the images to scale for emphasis. "The derelict is far larger than our transports. There just isn't any practical means of shielding a vessel that huge from the field. Also, when we talk about the amount of exposure that our transports can tolerate in the field, we're talking about vessels that can travel at speed. The derelict would just drift through, which would increase its exposure time by a huge amount."

"Why can't we just attach thrusters to the derelict and accelerate it through the field?" Austin asked.

Yabuno brought up a map of their system and gestured as he explained, "The approach to our solar system is all wrong. If we accelerate it along its present path, it will be pulled in near the seventh planet. There's a good chance it would collide with the planet instead of fall into its orbit, which would be the end, even for this ship."

"What if we use a different course?"

"Gravity will play hell with any other course," Yabuno replied, pointing to other places on the map. "We'd just end up sending the ship close enough to another planet that we might end up with a collision. Even if we're lucky and avoid a collision, we'd likely end up with the ship stuck in orbit around one of the planets. We're not sure we could ever get the derelict out of orbit if that happens. The only way to bring it into our system is to let it drift. The larger planets will have shifted enough by that time that they won't just haul the ship with them."

"This brings us to the question of whether the ship can handle the radiation on its own."

They stared at a close-up of the ship's exterior. Yabuno continued, "We've done the best we can to analyze the ship's hull. There's a good chance the ship's been exposed to plenty of radiation during its time as a derelict, although we can't find any sign of damage to the hull. We've tried practically everything we can think of to at least scratch it. Even when we've used our most advanced tools and probes, we can't affect the surface at all, let alone penetrate it. We've also tried directing radiation at it."

"How did it react?"

Yabuno brought up two images. "These images were taken before and after the tests. As you can see, it was as if the radiation had never been there. It could be that the material is too dense for the radiation to penetrate it."

"What does that mean for us?" Austin asked, the interest plain on his face.

Yabuno pointed to the second image. "We think there's a good chance that the radiation field would be no more successful at penetrating that hull than we've been."

Austin's interest hesitated for a moment. "Doesn't allowing the derelict into our solar system present its own risks?"

"Yes." Yabuno nodded. "Even in its current condition, the derelict isn't drained of energy. It was able to react to our probe. I'm going to assume that lack of energy isn't the reason why it's ignoring our efforts to repeat that experiment. For all we know, it might even now have energy reserves that could overwhelm us. We don't know whether its resilience to the radiation we've been able to direct toward it is a property of the materials from which it was made or because of an internal energy field that it maintains. What we've been able to detect doesn't look like any traditional energy signature.

"Since we believe it still has energy, possibly substantial reserves, there are negatives associated both with an end-game scenario and with a fully repaired scenario. In the event of an end-game scenario, which is a fancy way of saying that it fails in such a way as to result in an explosion, we probably wouldn't want to be anywhere near it. We should be able to deal with this risk by positioning the derelict in our system, but far away from planet Citadel. As you know, we've nearly completed a special space yard to look after the ship, with sensors to monitor any problems."

"What are the concerns about repairing the derelict?"

Yabuno's face revealed his worries. "We need to keep in mind that we don't know the ship's purpose. Is it intended to be a cargo ship? Perhaps it's supposed to engage in deep-space exploration. It could even be a warship. If we bring it back online, we might resurrect an activity that could spell trouble for us, especially since we wouldn't register as its original masters. If something really bad happens, we may be stuck with trying to leave this solar system through the neck of the bottle, meaning the safe path through the radiation field, at a relatively slow pace."

Austin turned to Liz, who had handled a lot of the organizing for large-scale activities, including the planning and execution of the original landfall with the first settlers, and for each subsequent group of settlers. "What do you think, Liz? How manageable would the risk be if we brought that ship into our solar system?"

Liz made a gesture as if weighing items on a scale. "First, if we're talking about a catastrophic event, I'm not sure any amount of planning would be sufficient. However, unless we're talking about a situation where the ship is out of control and determined to destroy planet Citadel, we should be able to manage the risk. We've already taken an important step in constructing a separate space yard for the ship to keep it a good distance away from Citadel. We would make emergency plans to get off-planet to a safe region elsewhere in this solar system. We should also consider a plan where we try to leave this system with the warp-field generators."

Before the usual concerns were raised, Liz raised her hand and said, "Yes, I know, the combination of planets with their gravitational fields would make it difficult at best to get out without something going wrong. Also, it won't be much longer before the size of our population would overwhelm any efforts to use the transports in a mass evacuation, even when most of them are available. I'm only suggesting that we consider this approach as a last resort, to be used only in the event of a system-wide catastrophe."

Austin turned back to the group. "It seems to me that the risk of letting the derelict enter our solar system is acceptable. On top of that, the benefit to our having it in our solar system is that our right to claim it for our purposes is pretty much absolute. We don't need to have any further discussions about whether we can extend our jurisdiction over something beyond our solar system; this thing came to our system unasked."

Austin looked around with a wry expression. "Of course, once it enters our solar system, we don't want it to drift *out* of our solar system someday, so locating it at a permanent facility makes sense."

Austin's tone turned serious. "Let's talk about something else that's been on our minds. Melody, What do we know about the communications situation with Earth's solar system?"

Lambert spoke up. "We did some upgrading to the system after we were able to get it up and running a while back. It used to be the case that if the link back to Earth's system failed at any point, no communications would work and we wouldn't know where the failure took place. It's taken us a lot of work to eliminate possible reasons. We now know where the failure has occurred. The beacon just outside their solar system has been disabled."

Austin frowned. "What do you mean by 'disabled'? Don't you mean that it has failed?"

Lambert shook her head slightly. "No, I mean disabled. Someone has disabled that beacon. The method used would have been sufficient to keep us in the dark over the entire status of the system previously. While we don't know who was responsible or why, we know it wasn't an accident."

Austin thought for a moment before asking, "If we think back on when the messages stopped arriving, wouldn't that have been around the time that *KT-2*, Sara Albretti's ship, was due to arrive there?"

"Yes, that's right." Lambert nodded. "We've heard nothing from any of our transports since that time. In addition, none of our transports has arrived from the other solar system."

"There are several possible reasons why the beacon has been disabled." Austin then said the chilling words that no one wanted to hear: "The first is that the alien invaders have returned for a rematch."

"If they have," Yabuno replied, "they'll have a much tougher time of it than the last time they were there."

There was a skeptical look on Austin's face as he answered. "I'd feel better about that statement if our counterparts had been willing to put the security measures in place that we recommended."

"Even without them, Earth, Mars, and the Moon have upgraded their defenses," Yabuno countered.

"I can think of ways around those upgrades," Austin said pointedly. "I'm sure you can too."

"Yes, you're right," Yabuno admitted. "However, by my count there are at least ten of our transports unaccounted for. I'm assuming that they're all in that solar system, able to work together to take on an alien invader. While their torpedoes still need some work, their EMP weapons are pretty nasty. It may be that things aren't in the best of shape there, which is why we haven't heard from them. It may even be that we've lost some of them."

"What if more than one alien invader paid them a visit?" Austin asked. "Two or three of those ships could be a game changer, even with our improved transports. It may be that they've taken out everything in that system and trashed the beacon for good measure. Remember what they did to the beacon at this end when they were here."

Liz spoke up. "If that's the case, then I hope some of our ships were able to get away. I guess we'll know for certain once the next one arrives. In the meantime, it isn't safe for our ships to stay near the derelict. We might not make it into the safety of our system in time if an alien invader arrives. We already know they can't send a full-size ship through the safe path. Even if they send several of their scout ships, our defenses should be able to deal with them. Our space yard is better defended this time too."

Yabuno continued with the thought. "We've already decided to let the derelict just drift into our system anyway, so there isn't any need to keep ships near it. We can leave a few remote probes just to monitor the situation. We can wait until the derelict is in our system before we have to worry about attaching remote thrusters to maneuver it to its own space yard."

"What if an alien invader shows up before the derelict enters our radiation field?" Austin asked.

Yabuno stared back at Austin with hard eyes as he said, "If that happens, we're screwed. We can't fight them out there with what we have, which means they'll be able to claim the prize, damn them. Fortunately, in a few days, it won't matter. Let's hope that someone will show up soon to fill us in on what's happening."

"I'm not sold on the idea of just abandoning the derelict entirely," Austin said. "I want to keep some of our ships in the area, to keep an eye on things." He anticipated the comments from his wife and Yabuno as he continued. "Don't worry; we'll keep the ships far enough away that they can haul ass through the radiation field if necessary."

After the meeting was over, Liz took Austin aside and asked quietly, "Sam, what if we're wrong about what's happening back there?"

"What else could it be?"

"What if someone else is screwing with the beacon?"

"Who?" Austin asked in a puzzled tone. "I can't believe anyone from the Citadel Group would be responsible. Besides, we have enough good people there to deal with anyone like that."

"What if it's someone outside the Citadel Group?"

"It's hard to see how it could happen. As Bret pointed out, we have plenty of transports available to look after the beacon, even if someone were to screw with it."

Liz looked somber as she said, "There's another scenario that fits, although it would be horrible in a different way from an attack by the alien invaders. We've been hearing about how Harrington has been trying to scare people during her reelection campaign into focusing on a phony issue involving Citadel instead of her own shortcomings. Could screwing with the beacon be part of that campaign?"

"It would be a pretty risky campaign strategy," Austin said. "Strictly speaking, the beacon belongs to Citadel. Now that Citadel has been recognized as an independent nation, screwing with it is an act of war. It's hard to see Courtney being that consumed with her desire for reelection that she'd be willing to risk war. Besides, the rest of the international community would be outraged by those actions."

Liz stared hard at Austin's face. "Is she the type of person who would let that outrage get in the way of being reelected and then dealing with whatever she has to deal with later?"

A new worry rippled across Austin's face as he answered. "Until recently, I wouldn't have thought so. Now, I'm not so certain."

CHAPTER TWENTY

President Harrington and her campaign team had been hard at work explaining the actions the United States had taken against Citadel. Harrington had released carefully doctored excerpts from her communications with Austin to convey the impression that Austin was ready to sell Earth out in order to maintain a security advantage over them. Her team was reviewing the status of their efforts.

"Where do we stand on the domestic side, Henry?" Harrington asked the campaign weasel.

"We're dealing with a lot of disbelief over the notion of Sam Austin being hostile toward Earth," he replied. "There's plenty of history with Austin, where people see him as someone who's done everything possible to help this planet and this country. Fortunately, there are also people who are prepared to give the president of the United States the benefit of the doubt, no matter who he or she might be. While we know we won't win over everyone who's a fan of Austin, we don't need to. We just to win over enough of the people who tend to support the president, and keep that support until we get their vote on Election Day. After Election Day, we can work on the next message."

"Will it be enough?" Harrington asked with a look full of desire.

"It will be close," the weasel said with a shrug, "which is a hell of a lot better than where we were a few months ago. If we can keep going with the message that we have captured files that confirm our claims and are working on deciphering them, we have a good chance of moving the needle enough to get the electoral votes we need."

"Where do we stand internationally, Ned?"

Chambers replied, "Much of the international community is opposed to our actions, Madame President. The AN Security Council is demanding to see the intelligence that supports our claims against Citadel. There are threats of a formal resolution to this effect."

Harrington dismissed the concern, saying, "The Security Council won't get anywhere, since we can veto any action it proposes. What else?"

"Mars is denying US vessels a right of entry into their space so long as the US occupies any Citadel facilities. There is even talk of breaking of diplomatic relations if the US doesn't discontinue its actions, and the threat isn't coming just from Mars. The matter is so serious that several of our traditional allies are being very open in questioning whether this is a ploy to keep this administration in office." He stated the obvious: "This isn't good news, Madame President."

"Fortunately, as usual, much of the domestic population doesn't give a damn about what happens elsewhere in the world or our solar system," Harrington replied cynically. "I'm not worried about Mars—they've barely finished rebuilding after the last attack. As far as the international community overall is concerned, let's remember that this is the United States. We are the pre-eminent nation in this solar system. All we need to do is push out until after the election any serious effort to meet anyone's concerns. If it becomes necessary, we've already discussed the possibility of claiming that the intelligence was faulty and firing a few of Bering's low-level flunkies. We can even appoint a commission that is stacked with people who will ensure that it gets nowhere and will conclude that no one did anything wrong."

Harrington turned to her vice president. "Where do things stand with Congress, Rhoda?"

Molder said, "Congress is unhappy as hell over what's been happening and has been trying to get us to send the top people in the administration to appear before their committees to answer their questions. We're much better off putting things off as long as possible and only sending over lower-level people who either won't have direct knowledge of events or can be counted on to paint whatever picture we want painted for now." With a smirk, she continued, "Although Congress has asked for documents as well, we can keep stonewalling their requests by giving them lots of documents that don't really say anything and then claiming we've been cooperating with them fully."

Harrington nodded her approval and then turned to the attorney general. "Where do things stand as far as keeping the Citadel Group people on ice?"

Walker looked pained as he replied, "The effort to round up everyone associated with the Citadel Group has run into some major roadblocks, Courtney. Let's first keep in mind that the Constitutional amendment that recognized Citadel also declared that everyone that was part of Citadel who had been a US citizen is still a US citizen. These people are entitled to their rights under the Constitution. That means that we can't simply lock them up for the duration. The matter is being pressed in the courts right now, with several judges issuing orders that these people be set free. Some of the judges have allowed for exceptions where the government can show that specific individuals had engaged in unlawful actions. We have therefore made the argument in these cases that everything is motivated by national security, which is why we need to keep these people locked up.

"While some judges often can't move fast enough to defer to the government in such cases, not every judge is buying it this time. Some of them won't drop the cases without seeing some of the underlying intelligence privately." Walker nodded at Bering with a rolling of the eyes as he said, "Since the government's intelligence is suspect, we have appealed those decisions. We're doing everything we can to slow down the appeals process so that nothing final is decided until after the election. There have been some noises to the effect that some of the plaintiffs are seeking expedited review by the Supreme Court on an emergency basis. If the Supreme Court agrees to hear any of those appeals, we'll have to hope that it won't rule on them for a while."

"We can also mount a campaign to the effect that the Supreme Court shouldn't meddle in these matters by getting into the inner workings of the government, which it isn't equipped to do." Harrington turned to Dormer and said, "Make sure it happens right away, Henry." The weasel nodded back at her.

Her displeasure was evident as she asked, "What's the story on that old fox Preacher? I thought we had him locked up."

Chambers said, "We overlooked the fact that the old fox has a son who is a younger fox, Madame President. J. W. Preacher IV, who took over his father's law firm when the old fox retired, presented evidence of having a power of attorney on behalf of Preacher III and was in court seeking an order for the release of his father."

Chambers looked around the room in resignation as he continued, "It's one thing to lock up people who can't claim diplomatic immunity and don't have the resources to fight the government. It's another thing to lock up an accredited ambassador who has the resources and skills to fight back. Preacher IV has already obtained an order from a federal judge for the release of Preacher III. When we sought to appeal the order, Preacher IV was sharp enough to maneuver for a direct appeal to the Supreme Court on an emergency basis."

The smug looks were wiped from their faces as Chambers continued. "We have just received word that the Supreme Court has agreed to hear the appeal on an expedited basis. In an unusual arrangement, the court has also agreed to allow Preacher III to appear before the

court to argue his case with his son. We have therefore
been given an order from the court to produce Preacher
for the hearing.

"Many of the justices know and respect Preacher
from his days appearing before the court as a litigator,
and they would be highly motivated to give him the
benefit of the doubt. It is very likely that this means that
the court will order Preacher's release while the case
continues. We should assume that the ambassador will
be released within a few days at most and will be largely
untouchable."

Harrington said, "OK, so Preacher buys a few days of
liberty while we seek to lock him up on national security
grounds. That hardly seems like he is untouchable."

Walker shook his head as he spoke up. "Our option
under the law is to expel him from the United States if he
has been acting in a manner not consistent with his status
as a diplomat. Once again, our problem is that Preacher
is also a US citizen, so he is entitled to the same rights as
any other citizen. He is too prominent for us to get away
with making the same national security claims without
clear proof behind them, and we can't just expel him
because we don't like him."

The campaign weasel explained some political facts
to the group: "The problem is that once Preacher is out
of our custody, he will become what Citadel hasn't had
yet, which is a voice. No one has heard from Austin in a
while, and no one else with the Citadel Group has a major
following in the US. Preacher is well enough known that
at least some people will listen to him. The only other
exception would be Sara Albretti, who was the captain of

the transport that worked with Austin to defeat the alien invaders. But while she is known and respected, she has been taken into custody and is safely out of reach while she's taking her transport back to Citadel."

Walker spoke up. "In view of the legal situation as I've described it, with Preacher free, we should expect that the rest of the Citadel Group people will be set free. It would be entirely in character for Preacher to argue some of these cases before the Supreme Court in person. In view of the likely outcome of Preacher's own case before the court, it isn't hard to predict the outcome of these other cases."

The campaign weasel continued. "Getting back to my comment about Preacher becoming the voice for Citadel, we'll just have to hope that the majority of the people won't start to pay attention to him until it's too late."

Harrington turned to Bering. "What success have your people had in getting access to Citadel's core technologies?"

Bering's face revealed little emotion as he replied. "We haven't had the success we had anticipated, Madame President. Citadel had in place some emergency protocols that locked down all of their key technology files before we could get to them. The technical brains within the organization have all refused to cooperate with us, and now that there is controversy about our actions with those people, no reputable scientist has been willing to work with our people in any of the interrogations. Without that assistance, our interrogations will be useless. Now we're hearing from others in this room that the

Citadel people will be set free shortly, which means that the interrogations will cease as well."

"You told me you'd find something on Austin. You said everyone has something to hide. What has Austin been hiding?" Harrington demanded.

"We haven't found anything," Bering admitted.

"What about that ranch of his?" Harrington asked. "He's always been so damned touchy about anyone setting foot there without his permission. Haven't you checked it out?"

"Austin could give *us* lessons in keeping out people he doesn't want around." Bering's tone hinted at respect for his target. "We don't have any pretext for entering the property, and his armed guards seem to know immediately when we try to probe around the boundaries. Besides, the law is explicit that even the government must respect his privacy where his ranch is concerned, thanks to some past transgressions by various government employees."

Walker gave Bering a hard look. "We should also assume that Austin's people are good enough to have proof of your attempts to get access. With that proof, Preacher won't have any difficulty getting an order from the Supreme Court backing up the law and telling us to stay away." Walker shook his head. "It's better to back off quietly than to give them an opportunity to go public with what we've been doing and hurt us more politically. Let's face it; we've lost that one."

Harrington's frustration level was rising. She turned back to Bering and said, "All right, let's get back to their ships. Why can't we analyze them to get what we want?"

"There are no ships to analyze," Bering replied. "We sent all of the transports we seized to Citadel to capture the derelict. We didn't worry about it at the time because we needed them to be sure we could overwhelm the ships in the Citadel system with greater numbers, and we knew there were other ships in our solar system available for study."

Bering nearly sighed as he continued. "We misjudged the situation. While there were ships under construction at their space yard in this solar system, they managed to take them and crash them into Jupiter before we could take control of them. There isn't anything else of value to retrieve. They also destroyed everything in their research facilities that was useful, and their files are also encrypted beyond our ability to decipher.

"The one ship that we'd hoped we could capture was a transport that arrived from Citadel after our 'fleet' departed. We thought that we could capture it and take it apart. But somehow, they were warned and managed to elude our ships and find refuge on Mars. In view of Mars's denial of access by US ships to Mars space, we haven't been able to get close enough to capture that ship."

Harrington had a dismissive look on her face. "I would think we're past worrying about what the people on Mars would think. Why can't we launch a raid anyway?"

Bering managed to keep a patronizing look off his face as he said, "Mars has placed several of its ships at strategic locations around the Citadel ship, Madame President. They have made certain that the press is nearby and aware of what has been happening. We can't reach the ship without violating Mars's space in a very clear and public manner." Bering gave a cynical nod to Chambers. "We've been given unofficial messages from our counterparts on Mars to the effect that entering into their space would be an act of war."

Chambers added, "I've received the same messages, Madame President. It is one thing to claim Citadel is placing our security in jeopardy. It's another to claim that it justifies going to war with Mars, especially when we can't show any direct evidence of any aggressive actions by Mars. Mars is the tipping point that would undo everything. Enough people would notice that we'd be forced to explain ourselves further. That would include Congress, which would insist on investigating why we were at war with a friendly neighbor, especially without a declaration of war from Congress. To paraphrase Abraham Lincoln, 'One war at a time.'"

Unusual for Bering, he now had a trace of emotion on his face as he looked back at Harrington. "In short, we'd better get our hands on the derelict, Madame President, because we haven't been able to get what we want from other sources."

Harrington looked toward the campaign weasel and asked, "Can we still win, Henry?"

The weasel said, "Yes, Courtney. Although we've had some setbacks, we still have a message that's been working for us. We will continue to claim that we can't reveal the specifics of our intelligence and that the Citadel people are being disingenuous in holding our own desire for ensuring our national security against us. Preacher is Austin's mouthpiece, so anything he says has to be discounted.

"We need to maintain this message for only a short while longer, and we can win. It'll be an ugly win, but it will still be a win."

Harrington looked around the room and said, "I'll take *ugly* any day."

CHAPTER TWENTY ONE

Transport *KT-2* had nearly completed its journey. Although Roetter hadn't killed anyone else, the horror of his actions hung over everyone. Sara knew that Roetter's actions meant that he wasn't planning on letting them live once they'd achieved their objective. He would probably find a way to report the unfortunate demise of all of the transport crews. She wondered where the man's bosses found such people.

Although Roetter's people kept a close watch on the Citadel crew during the trip, Sara had managed to meet secretly with her chief engineer.

"Chief, we have to find a way to stop Roetter and his people when we arrive at Citadel. If the people on the other transports are anything like him, Citadel will have to deal with a bunch of monsters. The question is how to do it."

"The question is also *when* to do it, Captain," the chief replied. "They've always had people in engineering, so I haven't been able to get the access I'd need to do anything. One time that I have to have complete access to everything is when we bring the ship out of its warp-field bubble. I can try to freeze out other systems at the same time."

"Can you do it without their knowing what you're doing?"

"They'd know pretty quickly what we're doing," the chief said with a skeptical look. "The problem is what systems to freeze. Roetter's people are spread throughout the ship, so there isn't much we can do to them directly without affecting the rest of the crew. What about screwing up the alignment of the ship's maneuvering thrusters?"

Sara gave the chief a worried look. "We need to consider our objectives, Chief. If we screw up the ship's ability to maneuver properly, we run the risk of a catastrophic collision. Do we plan on killing everyone, including our own people?"

The chief thought hard for a moment before asking, "What about screwing up the sensors for the remote thrusters, the ones that would be used with the derelict?"

"That would be helpful, but only temporary," she replied. "We need to ensure that the ship can't do what Roetter wants to use it to do, while trying to protect as many of the lives of our crew as possible."

"We could try something with the environmental controls," the chief suggested. "I can arrange for the system to be compromised in selected areas. If some people could get access to survival suits, they might be able to retake control of the ship."

"How quickly would people feel the effects?" Sara asked.

"Depending on how we do it, it shouldn't take more than a few minutes to take people out. We may have a little luck on our side, as sick bay has a set of containment compartments for dealing with infectious conditions as well as to ensure an uncontaminated environment for certain procedures and for patient recoveries. Engineering also has a double set of hatches to deal with catastrophic failures."

Sara shook her head. "They'll be expecting something in engineering. They might not think about sick bay, since no one's needed it during the trip. In addition to the containment compartments, sick bay has isolation suits that will work in shielding people from the environmental conditions. Work it out with Doc so that he'll know what to do when the time comes. I hope to God this works!"

A day before they were due to arrive just outside the Citadel solar system, Roetter met with Sara in her cabin. He began by saying, "I want to explain what will happen tomorrow, Captain, so that there won't be any unnecessary problems. The first is that one of my men will be standing next to your chief engineer when we are taken out of the warp-field bubble. If my man doesn't like anything about what your chief is doing, he will shoot him on the spot."

"If that happens, Major, you will have signed all of our death warrants," she replied. "Since you killed my assistant chief, the chief is now the only one aboard this ship who can take it out of the warp-field bubble safely."

Roetter's face darkened. "Then your chief will be shot the moment we are out of the warp-field bubble."

"That's not the way it works, Major, if you want to stay alive. He has to keep monitoring the generators to make sure they remain stable. Because we turned right around to come back to Citadel, the generators didn't get the inspection and any needed adjustments they were supposed to have, so they're a lot more likely than usual to have some stability issues." Her face had a hard look as she said, "If you've ever seen any pictures of what can happen around an unstable warp-field bubble, you wouldn't even think of messing with the only one who can deal with it."

"You're raising false objections, Captain," Roetter warned. "While your chief might not mind sacrificing himself for a cause, I doubt either of you wants any further bloodshed. My man will shoot two of your chief's people if he doesn't like anything about what your chief is doing. That will include any mysterious equipment or system malfunctions. In addition, if the word will be sent around, and each of my people will shoot some member of your crew who's nearby, at random, just to make the point." Roetter's face took on an inhuman look as he asked, "Do you understand?"

Sara gave a stone-faced look back at Roetter as she replied, "Yes, Major."

"Good. Since you will have a part to play, I need to be sure you know what you'll be expected to do. When we show up, you will inform Austin that the alien invaders have returned and laid waste to much of our solar system. This will be the reason for the communications beacon being disabled and for the transports being delayed. You'll tell them that the aliens are after you, and you will stand guard over the derelict until it drifts into the solar system. You will also tell them that your files were encrypted due to a mistake and that you need Austin to release them.

"As the captain of this ship and with your history with Austin, he will believe you." Roetter's eyes narrowed as he continued, "In fact, you'd better make sure he believes you. If he doesn't believe you or if you attempt to warn him or anyone else about us or try to interfere in our actions, I will consider your actions to be hostile acts in time of war, and I will order the executions of you, your chief, and at least half of your crew."

She gave Roetter a cold stare. "Murdering prisoners doesn't have anything to do with the rules of war. It's just murder."

Her head snapped back from a hard slap to the face, which was the only response to her words.

Sara thought with bitterness on Roetter's threats as she'd gotten the word to the chief not to go through with the planned modifications to the environmental system until he heard from her directly to do it. Although he'd protested strongly, she reminded him that if it happened at the wrong time, too many people would die. Although she believed that they were all destined to die anyway, she wanted to be sure their deaths would have some meaning. It was more important to try to warn Austin about what was happening than to screw up the operations of one ship out of eleven.

It was time for them to complete their journey and cancel out the warp-field bubble. The chief always performed this task from engineering. The difference this time was that he had company that was armed and watching over his shoulder. As the bubble finally collapsed gently, the view from the screen changed into something that was recognizable. They'd been right on target.

She took note of the rest of the ships as they materialized into normal space as well. Once they had all arrived, they proceeded at top speed toward the derelict. She had her bridge open communications with *Pathfinder*, which was the nearest ship. She was surprised to see both Joe and Austin on the bridge.

Austin spoke first. "Sara, what's been happening back on Earth?"

She took a mental deep breath and began with her performance. "Thank God we made it, Sam! There's been an invasion with three alien invader ships. No one saw them coming, and they've taken out pretty much everything this time. Earth, Mars, the Moon, everything, are all gone. We fought them as long as we could, but once their weapons finished trashing everything, there wasn't much point in staying around. They were able to use two ships to hold everyone off while the third ship took out the target. We've underestimated how powerful those ships are when they aren't split into a mother ship and a scout ship. At least we were able to take out one of their ships."

The shock from the news rippled across *Pathfinder's* bridge. Austin spoke. "Where are the invaders now?"

"We think they're heading this way. They might be right behind us."

Austin's face showed alarm as he said, "If that's the case, then get the hell into the inner part of our solar system now, and we can talk some more about where things stand."

"I don't think that's a good idea, Sam."

"Why not?"

"Remember when we talked about the possibility that they were looking for the derelict? If they show up before the derelict has drifted past the radiation field, they could take control of it. They might even be able to understand the technology, even though we haven't."

"If it happens, then it happens," Austin replied with a shrug.

"It doesn't have to be that way," she said pleadingly. "We'd like to stand guard around it until it is within the radiation field. If nothing else, if the alien invaders show up, we can keep them occupied until it doesn't matter anymore."

Austin spoke gently as he said, "I don't mean this as a criticism, Sara, but it doesn't appear that you were able to take them out before. I don't see how you expect to be able to do things any differently if they show up here, except die."

"One thing that hampered us hugely, Sam, was that someone at the Citadel Group initiated the emergency encryption protocols, and all of our weapons were locked down before we could complete the job. If we'd been able to keep using our weapons, we might have had more success against the invaders."

Austin was shocked. "Who the hell would do something like that to cripple you when you needed every possible advantage?"

"We never found out. Everything on Earth is trashed, so there's no way of knowing. If you can issue the command to lift the encryption, we'll be able to protect the derelict from capture by the alien invaders."

Austin spent a moment at a control panel and then said, "There, the encryption is cancelled. You now have full access to your weapons. Go ahead and take your positions around the derelict. I'll order the other ships to return to our solar system."

Joe stood up and said, "How was it there, Sara?"

Sara looked at him unblinkingly and said, "It was like a witches' brew, Joe." Joe didn't react as she broke communications and the screen went dark.

Roetter stepped onto the bridge from a passageway. He was pleased. "That was well played, Captain. You improvised in a way that seemed very logical. You will give me the command codes for the weapons now, before any surprises show up."

Without a word, she entered the codes into the panel. Roetter checked them to confirm that they were valid and then nodded.

"Notify the other ships that we will head toward the derelict as you have discussed with Austin," Roetter said. "Anyone who is listening will assume that you are just doing as you told Austin you'd do. Once we arrive, you will wait for further instructions."

Once contact with Sara's ship had been broken, Albretti turned to Austin and said, "Something is wrong with this setup, Sam."

"Yes, I know," Austin replied.

Albretti was surprised. "How the hell did you know?"

"First, why don't you tell me how the hell *you* knew?"

"Sara told me about a term her mother used to use when she thought someone was trying to pull something past her. Her mother called it a 'witches' brew.' Sara said things were a witches' brew back on Earth. It couldn't have been a coincidence. Now, how the hell did you know something wasn't right?"

Austin gave a humorless snort. "Several reasons. The first is that all of the transports that were in their solar system made it here, even though they fought the alien invaders. I would have expected at least some of them to have been either damaged or destroyed. There wasn't a scratch on any of them. The explanation about having to bail after their weapons were locked out was bullshit." Austin nodded toward the display. "I mean that with compliments to Sara. She knows that I can check out the encryption lockdown and learn who initiated it. I did a quick check when I cancelled the encryption. J. W. Preacher initiated the encryption. He would only have done it to protect Citadel from a different kind of adversary, one much closer to home."

"Who the hell would hate us that much?"

Austin's expression turned cold as he answered, "Almost certainly the United States, or more specifically, President Courtney Harrington. The bullshit we heard before communications with their solar system were cut was bad enough. She must have become unhinged to take it to the next steps, which would be some kind of formal action against Citadel, perhaps even a declaration of war. She'd be relying on the notion that some people will always believe a lie if it comes from the president of the United States. While I hope there aren't very many people like that, she must think there are enough of them to get her reelected. After that, she probably plans on finding a fall guy to take the blame, while doing everything she can to screw us.

"People like her are one of the reasons why we implemented the emergency protocols in the first place. If we hadn't, right now they'd have all of the knowledge that we've spent huge resources to develop, and they'd probably try to use it against us.

Now Albretti was puzzled. "If you knew something was wrong, why did you release the encryption?"

"I didn't know for sure until I had committed to releasing it. I expect that there was someone just outside viewing range with a weapon ready to shoot Sara if she didn't convince me to do as they wanted. I had to make them believe that she'd been successful, or she'd probably be dead by now."

"What good would it do them to take charge of the derelict? They can't take it back with them."

"They probably want to be able to claim that it is within their control and that they've learned horrible secrets about us that they're trying to decipher. They'll promise to let everyone know what they've found after the election. We already know what will happen at that point. Anyway, so long as the derelict isn't within the Citadel solar system, they have as much right to it as anyone else. Once into our solar system, they can't make the claim."

Austin's face took on a wry look as he added, "They don't realize that they've made a big mistake, since the derelict is *already* within our solar system. Our claims to the system don't start at the outer boundary of the radiation field; that's just a natural phenomenon that contributes to the security of our system. We only use the term 'entrance' to refer to the point where the safe path to the inner part of our system starts at the outer part of the radiation field. Even *we* sometimes use that 'entrance' as shorthand for the beginning of our solar system, but our formal claim is clear about the outer boundary.

"While they might try to bluff their way around the boundary issue, one lie they absolutely have to avoid making is claiming control over the derelict if they don't really have that control. They're screwed if we can show the other people in their solar system that we have the derelict and that there isn't anything that's been shown to be a danger to them or that could be used for their defense.

"Ultimately, they probably plan on destroying the derelict, once they've done what they planned from a propaganda perspective. As we've already noted, they'd never be able to take it back to Earth, and they have to assume that we'd be able to recover it at some point."

"What do you intend to do?"

"I intend to send out our three transports with *Pathfinder* and tell Sara that we are adding them to the 'armada.' I'd like to tell them that we have volunteers ready to man their ships so that they can get some rest, but that will force them into action that we might regret."

"They might not allow our ships to approach anyway," Albretti said, worried. "I assume that they're getting organized right now to attach remote thrusters to move the derelict."

A grim look returned to Austin's face. "Why don't we find out?"

CHAPTER TWENTY TWO

As Joe had predicted, the captured transports had preparations underway to take control of the derelict. One of them sent a signal to Sara's ship, alerting them to a scene taking place near the entrance to the Citadel solar system. *Pathfinder* and three transports were heading toward the alien ship. One of the transports was towing an unusual piece of equipment. The other two were towing asteroids.

Roetter told Sara to make contact with *Pathfinder* to find out what was happening.

"*Pathfinder*, why are you and your transports heading here? We didn't talk about needing any additional ships or equipment."

Joe's image appeared. "It was Sam's idea, Sara. He thought it would make sense to bring out some additional weapons in case the alien invaders show up. We already know what can happen to their ships when we blast them with asteroids from a rail gun. We happen to have the latest and greatest version ready, on a mobile platform, along with some ammunition. Stand by for us to join you."

Roetter stepped into view. "I guess the game's up, Albretti. Stay where you are, or your wife dies in front of you. I'm surprised Austin would let you lead this group here in view of such an obvious weakness."

Austin walked into view on *Pathfinder's* bridge. He looked grimly at the shocked look on Roetter's face. "What makes you think I'm not in charge, mister? Who are you and what the hell are you doing on our ships?"

"My name is Major Roetter. I am here pursuant to a national security directive authorized by President Harrington that finds that the actions of Citadel constitute a national security threat to Earth, justifying preemptive measures that include the use of force."

Austin stared at Roetter for a full thirty seconds before replying. "I'm guessing, Roetter, that you're one of those people who owes his commission to a political posting rather than to more traditional military service. I think you knew before you ever departed for Citadel that there was no basis for the use of force against Citadel, but I'll give you a chance to prove me wrong. Now that you're here, it's obvious that the basis for the national security directive is a bunch of bullshit. The fact is that we haven't learned anything about the workings of the derelict. We don't even know how to get inside the damned thing.

"That being the case, you know that the national security directive is invalid. Since it is invalid, there is no basis for the use of force against Citadel. I therefore order you to surrender all of our transports to their Citadel crews and for you and your people to submit yourselves to questioning by our people. If you do these things and no information comes to light showing me to be wrong, I will treat your presence here as merely being one of an officer following orders from a superior."

"Sorry that you had to make a fine speech for nothing, Austin", Roetter replied. "We have our orders, and we will carry them out. If you interfere, your crews will die." He paused for a moment as he studied the display. "There will be one change of plans, however. Since you've gone to the trouble of bringing out an interesting new weapon, you will leave it there to be retrieved by my people. You and your transports will return to your solar system while we carry out our orders."

He continued, "You already made the mistake of releasing our systems from the encrypted lockout, Austin. We've seen to it that the systems won't accept any new encryption commands, just in case you were planning on doing something like that. Don't forget that we outnumber you more than two to one. We can still move the derelict while defending it against your ships."

"Do you really think so?" Austin asked quietly.

Roetter gasped at the reply. With a quiet nod of his head, Austin continued, "I'm sorry to say that you've proved yourself to be everything that I had guessed about you. You and I are going to have a most unpleasant talk, Roetter."

Before Austin could continue, the visuals became far less stable. He thought he could make out signs of a struggle on board Sara's ship, but he wasn't sure. At the moment, he was much more interested in the horror that had appeared out of nowhere behind the captured transports. A ship similar to the one that had tried to wipe them out over a year ago had filled up most of the screen. In rapid succession, it had targeted three of the transports with its deadly EMP weapon.

Very quickly, the dull glow from the weapon generated a horrific response from the first transport in the form of massive overloads and system failures. Two emergency hatches blew out, venting equipment and people into space. The next transport fared little better, as the attack had been completely unexpected. By the time the third transport was under attack, Austin was trying to rally the remaining transports into a semblance of a defensive force.

A key problem was the fact that the US personnel aboard the captured ships weren't responding to Austin. They weren't doing much of anything at the moment, since they hadn't been trained for this situation. As Austin had noted, their commissions were based more on political considerations than military ones. Although some of them eventually started to engage in a few basic maneuvers, they weren't nearly what Austin's own people would be doing if they'd had control of the ships. Austin ordered them to turn the controls over the Citadel people so they'd at least have a chance of surviving. He might as well have been talking to asteroids for all the good it did him. He watched in helpless frustration as more of their transports fell to the alien invader.

He finally had no choice but to work solely with the ships that were under Citadel's control. While the alien invader continued to focus on the other transports, Austin rallied their transports and *Pathfinder* into a double flanking maneuver so they'd have shots from multiple approaches at the same time. The question was whether they could reach the alien invader while there were still any transports left to save.

As the eighth of the captured transports fell to the weapon, Austin ordered *Pathfinder* and all of their transports to bring their EMP weapons online. Although they were still out of effective range, Austin hoped that they could distract the aliens enough to save some lives.

Austin cursed as he saw it wasn't going to be enough. The ninth ship fell to the alien weapon, and they were still too far away to do anything about it. Suddenly, the last two transports broke away from the cluster of shattered hulks that littered the area and maneuvered out of range of the alien weapon. As they tried to bring their EMP weapons online, the alien ship turned back to the derelict. In short order, the aliens attached towlines to the derelict and began to move away from the Citadel solar system at high speed. So quickly had they moved that they were already out of range of the transports' weapons.

As Roetter was reacting to Austin's threats, Austin's image on the screen deteriorated suddenly. Someone on the bridge called out, "Holy shit, we're under attack!"

As Roetter turned, Sara moved and tried to subdue him, but he managed to keep his weapon pointed at her and slapped her hard across the face. Another hit to the torso put her on her knees. Roetter looked back toward the person who had made the announcement and said,

"If you were lying to me just to cause a distraction, you're a dead man."

The man pointed at the screen, and they could make out a familiar horror in front of them. Roetter tried to notify the rest of his team about the attack but wasn't sure he'd gotten through to anyone.

Sara got off her knees. "Let us take over, Major. You don't know what to do, and we do."

Roetter just looked back at her. "If you think I'm turning this ship over to you, you're crazy."

Sara replied, "If you don't, we're all dead."

Roetter stared at the screen, unsure what to do, as they saw transport after transport taken down by the aliens. Roetter screamed at his team through his link, but the entire communications system was being affected by all of the EM pulses, and he couldn't raise anyone. They couldn't raise any of the other ships nearby, either. Sara realized that if Roetter's team couldn't hear him, he couldn't order anyone to undertake reprisals. She looked at two of her people, and they nodded at her in silent agreement.

She waited for her moment and then moved toward Roetter with the speed and grace of a panther. As he brought his weapon toward her, he was distracted by movement from another direction. Sara managed to knock the weapon away from her tormentor. While he tried to slap her again, without his weapon she was free to push his hand away and smash him in the mouth, hard. Three months of frustration and humiliation boiled up inside her and burst out through her arms and legs. She followed with an elbow that wrenched his head to the side and then kicked him in the ribs. As he dropped to his knees, she placed several more kicks to his head and then slammed his face into a console. Her former captor sank down without another word.

While Sara had been pounding Roetter, her crew had jumped his two colleagues and vented their frustrations on them until their former captors were sprawled on the deck, as senseless as Roetter. Sara motioned to her pilot and said, "You and I need to stay on the bridge to get us the hell out of here if we can. Maybe we can even try to give it back to the aliens. For the rest of you, we know that communications are screwed up, so these bastards can't talk to each other. We may never have another chance like this again, so do whatever you have to do to get the ship back under our control."

She nodded toward the figures on the deck. "Take these bastards with you and lock them up somewhere. Use their weapons and go from compartment to compartment and take them out. Start with a small compartment, secure it, and then work your way through the rest of the ship with our crew as you free them. Good luck!"

The pilot pointed to what little they could see on the screen. "It looks like we're next in line for the feast and we're on the menu, Captain."

"Take us straight toward Sam, as fast as she'll run." Sara swore as she looked at her console. "Damn it, we'll have to reboot to get our EMP weapon online. I've started the reboot, but it it'll take a while. I hope they don't catch us before then. Get ready to come about once we're online with it. I want to hit them back with some of their own medicine."

A minute later, the pilot reported, "Captain, I'm not sure from what we can see onscreen, but I don't think they're following us anymore."

Sara looked up from the reboot. "What are they doing?"

He pointed to the screen, and they looked at a blur of broken images as he said, "The image is still lousy, but it looks better than it did when we were closer to them. They seemed to have moved back toward the derelict. It looks like they're putting lines on it for towing." He couldn't keep the revulsion out of his voice. "God, it looks creepy. It's like the lines are growing out from their ship."

"Come about now, then," she ordered. "We can't let them take the derelict. Sam will be here soon, and then we can take them on."

"They'd better hurry, Captain," the pilot warned. "The aliens are practically spewing those lines out."

"It'll be a different story once Sam gets here," she said with heat. "With him in charge, we'll be able to kick some ass."

The pilot shook his head. "They won't be here in time. The aliens are leaving with the derelict, and they're moving pretty damned fast."

Sara swore in frustration. They could just make out a grainy image of the two giants shrinking into the distance.

SHOWDOWN

CHAPTER TWENTY THREE

The impact from the multiple EMP weapon discharges began to fade, and visibility improved on the screens. As Austin ordered rescue efforts for anyone who might still be alive on any of the ruined transports, he took note of the ones that had finally broken free instead of facing their own destruction. He saw that one of them was *KT-2*, which was Sara Albretti's ship. Although he mourned for all the lives that were lost, he was glad that at least he wouldn't have to console Joe over the loss of his wife.

Austin contacted *KT-2*. Sara's face was a welcome sight, although it was nearly overwhelmed by sadness at the moment. "I'm so glad to see you, Sara," he began. "Where is that piece of shit Roetter?"

The sadness on her face shared space with triumph and loathing as she replied, "He's under restraints at the moment. The rest of his people are as well." The sadness took over again as she said, "We lost some of our people when we regained control over our ship. I'm not sorry to say that some of his people are dead as well."

Austin didn't allow himself the luxury of speculating over how it would feel to initiate some additional deaths among Roetter's people; he would leave their fates to be decided at the appropriate time. "We'll talk further when you feel up to it, Sara, but how did you take them out?"

Sara motioned at her screen. "If your screen is anything like mine, the images haven't yet returned completely back to normal. At the time of the attack, the interference from all the EM discharges wreaked hell with our external and internal communications, which is one of the reasons why none of the other transports was able to coordinate anything.

"Once it got bad enough for the internal communications, we had a chance to take out Roetter and his people on the bridge before they could alert anyone else. After they were restrained, I sent most of our bridge crew to go through the ship and capture the rest of Roetter's people, while we tried to get the ship out of harm's way and bring our EMP weapon online. *KT-7* was able to do the same, but you know what happened with the derelict."

Austin was pleased. "That's terrific initiative, Sara, and obviously saved lives that would have been lost otherwise. We'll talk some more after I take care of some other pressing business."

Austin disconnected and made contact with their space yard. Curly Stephens was openly weeping as her face came into view.

"Curly, you're doing what I feel like doing as well, but we need to put it aside for now and focus on what we need to do next. How many of the new transports in your yard can you get ready for action within twenty-four hours?"

"What kind of action, Sam?" Stephens asked. "They're designed to do plenty of things."

The sadness in Austin's face gave way to grim determination. "I don't give a damn about whether they can transport settlers or support colonization activities. I want them ready to hunt down that alien ship and use their weapons to tear it to shreds. That means we need the warp-field generators operational, since we'll never catch up with them using conventional propulsion. Bret and Alan will work with you to get the weapons online. We're also going to take a mobile rail gun, so at least one of the transports will need to house it."

"I only have one transport that can be ready that soon, Sam, and we'll be pushing it on whether everything will function properly, even with help from Bret and Alan. In a week, I can have three more completely ready." Stephens's gaze clouded up as she continued softly, "I won't have time for salvage if we're going to get ready, Sam. I need every hand to do what we need to do."

Austin's voice was equally soft as he replied. "Focus on what you need to do, Curly. We'll take care of things out here. We'll get together when everything is over and shed some tears."

CHAPTER TWENTY FOUR

True to predictions, J. W. Preacher III was a free man. His appearance before the Supreme Court could only be described as triumphant. Preacher pointed out that Citadel was a sovereign nation and that no hostilities against it had been declared by Congress. While the court was usually loathe to step into what were often called "political" disputes, there wasn't a line of questioning from any of the justices that suggested the government would be able to continue to keep Preacher locked up. In an extremely unusual move, the court issued its ruling from the bench and ordered the immediate release of the ambassador.

Preacher had a laundry list of additional actions that he requested be included in an order. The court was happy to oblige, ordering the government to return control of the Citadel embassy to Preacher, considering the sovereign status of any embassy. The government was ordered to identify everything that had been taken from or copied from the embassy and to identify any form of monitoring or other technology that had been installed within the embassy at the direction of the government.

All information captured was to be destroyed. All embassy staff was to be released from custody immediately.

The court was somewhat more circumspect regarding the members of the Citadel Group that had been taken into custody by the government. The justices ordered the government to show cause why the other members of the Citadel Group shouldn't be granted their release. The government was warned that it should be prepared to return any captured information, monitoring devices, et cetera, relating to those people. The government was given twenty-four hours to comply with the court's orders concerning the embassy and its personnel. The court made it clear that failure to comply with the orders relating to Citadel personnel would result in an automatic order for their release, with severe consequences for the government in violating the order.

Preacher wasn't done, however. He made a direct petition to the court to have General Choi released, since his only "crime" was having been visited by General Buck and then visiting Preacher. Preacher reminded the justices of Choi's advanced age and extraordinary reputation in service of his country. The court granted Preacher's motion, ordering Choi's immediate release and giving the government twenty-four hours to turn over all evidence justifying holding Choi in the first place. The justices made it clear that if the evidence wasn't produced, the charges against Choi would be dismissed and Choi would be within his rights to pursue action against the government.

As bad as things were for Harrington's administration following the debacle with the Supreme Court, things only got worse after Choi appeared before the press. The government sought an emergency order prohibiting Choi from talking to the press on national security grounds, but the request was denied, in unusually blunt language.

Choi appeared in his dress uniform, his many decorations on prominent display. He read from a prepared statement.

"My fellow Americans and friends throughout this solar system, I stand before you as an example of what happens when a government becomes beholden to the personal ambitions of one person, instead of remembering that it is in place to serve all of us..." The statement went on to condemn Harrington in forceful terms. Choi's dignity and stature, the result of having spent decades of his life in service to his country without regard to partisan politics, made the condemnation especially damning.

"Choi is crucifying us, Courtney," the campaign weasel said. "Also, Preacher is hurting us more than we thought he would. That appearance before the Supreme Court keeps showing up on the news."

Harrington was royally pissed and let her team know it. "Preacher is bad enough; why are we being sandbagged by General Choi?"

Walker said, "It goes back to Preacher again. No one could have predicted that he'd be able to get the Supreme Court to order Choi's release from the bench. While we knew it might happen eventually, no one thought it would happen this soon. We thought the court would do what it usually does, which is to take its leisurely time in addressing the matter. This should have meant sometime after the election. In view of what would happen if we were to play the 'national security' card again, we've had no choice but to drop the charges against Choi."

Molder spoke up. "That's not the only thing that might not wait until after the election. Things are heating up in Congress, and hearings will be called shortly to investigate the government's actions against Citadel. At the very least, the national security oversight committee members will repeat its demand to see the intelligence behind our actions."

Walker looked at Bering with a sneer. "Whatever intelligence you have to back up your claims had better be convincing, because without it we've lost control of this situation."

Bering was calm as he replied, "That's not correct, Walker. All we have to do is show proof that we have captured the derelict, and the rest will sort itself out. We can explain away everything else as perhaps an overreaction to the initial intelligence. While overreactions may be embarrassing, they won't be fatal, especially if we characterize them as being motivated from a sense of protecting the security of our solar system. As the president has already pointed out, if we destroy the derelict after capturing it, then there won't be any proof that it doesn't have technology that would either help us or be detrimental to us if used by Citadel."

Bering turned to Harrington as he continued. "In fact, Madame President, we need to keep in mind the Supreme Court's orders. They probably include restoring functionality to Citadel's communications beacon. For obvious reasons, while we will need to restore the link at some point in order to have any confirmation from our people of our activities at Citadel, we would want to do so in a way that would minimize what are significant risks."

Harrington was wary. "Isn't one of those risks the fact that others will be able to see everything as well?"

"Yes," Bering replied, "we took it over because it's the only point in the system that we can use to control the flow of information. We know there are plenty of other paths for the information to travel into this solar system once it reaches the beacon. It is also, obviously, the key point for information traveling to Citadel from this solar system."

"Can't we do something to the beacon to ensure that that only we see any messages coming from Citadel, so that we can screen them?"

Bering shook his head. "Everything is encrypted, so we can't see the content before anyone else. It has to enter the system for distribution through the Citadel Group before we, along with plenty of others, see it. We can't try to fool it into believing that this has happened while rerouting it to a secure location, because we don't have the proper encryption keys. We had expected to get those keys and do as you've suggested, but we've been stymied by events we didn't anticipate.

"However, we've had a bit of luck. Just before he was captured, Preacher mentioned that there was an alternate beacon that was ready to be launched. We finally found it stashed inside the embassy itself. It had the ability to decrypt messages. It appears that that feature would normally be deactivated, but that would have happened as it was being readied for launch."

Harrington's face lit up with greed. "Does that mean we have their encryption keys?"

"No, but it means that once we launch this beacon, we will have the ability to read messages from Citadel."

"Can we send false messages to Citadel?"

"No, because they wouldn't have the proper identifications needed for the beacon to accept them as genuine. Still, this is huge, because we will know the status of our mission to Citadel before anyone else does."

"Aren't you forgetting about the beacon we have to bring back online?" Harrington said in a challenging tone.

Bering deflected the challenge calmly. "No, because we've never acknowledged having done anything to the beacon. We can still keep other ships away from it until we're ready to release official word about the capture of the derelict. We'll already know about it from using their alternative beacon, but we can't acknowledge having it in view of the Supreme Court's order to return everything we removed from the Citadel embassy."

Harrington was long past worrying about complying with laws or orders that she considered to be inconvenient obstacles to her objectives. "Launch that beacon at once," she ordered. She gave Bering a hard stare. "We haven't discussed what happens if the message comes through that they've failed."

"That is still very unlikely," Bering replied with his usual expression. "Our transports outnumber theirs by more than two to one. If necessary, our people will launch a surprise attack on the Citadel-based transports to make the odds even more in our favor." Bering's look became scarier as he said, "About the only thing that could go wrong would be if the aliens returned to Citadel. Considering what happened to them the last time they visited, that isn't likely. However, even a visit from them might be good for us, especially if they kill everyone back there. We'll just blame it on Austin!"

An irrational concern had been nagging at Harrington. "What if our people *can't* destroy the derelict?" she asked.

Bering still had the answers. "If all else fails, they have orders to attach multiple remote thrusters to the derelict and set it on a course for the Citadel star at high acceleration. Not even that ship can withstand a one-way ticket like that, Madame President. Once that happens, we can write whatever story we want, and everyone else be damned. Even General Choi's press conference won't make a difference in time."

CHAPTER TWENTY FIVE

Roetter had been transferred from *KT-2* to *Pathfinder*. He stood before Austin, wearing restraints and looking worse for the wear. Austin suspected that Sara Albretti had had something to do with the bruises around Roetter's face that spread out in angry blotches. They looked something like a fist or a boot, although they could just as well have happened during the time that Roetter was captured. Regardless, after listening to Sara's initial report, Austin wouldn't have blamed her.

There was a cold blue fire in Austin's eyes. "Major Roetter," he began. "I told you we would have an unpleasant talk. I have received an initial report from Captain Sara Albretti that damns you. What we have learned so far from the other survivors is equally damning for you and your people. While I suppose that you must have sworn an oath at some point when you received your commission to defend and uphold the US Constitution, your actions have been a disgrace to the uniform and your country."

"What you think doesn't matter, Austin," Roetter answered. "What Albretti claims doesn't matter, either. I was just following orders from my superiors, going all the way to the president of the United States. If you have a problem, take it up with her."

Joe Albretti stood and said to Austin, "With respect, before we continue we should ensure that the prisoner has had a chance to make a trip to the head. It's the proper thing to do."

Without expression, Austin gave Albretti permission to escort Roetter out of the room. After a few minutes, they returned. Some of the starch had gone out of the prisoner. There was something on his face that looked like the mark from another fist. Also, the way Roetter walked suggested he had taken some shots to the balls as well. A grim twinkle appeared in one of Austin's cold blue eyes for a moment before it vanished. He continued, "You were saying, Roetter?"

Roetter stood at attention as he said, "Mr. President, my response to the issues you have raised, as well as the claims from Captain Albretti, is that I was following orders issued to me by President Harrington. While you have disputed whether there was a legitimate basis for those orders, they were nevertheless ones that I was duty bound to obey."

"Did your orders include killing unarmed prisoners?" Austin demanded.

Roetter appeared to take some time to swallow before he answered. "My orders were that we were in a situation where hostilities were present and that I needed to do whatever it took to accomplish my mission."

Austin didn't bother hiding the look of revulsion on his face. "I guess your political commission meant you didn't bother to learn about military rules and regulations where prisoners are concerned, Roetter, especially in time of war, even if the war is one of your own creation. You probably didn't have to worry about such things when interrogating people during some of those political assignments. You probably also didn't bother to learn about your duties where unlawful orders are concerned. Fortunately, my commission as an officer in the United States Navy, serving the same government you claim to serve, required that I learn about these things.

"However, we are pressed for time for now, so we will continue this conversation at another time. When we do, I will tell you some of my thoughts about the lives on nine of our transports that were lost when you and your people refused to yield control of those ships to their proper crews in order to deal with the emergency. Thanks to your actions, we have to go after the aliens to retrieve the derelict and make the loss of those lives mean something."

There was a slightly smug look on Roetter's face. "You realize, Mr. President, that President Harrington considers you to be an enemy of the United States. Going after the alien ship might well eliminate that enemy."

An unpleasant look played across Austin's face as he said, "It's very tempting to give you the opportunity to see up close whether we succeed, Roetter, by bringing you along with us on *Pathfinder*. You could have a front-row seat when she helps to blast the hell out of the alien ship. However, as I've already stated, I have a much better understanding of my responsibilities than you do when it comes to the proper treatment of prisoners. Besides, you won't need to be aboard *Pathfinder* to worry about life-and-death issues on a personal level."

Roetter paled. "What do you mean?"

The look faded from Austin's face into something hard as he said, "Regardless of the specious nature of some of your arguments that your orders were lawful, you and your people have committed multiple war crimes. You will appear before a tribunal on Citadel that is very much based on the military tribunals I established a century ago on Earth. Good luck trying to use some of the excuses you've given so far. War crimes and crimes against humanity are capital crimes on both Earth and Citadel. If you are convicted of such crimes, you will likely face execution by hanging. It is in your best interest to cooperate with us now instead of continuing to stonewall and lie. You aren't likely to find much mercy otherwise."

CHAPTER TWENTY SIX

True to her word, within twenty-four hours, Curly Stephens was giving Austin an update on the transport she had added to the other five that were ready to recapture the derelict. She stood before a giant screen as she pointed out what was working.

"Like I said earlier, this transport hasn't gone through a final shakedown. We focused on getting the systems up and running that are needed to handle the weapons, environment, gravity, communications, sensors, and propulsion, including the warp-field generators. Forget about the rest of the creature comforts, because they aren't worth a damn right now."

Stephens brought up a familiar image as she continued. "While the aliens' EMP weapon is too powerful for our transports to handle individually anyway, this particular transport would probably fail before the others. We haven't had the time to 'harden' it as much as we would have liked. That means that once EMPs start being bandied about, sensors and communications will suck on this ship even more than on the others."

"What about a rail gun, Curly?"

For just a moment, her expression brightened. "A bit of good news is that we've managed to set up several of the transports with rail guns. There hasn't been any time to check them out for effectiveness, though, so tracking and aiming functions may be subpar. We also know they aren't as powerful as what we've set up elsewhere in our system for protection, although they can still pack quite a punch."

As Austin nodded his appreciation, Stephens continued in a subdued tone. "One other thing we've tried to do with this transport and the rest of the transports is to set up some more effective manual systems for the crews to use in case their ships are trashed. That way, they'll have a better chance of surviving until they can be picked up by another ship."

Stephens looked melancholy as she added, "We're hoping, of course, that there will be ships left from the assault that can pick up survivors. We stripped everything we had to get the one transport ready to join you, so you know that there won't be any way for us to get to you otherwise until we can finish getting more ships up and running. It isn't likely that these systems will sustain you if they are trashed. If that happens, you can take your pick how you will die as your environment fails."

Austin was equally melancholy as he said, "Thanks for everything, Curly. With luck, we'll come back to you under our own power." Stephens's face disappeared from the screen.

Austin thought back on a message he'd delivered to the other transports shortly after Stephens had gone to work at the yard on the extra transport. Austin had opened a link from *Pathfinder* and begun, "First of all, I want to stress that only volunteers are going on this mission. I'm proud of and very grateful for everything that you've done to deal with an impossible situation. As much as Citadel needs you, so do your families. Nothing will be said about anyone who wants to be with his or her family.

"I have some special words for the crews of *KT-2* and *KT-7*. I won't begin to claim I understand what it's been like for you over the past three months. It goes without saying that you've all acquitted yourselves admirably during this time. While most of you don't have families here on Citadel, you still have families back in Earth's solar system. You are also part of the Citadel family. In view of what you've been through, I want to stress and even advise that it is OK to stand down and let someone else in the Citadel family take on this next mission. You have nothing to prove to anyone. Whatever you decide, it's been an honor to know each of you."

Austin also thought back on the conversation he had had with Sara Albretti not long afterward.

She got right to the point, pleading, "Sam, please don't order us to stand down."

"I'm *not* ordering you, Sara," Austin replied wryly. "It's probably a good idea for you and your crew, though, considering what you've been through."

"It's because of what we've been through that we need to do this."

"Why don't you tell me about it," Austin said gently.

Sara seemed to be talking to herself as much as to Austin. "It isn't just that we were prisoners for three months, although that was bad enough. Citadel itself was being called into question, which meant that *we* were being called into question. It was hard being told that we had done something that was so bad that another nation felt justified in waging war on us.

"That was only the beginning, though. Roetter went out of his way to humiliate us and prove that he was in charge. He went out of his way to humiliate *me*."

Austin said, "Sara, this is a difficult question, but I need to ask it. Aside from the murders, did Roetter or any of his people mistreat you or any of your crew in any physical way, including sexually?"

Sara shed a tear as she said, "He slapped me more than once in the face to show me who was boss, usually when he wanted to get information from me or force me to show him respect as a superior officer. The first time he slapped me was right after we'd been captured and I was still tied to a chair with my arms behind me. The front of my jumpsuit had been ripped open at some point. No one made any effort to cover me up. After he murdered one of my people in front of me, he told me that if I didn't cooperate, when he was through with me, Joe wouldn't want me anymore." Sara's expression was stony. "He never actually touched me sexually, though his look was revolting. I wasn't the only member of my crew to take a beating from Roetter or one of his people. While they didn't do it every day, they did it from time to time to remind us that they were in charge."

She flinched as Austin's eyes turned colder than she'd thought possible. She was grateful for Austin's fierce loyalty to his people and knew it meant Roetter was in even more trouble than he might have guessed. She continued, "Anyway, while all of that was bad enough, it was worse when the alien ship attacked us and Roetter wouldn't let us take control of our ship to try to defend ourselves. I think he froze from not knowing what to do in that situation."

"I'm not surprised, Sara," Austin said with disdain. "If his commission is a political one, I doubt he's ever actually seen combat. Please go on."

"All we could do was watch the other ships fall to the alien weapon while we didn't do anything. We were helpless because of that asshole's actions," she said, her eyes welling with angry tears.

"You didn't stay helpless, though. You looked for your chance and took it,"

"It occurred to me that we had a chance when visuals and communications were so bad that we couldn't tell what was happening anywhere. While Roetter was distracted, we jumped him and his people and took them down."

A little color appeared in her face as she continued. "Roetter took some extra hits before he was subdued, I'm happy to say. We confiscated their links, and I sent most of my bridge crew to round up the rest of them while we tried to do something." Sara shed another tear as she said, "We didn't do anything, though. We couldn't even get our EMP weapon online in time before the aliens headed out with the derelict."

"You're wrong if you believe you didn't do anything, Sara," Austin said emphatically. "Because of your actions, you saved the lives of your crew. I'll bet their families would agree with me that you did plenty."

Sara's face showed some doubt over Austin's comment as she said, "Anyway, Sam, we've been forced to be helpless for three months, and we're tired of it. Going on this mission means that we finally get to be in charge of our destinies again. I've spoken with my crew, and they have asked me to let you know that it is their unanimous desire to remain on board *KT-2* for this mission."

The admiration was plain on Austin's face as he replied, "Captain Albretti, please inform your crew that their request to remain at their posts for this mission is granted. The same goes for their captain."

They'd been making and refining their plans for dealing with the alien ship practically since the countdown had begun. The people linked into the conversation included Austin, Yabuno, Turner, and all of the captains.

Austin continued, "Thanks to the long-range sensors that Joe has been depositing around the neighborhood, we have a reasonably good idea of their course and speed as they headed away from here."

One of the transport captains asked, "Why don't we just go after them at our top speed, Sam?"

Austin shook his head. "We'd never catch them. In a regular foot race, they'd win."

"They didn't do so well when they were attacking Earth," the captain countered.

Sara spoke up. "That was because we had already pounded the hell out of their ship. Also, they may have used up something in pulling a scout ship out of the main ship back when they were in the Citadel system. They didn't have to do that this time."

"Sara's right," Austin said. "We have to assume that we won't have any of those advantages this time."

Another captain asked, "They'll have the same problem with the derelict that Earth did, won't they? Even *they* can't transport it with warp-field generators. That means that they'll have to stop if they want to analyze it. Why not just follow them until they stop and then attack?"

"They'll be able to track us long before we reach them if we're traveling under normal propulsion," Austin replied. They can just keep putting more distance between us and them until there's no way to ever catch up. Also, we're only set up to track them for a short time. It won't be long before they're out of range of our sensors, and then we won't have any way to track them."

A predatory look appeared on his face as he continued. "Fortunately, that's where our warp-field generators come in. If we do this right, we can use them to get ahead of where we think they'll be and catch them off guard. We can do to them what they did to us. This only works if we're right on top of them, so there won't be any time for us to get accustomed to the surroundings."

Yabuno said, "Another reason we need to do this quickly is that we don't know whether they've contacted another one of their ships. We need to get this over with and get the derelict deep inside our solar system where they won't be able to reach it. We might even be able to use our mobile weapons platforms to hassle them if they get too close to the entrance."

Austin continued, "We'll want to approach them from at least two different directions. Their EMP weapon is nasty, but it can only be aimed in one direction at a time. We have mobility on our side, and we need to take full advantage of it."

"What about their other weapon, the lasers?" Sara asked. "Their lasers took out every physical weapon we launched at them from Earth."

"We're not sure how powerful those lasers are," Yabuno admitted. "While they were able to take out Earth's nuclear weapons and satellite-based projectiles, you don't really need a lot of energy to do it. We'll have to be ready to adapt to the situation if they use them and they turn out to be strong enough to affect our ships."

Turner spoke up. "There's another potential weapon that we have. The reason I say 'potential' is that we don't even know if it will work, so it's hard to make a plan around it. However, if you get the order to haul ass, do it right away because it means we're going to try it. If it works, you won't want to be anywhere near the alien ship or the derelict."

As they continued with their preparations, Austin had a private conversation with Bret, Liz, Alan, and Joe.

"Sam," Turner began, "you know I'll support whatever we do, but let's understand that going after the derelict means that more of our people will probably die. Are the lives worth it? Is the derelict really worth it?"

Austin looked at everyone for a moment before he answered. "I hope so, Alan. While we're dealing with a phony war thanks to Harrington, we also have to deal with a real one. We might not have lost the lives we lost today if we'd had all of our ships arranged around the derelict. We'd have been in a position to take on the aliens with our weapons and perhaps destroy them or at least drive them off. We have to show them that we aren't afraid of them and that the price of attacking us is too great for them to try again."

"What if the aliens aren't really at war with us?" Turner countered. "What if their only objective all along has been to find and claim the derelict and then leave us alone?"

Austin was skeptical. "If that's the case, then why did they invade this solar system the last time and try to destroy Citadel after taking out the yard? For that matter, why did they attack Earth's solar system after we drove them out of here before?"

Turner shrugged. "I get the question about attacking this solar system and I don't have an answer for it, but as far as attacking Earth and Mars is concerned, once fighting starts it's pretty hard to stop it. Why should that be any different for aliens?"

"Their approach to getting what they want includes killing our people," Austin said with some heat. "That means I don't really care about the rest of it. They need to understand the high price they'll have to pay for their approach. If that doesn't work, then vengeance is a good enough reason to go after them," Austin concluded.

Albretti spoke up. "If we just give up now, it would be an insult to Gina and the others who died a year ago while trying to protect us. It would also be an insult to the people who died this time."

"I don't claim to have analyzed this matter perfectly," Austin said deliberately. "I believe that vengeance is sometimes worth it, so long as you don't become consumed by the desire for it. This is one of those times where I have to make a command decision and hope I can live with the consequences. That's one reason why only volunteers are going after the aliens. While I've ordered men and women to their deaths in combat more than once, our lives are too few and precious here on Citadel to order anyone to give up his life. I pray that whatever happens to those lives, they won't have been wasted."

Austin gave Turner a hard look. Turner shook his head, but didn't say anything.

CHAPTER TWENTY SEVEN

After further refinements to their plans, they were ready to go. From the information provided by their long-range sensors, it didn't appear that the aliens were much worried, or at least they hadn't seen any reason to change their course. Within seconds, the ships vanished into the blackness.

Austin, Yabuno, and Albretti discussed the latest information just after they'd headed out. "The aliens have put a good day's travel between themselves and Citadel," Albretti said. "Fortunately, the distance isn't significant when using a warp-field generator to catch up with them."

Yabuno said, "The good news is that they seemed to have reduced their speed substantially, which suggests that they've decided that there won't be any pursuit. They might even be planning on coming to a complete halt and inspecting their ill-gotten cargo."

"We can't use our EMP weapons while in a warp-field bubble," Austin noted, "which is why we need to bring them all online as quickly as possible once we materialize into normal space."

Albretti looked at a display as he said, "That'll be in about five seconds." Seconds after the pursuers materialized into normal space, Albretti and the other captains looked for their quarry's location. "Got you!" Albretti said with satisfaction as they moved toward their enemy.

While they were waiting for their EMP weapons to charge enough for use, they saw their enemy's familiar EMP probe extend itself, already primed for action. Before the communications became too degraded, Austin sent a message out to the group: "As planned, *KT-8, 10,* and *12* split off to port; *KT-2, 6,* and *7* split to starboard. Let's make those bastards commit to one side or the other so that we can pound the other side!"

Almost immediately, the probe sent out its EM horror, and visuals and communications near the ships took a hit as well. Yabuno looked at the display and said, "Shit! It looks like *KT-8* and *12* are already affected. Although they can still maneuver, much of the power from their EMP weapons has been reduced."

Austin spoke to the display: "*KT-10,* keep that side engaged if you can, while the other side does its work." In response, *KT-10* brought its own weapon to bear on the alien ship and opened fire.

Austin looked to Yabuno, who said, "While it looks like there's some damage, we'll have to add to the damage from our other weapons if we're going to take out these creeps." Yabuno paused for a moment as he looked back at a display. "They're trying to move to lock their probe onto *KT-10*, but our guys figured it out and are moving out of the way."

Austin had been splitting his attention between both sides of the attack. The three transports on the other side used their EMP weapons as well, but the alien ship took the brutal punishment. Austin had to strain to make out the degraded images on the display. He pointed to it as he said, "Joe, the aliens are attacking the transports on that side with lasers. It looks like they're targeting our own EMP weapons." Austin had an inspiration. "While the lasers are being used, let's get into position and use our own EMP weapon against them."

As they maneuvered, Yabuno called out, "They've taken out *KT-6*'s EMP weapon."

Albretti said, "We're in position, Sam."

"Take out everything you can," Austin replied. *Pathfinder* launched its own EMP weapon and blasted the enemy lasers. Austin asked Yabuno for an update.

Yabuno grinned fiercely. "Although they're still using their lasers against us, it looks like there's now a blind spot where they can't reach us. The interference makes it hard to be sure, though."

"That's good news, Bret. Joe, *Pathfinder* is a hell of a lot more maneuverable than the transports, so let's use that to our advantage and use our EMP weapon as a distraction for their lasers. Let's try to keep our weapon shielded from them, though, until we're in a better position to use it."

Austin called out to the transports on the starboard side. "While *Pathfinder* is serving as a distraction for the lasers, switch over to your regular torpedoes and launch them."

As the torpedoes were launched, Yabuno said, "Too bad we haven't punched any holes in their hull yet, or we might be able to use some modified torpedoes with warp-field generators and rip them apart from the inside." He looked back at a display as he said, "I just hope that their lasers are tied up worrying about us and not able to deal with the torpedoes."

All of the faces in the room showed disappointment as they were reminded that as fast as the torpedoes were, they weren't too fast for the lasers to deal with. In moments, the torpedoes were nothing more than insignificant debris.

Yabuno pointed to the display. "What the hell! Somehow, they've managed to lengthen their tethers to the derelict enough to do a little maneuvering. Shit! They've caught *KT-8* and *12* by surprise." They watched in horror as the two transports were blasted by the EMP weapon.

The looks of horror changed to confusion as something streaked by the enemy ship, obscured within the degraded image. "That came from a rail gun!" Yabuno said, elation written over his face. They looked back to see *KT-10*'s newly deployed rail gun. The elation was only momentary, as the rock passed by without making contact. Austin didn't waste any time. "Joe, take us back toward that side, fast! Target them with our EMP weapon as a distraction to give *KT-10* some breathing room."

As *Pathfinder* began to move, a major hole appeared in the alien ship's hull, courtesy of another rock from

KT-10's rail gun. Unfortunately, in order to lessen the margin for error with his second shot, the captain had made the mistake of getting too close to his target. Austin saw the danger first: "*KT-10*, get the hell out of there!" They watched helplessly as the EMP weapon shifted and made sure the rail gun was no longer a threat. Austin ordered *Pathfinder* back to the other side. With the threats on one side neutralized, the EMP weapon began to shift toward the other side, where the fighting was still raging fiercely.

On the other side, the captain of *KT-7* wasn't making the same mistake with his newly deployed rail gun; he moved out of direct range of the enemy's weapon. Unfortunately, the lasers were still finding their targets, inflicting damage on *KT-7*'s weapon. The transport crew ignored the attacks and loaded a rock into their weapon and managed to launch it. The rock achieved extreme speed almost immediately, neutralizing the advantage of the EMP weapon and the lasers. Moments later, the alien hull was blasted, with the ancient projectile tearing another ugly hole in the enemy ship. Yabuno swore. "How the hell can they continue to function, with all the damage they've sustained?"

The aliens realized that they couldn't just stay where they were and hope that the Citadel ships would volunteer for destruction by venturing too close. While they had moved slightly to pursue two of the transports, they were still tethered to the derelict. If they didn't begin to maneuver more freely, additional holes would appear in their ship, causing catastrophic damage from which even they might not recover.

Austin called out to the ships, "Watch out, they're severing their lines so they can maneuver!" In rapid order, the ancient ship continued on its way as the aliens approached *KT-6*. The transport's rail gun had already launched a rock, but it missed. They managed to launch another one, with similar effect, before the EMP weapon found its target. The transport's rail gun was neutralized, and what was left of the ship began to drift.

The enemy turned its attention to *KT-2*, which had deployed its rail gun as well but was having difficulty getting a good lock on its target, thanks to earlier laser damage. *KT-2* was forced to move back as the EMP weapon sought it out.

Austin looked at Yabuno. "Can we launch any modified torpedoes, Bret, and rip them apart from the inside?"

Yabuno shook his head. "We could try, Sam, but there's so much interference out there it would be next to impossible to aim them properly."

Alan Turner looked at Austin while nodding at the display. "We'll have to try something else, then. Thank God some distance has finally opened up between the aliens and the derelict."

Austin nodded back. "I hope this works."

After sending a brief message to the two transports still in operation, Austin turned back to Albretti. "Joe, I want *Pathfinder* to pass between the two alien vessels." Austin pointed to the display for the course to take. The alien EMP weapon attempted to follow and lock onto *Pathfinder* for a clear shot, but the angle of the smaller ship's approach was too steep and the movement too rapid. The aliens were hindered further by the fact that the humans moved through the "blind" spot that protected them from the lasers that had lashed out at their sister ships.

As they passed between the vessels, Austin watched the display. "It's a pretty eerie sight to find ourselves closer to an invader ship than anyone has ever ventured before." While the holes in the alien hull were unsettling to see, their eyes were quickly drawn to the EMP weapon as it tried to track them in an attempt to bring forth more death and destruction. Austin's gaze was determined as he commented, "I'll be damned if they're going to catch us and bring an end to another ship with the *Pathfinder* name."

Austin looked at Albretti and said, "*Now, Joe.*" *Pathfinder* began to accelerate as it pulled out of the turn. Before the ship had even finished pulling away, it launched a torpedo, but not as the aliens expected. Instead of racing toward the enemy ship and useless early detonation, it moved toward the derelict. As *Pathfinder* completed its maneuver, the torpedo crashed into the ancient ship with an explosive charge that had been reduced to minimize damage. As this scenario played out, the other transports were racing away in opposite directions at extreme speed. For a critical moment, the aliens seemed unable to decide how to respond.

In that moment, the derelict came to awful life, with massive sheets of energy bursting from its hull, seeking the source of the attack. Unfortunately for the aliens, their ship shielded *Pathfinder* from the derelict. Ancient sensors concluded that the alien ship must have been the source of the attack.

Even a ship designed to absorb brutal punishment couldn't withstand contact with the energy that coursed through and overran every system. The holes that had been torn into the hull by the humans now served as pathways for endless waves of deadly fire. Many of the bizarre architectural structures on the surface of the invading ship either shriveled up and withered away or simply burst outward from the main body. In a shockingly short time, the ship was reduced to a twisted, burnt-out shape, devoid of life. The brutal surge of energy simply faded away, and the derelict again looked as it had for countless years, ignoring the other ships nearby.

The alien wreckage was no longer Austin's top priority as he looked at the display. "*Pathfinder, KT-2* and *7,* there are people on the other ships that need help. Let's get those rescue operations underway now." He knew he'd be shedding more tears later as they tallied up the dead.

In short order, they'd rescued everyone they could. Austin was grateful to note that the manual systems that Stephens installed had kept the fatalities to a tiny number. They attached remote thrusters to the derelict, which were ignored by the ancient ship. They did a brief survey of the burnt-out hulk of the alien ship. Yabuno looked back at Austin and shook his head. "There isn't any way anyone could have survived that destruction, Sam. For that matter, I can't recognize anything that looks like useful technology within those charred remains." He nodded at the display. "See, the glow from the fires is already fading."

Austin was uneasy and pushed everyone to finish as quickly as possible. As they headed back toward Citadel,

Austin ordered that the thrusters be brought up to high speed and had the transports match them.

"What's wrong, Sam?" Yabuno asked. "I know we won't have luxurious accommodations during the return trip, but we've retrieved the derelict and had the satisfaction of watching the aliens blasted into toast." Yabuno looked at Turner with admiration. "That was a hell of a piece of speculation, Alan. How did you figure it out?"

Turner replied, "It seemed to me that the derelict was still able to react to external forces. It could tell that our experiment with light was an inquiry, and it reacted accordingly. I assumed that it still had plenty of energy in reserve, so I wondered if it could make a determination that something was of a hostile nature and react accordingly. A torpedo couldn't have been taken for anything else, so if it was going to react at all, it would be to the torpedo. I was just hoping that the energy available was enough to take out the alien ship.

"Obviously, it was," Turner continued wryly. "We now have a reminder of the importance of not doing anything that could be construed as a hostile act against it. It's also a good reminder of why we don't want it too close to our planet."

"Speaking of our planet, I still don't see why you aren't happier about the outcome, Sam," Yabuno said. "We kicked their asses and are heading back home with our prize."

"I'm not happy about any outcome that costs us precious lives and more of our transports," Austin replied. "At most, I'm cautiously optimistic about the situation. While it's good that we've recaptured the derelict, I'm just not sure it's over. We still don't know if there are any other aliens in the area. If they're close enough, they can still catch us, and we aren't in any shape to take them on again."

"There isn't anything reported on the long-range sensors."

Austin frowned. "What if they blindside us again with an attack straight from a drop into normal space from a warp-field bubble?"

Yabuno's expression was hard as he nodded in the direction of the derelict. "At that point, we keep the thrusters going and scatter in separate warp bubbles. The thrusters are programmed to take the derelict to Citadel, and it wouldn't be a good idea for the aliens to try to blast the thrusters off the derelict. There's no reason to believe that they wouldn't suffer the same fate as their deep-fried friends we left behind, even if their aim was true and they took out the thrusters on the first shot."

He looked back toward a display as he continued. "That reminds me to revise the programming to ensure that the thrusters reduce speed as the derelict approaches the solar system, so that we don't have to try to reduce that speed from within our system."

"You'll want to make sure that if the aliens are about to capture it, the thrusters will haul ass into our system; we'll just have to deal with it at the time." Austin paused for a moment, deep in thought. "I have an idea that may buy us some time if we need it."

Hours later, Austin was still uneasy. Yabuno started to assure his friend that there was nothing to worry about, when he noticed that new information was coming in from the long-range sensors. His face turned pale as he said, "You were right to worry, Sam. Another one of those monsters just showed up. It didn't waste much time checking out what was left of its fellow ship; it's now heading after us at high speed."

Turner looked at both Austin and Yabuno as he said, "We may end up with a hell of a train wreck if we can't stop them."

CHAPTER TWENTY EIGHT

As the hours passed, they kept track of their enemy's progress. Austin looked at Albretti, who shook his head. "It won't be enough, Sam. I've compared our progress with theirs, and they'll overtake us before we reach Citadel."

"It'll be pretty close," Yabuno said, "but they might have enough time to neutralize the momentum from the remote thrusters and recapture the derelict. That would be pretty bitter to take, considering what we've already been through."

Austin wasn't about to accept that outcome. "We have to find a way to slow them down or run the risk of a disaster for our system. I doubt even Curly can pull any more miracles out of the yard." He ordered the transports to take positions behind the derelict, saying, "We'll force the aliens to go through the transports to get to the prize; there isn't enough time to try to do an end run around them."

"I wonder why they haven't tried to blindside us by using their warp-field generators to get between us and Citadel," Albretti asked.

"Originally, that might have been their best bet, but we were already hours closer to home when they found the wreckage of their sister ship. At that point, we were probably too close to the system to be sure of coming back into normal space out of range of our mobile rail guns," Austin replied. "The asteroids those guns can launch are massive and could easily rip to pieces even a ship as large as what the aliens have. Also, if they over-shoot their mark, they could end up in the radiation field, which they've always avoided. The best option for them now is direct pursuit."

More hours passed in the deadly race, and soon an image appeared on their rear displays. At first it was tiny, hardly distinguishable from the rest of the minor debris of space. With each passing second, the image seemed to grow slightly in size, gradually becoming recognizable as something other than a planetary body. As it continued to grow, they could make out individual features on its surface.

Eventually, despite the distance, the ship nearly filled up their screens. They began to make out the image of their old enemy, the EMP weapon, in more detail. Austin spoke to Yabuno. "I wish to hell we'd been able to trans-fer more of the survivors aboard *Pathfinder*, instead of aboard *KT-2* and *7*. It feels like they're still in the line of fire that way."

Yabuno replied, "That's the tough part about your plan; we have to wait until the last moment to make it work. One problem is that we don't know the precise range of their weapon. If that monster can be used before we're ready, we'll lose the race, the prize, and probably our lives."

"How are they coming along on the transports?"

"It's hard to tell. Both rail guns have taken some damage from the lasers and whether they'll be worth a damn isn't clear."

The alien weapon began to glow, signifying that it was beginning its attack. Austin ordered the rail guns to open fire, ready or not. The first rock missed completely, and the target was able to lurch slightly and avoid the other one. Yabuno cursed as he pointed at a display. "They're moving in an irregular fashion. We're already having a hell of a time with our rail guns; they've made it even harder to track and aim with them."

"How much distance have they lost through their maneuvers?" Austin asked.

Yabuno shook his head. "Although they've lost a slight amount, it won't be enough to matter."

Austin stared at the display as he said, "The rail guns need to end it, fast!"

Another rock was launched, ripping off one of the impossible structures on the ship's surface. The enemy didn't slow down. Another rock was launched and missed completely. Yabuno said, "For all we know, their EMP weapon could be affecting the rail guns, adding to the damage they've already suffered."

Austin nodded. "That could explain all the aiming problems we've been having. I just pray that we can get off at least one good shot before the guns fail completely."

Ahead of them a familiar solar system loomed in their screen, seemingly close enough to touch. Although the system beckoned with a promise of safety, the promise was a false one because they were still too far away.

As they continued to have trouble with aiming and firing, an urgent message came in from Stephens. "Sam! Get ready to move the hell out of the way!"

Austin looked at a forward display, and his eyes widened in shock. He did a quick calculation and broadcast an emergency message to the other ships. "Everyone! Get ready to do a quick jog off our course in thirty seconds. *KT-2*, move to port, and *KT-7* and *Pathfinder*, move to starboard. Start the countdown *now!*" Austin didn't need to add that there was no way to change the derelict's course.

When they got to zero, they all moved, sidestepping two massive asteroids that had been launched earlier from Citadel's mobile rail guns down their path. The behemoths passed within less than two hundred meters of the derelict, yet it might have been two hundred miles for all the derelict cared.

The alien ship began to move out of the way and might have succeeded in avoiding the massive projectiles, except that an asteroid from one of the rail guns finally found its target, followed by another. At the speed at which both the aliens and the rocks had been traveling, the damage was devastating and might have been enough to destroy the ship all by itself. For a brief instant, they could actually see a hole through one side of the ship, the ragged edges resembling lacerated tissue. Even more importantly, the ship's side motion was cancelled out for an instant by the collisions, holding it in place as the two giants smashed it into oblivion. The last they saw of their pursuers was a terrible fireball as the internal energy of the ship engaged in a hellish embrace with the energy from large and larger rocks.

The Citadel solar system now beckoned directly in front of them, but they were dangerously close to having the train wreck Turner had predicted. Austin turned to Yabuno and said, "Bret, we need to slam on the brakes!"

A moment later, Yabuno replied, "The thrusters are decelerating as quickly as possible; they'll burn out from the load, but I don't know how quickly." He pointed to the display. "There isn't anything else we can do. We sure as hell can't follow the derelict into the radiation field, and there isn't much of anything in place to stop it on the other side."

The ancient ship seemed determined to go right up to the radiation field and demand entry, but it finally decided that it could halt and wait for assistance. As Austin and the others in the bridge breathed a sigh of relief, he could have sworn he heard cheers even from the transports and beyond, in Citadel itself.

An image of Curly Stephens appeared on the screen. The tears that had been there earlier had been replaced with new tears over the new lives lost, plus a look of relief.

"Once the alien ship started closing the distance, you looked like you might need some help," she said, "so I figured sending a couple of jumbo-size asteroids after you couldn't hurt. I also figured that the thrusters would probably be toast by now, so I brought a few new ones to guide the derelict to its yard. After all, you can never have too many spares!"

She wiped the tears away and grinned broadly as she said, "Welcome home. You have no idea how good it is to see you!"

CHAPTER TWENTY NINE

As the derelict was finally escorted to its new home, Roetter and his surviving people were taken to Citadel and interrogated more fully. Although they'd tried to maintain the fiction about their actions, the full story came out eventually. All of the settlers' fears about Harrington and her ambitions were confirmed. As Roetter and his people were transferred to an orbiting prison to await further action, Austin discussed the matter with Yabuno and Liz.

"So we're at war with the United States," Yabuno said.

"I wonder if that's really true," Liz replied. "We seem to be at war with Courtney Harrington's ambitions, but are we sure those make us enemies of the United States?"

Austin was deep in thought as he mused, "Regardless of whether the hostilities are simply a reflection of Harrington's ambitions, she has ordered the United States government to engage in acts of war against another nation. I don't see how we can overlook those actions, especially considering the high cost to us. The Citadel Group's people may still be rotting in jail for all

we know. Our assets in that solar system have been confiscated, perhaps even destroyed. Most of our transports
have been destroyed. We've lost the lives of the good
people who formed the crews of nine transports. Other
people were murdered as well. We know that Roetter
would have tried to kill me if he could have found a way
to do it.

"I'm trying to figure out the next steps," Austin said,
the weight of the burden plain to see. "We'll have to
respond to the United States and Harrington. I'm just
not sure what the response should be. Do we send a
sternly worded message to the international community
condemning Harrington's actions? How much do they
know about what has really happened? I'm very tempted
to travel to Earth to have it out with her."

Liz was alarmed at the thought. "If Citadel has
been taken over by the US, you might find yourself in
custody, perhaps on some trumped-up charge as a war
criminal."

"I'm having a hard time believing that the people
would stand for such an outrage," Austin said, shaking
his head. "For that matter, I'm having a hard time believing that Harrington can keep the lid on everything until
the election is over. She must be pulling every dirty trick
and telling every lie possible to make it happen. If I'm
there to show the lies for what they are, her entire narra-
tive goes away."

Some familiar steel showed up in Austin's voice as he
continued, "However, I won't make the mistake of showing up without the ability to remind people about what
it means to have Citadel for an enemy. I need to have a

talk with Curly if I'm going to make it there in time for the election!"

Austin had been spending most of his time aboard *Pathfinder*, getting things ready for their trip. He and Liz hadn't been able to spend more than a few minutes talking to each other over their links. He was in a small cabin he'd selected for the trip when Liz showed up unannounced. He was surprised but pleased to see her. "Liz, I wasn't expecting you."

Liz leaned against a bulkhead. "We haven't really had a chance to talk lately, especially about the notion of your going to Earth again without me."

Austin's pleased look faded. "I thought you were going to stay on Citadel and look after Donna while we're gone."

Liz's face took on a wry look as she said, "Donna has informed me that she's perfectly capable of looking after herself and her kids. She also said she can look after our place again while we're gone."

Austin frowned as he rose. "Liz, we can't keep asking people to look after our place every time I need to go to Earth! It was incredibly generous of everyone to offer the last time, but they have their own places to worry about."

Liz shook her head gently as she replied, "You just don't get it, Sam. There are some debts that can't ever be paid. You were willing to die for Citadel."

"So were plenty of others," Austin pointed out.

"It was still different for you. You've always provided the leadership for Citadel. You've never asked anyone to do anything that you weren't prepared to do yourself. Now, you have an even tougher job, which is to avoid letting Courtney Harrington drag Citadel into a war, hopefully without the loss of any more lives. That means you may have to place yourself directly in harm's way to make a point." She got down on her knees in front of Austin as she continued, "I once told you I'd never again be apart from you when those times were at hand, and I meant it. I won't watch you leave, never knowing if I'll ever see you again. I love you too much."

She got to her feet. "My stuff is just outside this hatch. Matt and Luke are on board, taking a tour of the ship. We probably won't see them for a couple of hours before they are taken to their cabin, which is next to ours." With a mischievous tone, she continued, "If you want to put me off this ship, you'll need to lay hands on me to do it yourself. However, while you're laying hands on me, I plan on doing something else with my hands. There's no way we're going to go six months or longer without making love, and we might as well get started!"

Austin knew when he was beat. The same look came into his eyes as he said, "OK, Liz, you and the boys can come along." He took a quick look at the clock as they embraced, which she saw. With a giggle, she said, "We have plenty of time, Sam, and there won't be any interruptions—don't you think the crew knows why I told them to take the boys on a two-hour tour?"

One of the benefits on the new and improved Pathfinder was that the sound of their giggles didn't reach outside the hatch.

CHAPTER THIRTY

Harrington's eyes widened in shock as she read the message that had just been handed to her by Bering.

"They failed! Damn it, you assured me that this wouldn't happen, Bering. Now, Austin is onto us and looking for revenge!"

Bering maintained his calm. "We can make this work to our advantage, Madame President."

Harrington had a dangerous look on her face as she glared at Bering to see if he was mocking her. As usual, there was nothing to read. "I hope you aren't being a smart-ass, Bering, because this isn't the time for it."

"I couldn't be more serious," he replied. "Think about it. We now have proof that Austin is heading here to wage war against the United States. That moves us past the whole theoretical realm into the concrete. We can announce that hostilities have broken out and that we are preparing for an invasion and attack. Since it will happen around a week before the election, there won't be anything your opposition can do about it. Austin couldn't have taken a better move to ensure that you'll be reelected."

Harrington turned to Chambers with the message and said, "What about it, Ned? Is Bering blowing smoke at me, or does this give us a more solid basis for dealing with Citadel?"

Chambers finished reading. "This message isn't clear about hostilities, Madame President. It makes it clear that the effort to take over Citadel's transports and the derelict has failed and that you will be held responsible for your having ordered these actions and in ordering the unprovoked attack on Citadel." Chambers paused for a moment as he reread a part of the message. "Austin is expressing outrage over the loss of life aboard nine of their transports that were 'hijacked' on your orders. These are all expressions of outrage over *your* actions, not a declaration of war against the United States."

Bering said, "A threat against the president of the United States in her official capacity *is* a threat against the United States."

Chambers said, "You're talking nonsense, Bering. Madame President, we cannot take this message to Congress as the basis for a declaration of war."

"Let's take another message to Congress, then," Bering said.

"I agree," Molder said. "It wouldn't take much to make this into something that is practically a declaration of war against the United States."

Walker cried, "Are you out of your mind! What do you think will happen when Congress finds out that we've provided a falsified message in order to get it to declare war on Citadel?"

"What do you think will happen if Congress finds out we've already been lying?"

Walker all but sneered at Bering as he said, "So you admit that your *intelligence* was bogus."

Bering refused to be rattled by the outburst. "I think we're well past keeping score of everyone's part in this campaign, Walker. If you really had misgivings, you could have pushed the matter further."

As Walker prepared to make another comment, Harrington broke in with her thoughts and said, "In a sense, we don't have to go to Congress for a formal declaration of war. When Austin arrives, we can either wait for his attack, if that's his intent, or we can attack him and claim it was in self-defense. Once his ships respond, we'll have our hostilities, and that's what we'll present to Congress. Even if we don't get a formal declaration of war, we will have made our point about Austin and won reelection."

CHAPTER THIRTY ONE

As Roetter sat in his cell, he brooded over the relative ease with which his captors had drawn from him the truth about his orders. He still didn't understand why, in the end, they'd hardly been able to shut him up. He found that having always been on the other side of an interrogation up until now had done nothing to improve his ability to maintain his lies in a plausible form. He'd been especially unnerved by the fact that Austin himself had participated in some of the questioning. Austin's personality, magnified by his anger over the loss of life, was simply too forceful for Roetter to continue with the lies. To his surprise, he realized that he was afraid of the man.

While no one was in any hurry to explain to him what to expect next, he had some pretty good guesses, and they didn't make him sleep any better. He hadn't forgotten Austin's comments about the penalty for war crimes. More than once, he'd cursed himself for not having killed Sara Albretti when he'd had the chance. It didn't occur to him that keeping Albretti alive had kept *him* alive; he'd frozen at the critical moment when the aliens had attacked, and she'd taken over and gotten them out of harm's way.

With a start, he realized that a woman had entered his cell. He was disturbed by the fact that the woman didn't show the slightest concern about being alone in the cell with him. In fact, her body language said that she was quite capable of taking care of herself. That self-confidence, plus the fact that it had been that easy for someone to sneak up on him, made him feel vulnerable in a way that he hadn't experienced before. He wondered if this was how it would end for him.

The woman was of medium height and build. Although she had a pretty face, her expression was anything but friendly at the moment. Roetter noticed with a start that she was wearing a jumpsuit from one of the transports. With a slight gesture from her hand, she motioned for Roetter to stay seated as she said, "We don't have much time, Roetter, so keep quiet and listen to me. My name isn't important. What you need to know is that I work for Bering, and I was placed on transport *KT-7*. I'm going to get you out of here so that you can complete at least part of your mission."

"Which part is that?"

The woman showed her impatience at Roetter's lack of comprehension as she replied, "Use your head, Roetter. Since you failed in your primary mission to capture and destroy the derelict, I'm talking about the only part left, which is for you to kill Sam Austin."

Roetter's face flushed slightly as he said, "I don't like your tone, whatever your name is. You are here to support me, so you will follow *my* orders."

The woman stared hard at Roetter. "Let's get something straight, Roetter. When I said I work for Bering, I mean *Bering*, not you. Bering will know soon enough that you've already screwed up; the only thing that might redeem you in his eyes will be to hear that Austin is dead." The woman's head tilted slightly as she continued, "I wouldn't want to be in your shoes if you fail again."

Roetter paled at those words. "What about your own mission? Why didn't I know about it?"

"You didn't need to know," she replied in a matter-of-fact tone, which stung. He wasn't used to being on the receiving end of being shut out of information.

"Why the hell not?" he demanded in some fury. "We might have been able to work together if I had known!"

The woman looked at Roetter with disdain. "There wasn't any chance to let you know. I'd been trying to work my way toward getting access to the files on the core technologies of our ship. Before I could complete my work, you and your people descended on us. Like a bunch of morons, you used such a heavy hand that all access was cut off. There wasn't any opportunity to talk without being discovered by the rest of the crew. Besides, you were on a different ship from mine. Also, there was still a chance I could be more effective by staying under cover. As it turns out, I was right. Otherwise, you'd probably rot in this cell until they got around to hanging you."

The woman tossed a travel bag at Roetter. "Put these clothes on. Everything else goes into the bag."

As Roetter got out of his clothes, he asked, "What are these?"

"You'd be captured in no time if you walked out of here in your uniform. Fortunately, nobody notices a jumpsuit like what we wear aboard a transport. We'll walk out of here like two colleagues."

Roetter frowned. "Isn't the place monitored?"

The woman sniffed as she replied, "They're a little too fond of automation around here, probably because they don't feel like building regular jails, where someone has to sit on his ass and guard prisoners.

"That's a good thing for you," she continued. "This is a modified storage facility, rather than something that was built as a prison from the start. They have sensors to let them know how everyone is doing and programs that make sure everyone is fed, et cetera, but no one actually checks up every day unless there's a problem with something. This place is pretty good at keeping its prisoners from getting out, but not as good at keeping out people that want to get in.

"I've gotten access to their systems and made it seem that everything is fine here. There will be no surveillance that will tell them anything is wrong, nor will they know that anyone left here wearing crew jumpsuits. You just need to shut up while we walk out and let me do the talking."

As Roetter zipped his jumpsuit, he gestured around and said, "What about my people? We'd have a better chance with more people."

The woman scoffed. "We'd have a better chance of everyone getting killed if we brought them along. Just where the hell do you think we'd put them? This is a system where everyone actually works for a living. Your people can't just pretend to take on tasks they don't know how to do, and I can't stash them planet-side. They sure as hell don't know anything about running a transport, so I can't take the chance of trying to smuggle them aboard one. Besides, they'd be recognized anyway, since I don't have any more jumpsuits to hand out. If you want to die, I'll just leave you here. If you want to live and carry out at least part of what you were supposed to do, get up and walk out with me."

Even a man like Roetter was uneasy about leaving his people to an uncertain fate. He asked, "What will happen to them?"

Without emotion, the woman said, "They will die for carrying out your orders, Roetter. Deal with it and let's go."

Roetter and the woman, whose name was Powers, were aboard a shuttle to *KT-7*. He'd balked at the idea, and Powers had hissed at him to be quiet. There were only a couple of others aboard, so they were able to talk in low voices at one end of the shuttle.

He had to work to keep the anxiety out of his voice as he said, "Are you out of your mind, Powers? I'm a dead man if I return to a transport."

"Keep your panties on, Roetter," she hissed. "You're a dead man if you return to *KT-2*. We're going to my ship, *KT-7*, where no one knows you."

"What good will that do?"

Powers took a nervous glance around the shuttle and decided it was too dangerous to keep talking. "No more talking about it until we get aboard my ship. All you need to know for now is that we're going to walk aboard just like we belong there."

"Won't they know I'm not part of the crew?"

She shook her head slightly, saying in a low voice, "Not everyone is going back to Earth on this trip. Some people need to take a break, and others from the other transports have volunteered to go instead. That means it will be normal to have some new faces. Now shut the hell up!"

Before they'd boarded the shuttle, Powers had unzipped her jumpsuit enough to show off a great deal of cleavage, enough to confirm to even a casual observer that she wasn't wearing a bra. She gave a quick glance downward as she said, "Besides, no one will be looking at my face. Since you'll be with me, no one will be giving you much of a look either while my distractions are on display. The most anyone will remember is just another set of jumpsuits."

"That isn't what they'll remember, Powers," Roetter replied wolfishly, his eyes enjoying the view.

The only response was a cold, hard look.

Hours later, Roetter and Powers were in Powers's cabin aboard *KT-7*. Roetter couldn't believe their luck had held. Everything had worked out as she had predicted. She'd even made sure to lean forward as they were boarding to keep any eyes from glancing upward. Roetter was disappointed to note that the moment they were in her cabin, the zipper went back up and her demeanor became all business as she explained the next steps in their plan.

"We'll be heading out later today. Once that happens, there's no way anyone will be able to get the word to the group about your escape. If the word gets through to Earth's solar system, your trail will be cold by then."

Roetter was nervous about fulfilling his assignment. "How am I going to get to Austin if he's on board *Pathfinder*?"

"We'll have to play it by ear once we get back there. I assume that Austin will pause before dealing with Earth, which should give us the time to get close to him." Powers stared at Roetter and said, "That reminds me, you should let your hair grow longer. You should also grow a beard, without making it look like something that Moses would wear. The point is that you should change your appearance as much as possible. You may even want to change your hair color."

She gestured around her. "You'll have plenty of time for these changes, because for the next three months, you will stay in this cabin. I will bring in meals and anything else you'll need." She nodded toward to the bathroom. "Fortunately, each cabin has its own facilities, so you can at least stay clean."

"I'll go out of my mind staying in this cabin for three months," Roetter complained.

"You'll lose your head if you don't," she snapped. "We have a hell of a lot of reading and movie entertainment available online. Just make certain that you never do anything that could let anyone know that you're in here while I'm on duty, since I live alone."

"Where do I sleep?"

"You can sleep in the bed, since I'll sleep at another time."

Roetter wasn't happy. "That won't work."

"Why not?"

"It would mean that I'd have to be quiet while you're asleep, which will be part of the day for me."

Powers rolled her eyes. "What does it matter? You're not going anywhere for a while."

"If I'm going to be stuck in here, it's only right that I be able to move around for as much of my nonsleeping time as possible."

"You're saying you want to sleep when I sleep."

"That's right."

Powers's eyes narrowed. "OK, Roetter, but we need to get a few things straight. While the bed is big enough for two, we're not going to sleep like anything other than house mates. I'm not here to handle any sexual needs you may have. You're going to do everything possible to respect my privacy, and I'll do likewise for you. I'll give you a pass over the fact that your eyes were going all over my chest, because I set it up that way to get us onto the ship, but that's the last time. The first time you cross the line, you'll be sleeping on the deck with a sore set of balls.

"One other thing—while I hope it never happens, in case someone sees you, you'll need to have a name. Since you'll have to respond to it, you should be the one to pick it. What will it be?"

Roetter thought for a moment. He said, "A long time ago I had a mentor that I respected a lot." His faced clouded slightly. "He was a far better man than my dad. His name was Les Marsh, so let's use it."

"Where is he now?" Powers asked.

"He's been dead for years. I doubt many people even remember him."

"OK." After repeating the name a few times for effect, Powers said, "That'll work. In fact, we'd both be dead if anyone were to hear me call you 'Roetter' during this trip, so from now on you'll be Les Marsh."

"What's your first name, Powers?"

Powers sighed. "You're right, you should know my name. My name is Mara. Just make sure you don't try to use it to get into my shorts."

CHAPTER THIRTY TWO

When *Pathfinder* had been rebuilt, she'd been expanded to accommodate some additional features. One of those features was a stateroom that was somewhat larger than the usual quarters. When Albretti learned that Austin had selected another, smaller, cabin, he insisted that Sam take the stateroom, over Sam's objections.

"Sam, *Pathfinder* is the closest thing Citadel has to an official transport for the president of Citadel. I know that you don't use that title much, but it still belongs to you, and we need it right now in order to face our enemies. As the president, these quarters are for you to use. If you need another analogy, then consider that the captain always yields to the admiral. You are both our admiral and our head of state. Custom requires that you have these quarters."

Austin replied, "The hell with custom. Even though Liz is with me on this trip, we can stay anywhere. The cabin we've already moved into is fine. The boys are in their own cabin, so it isn't like we have to have enough room for everyone in one place." Austin took on a wry tone as he continued, "Besides, you and Sara are newly-weds and need space with more privacy than what your quarters provide."

Liz had walked in during the conversation and sec-onded Sam's comments. "I know what it's like to be a newlywed, Joe, and you'll never have that special time together again. Of course Sam and I will stay in our cabin."

Albretti's face turned a slightly different color as he said, "Truth be told, my quarters are where Sara and I stayed as we got to know each other. That's also where we were when we got engaged. In fact, we were in bed at the time. I guess I don't need to spell out the details."

Austin chuckled. "I figured it was something like that when the two of you called me to perform the wed-ding ceremony. You were obviously in your cabin, and it looked like you'd been celebrating for quite some time. I know plenty of couples who got engaged while in bed and then did some serious celebrating, so there isn't any-thing more for you to explain."

Albretti grinned. "Sara is quite a woman. She's both sentimental and earthy. She'd probably say that that cabin will always remind us of where we found our love. She'd then probably say if she was going to be in a cabin, she'd rather look at that cabin's ceiling than another's."

Liz had a sly look on her face as she said, "It's not the ceiling that matters, Joe; it's what a woman is doing at the time that matters." She looked over at Austin. "I don't mind saying that there are certain ceilings that I don't mind looking at either, especially because Sam was there with me. You're right, Joe, you must stay in your quarters and share them with Sara when you can." She looked at Austin and grinned. "Since the stateroom won't be used otherwise anyway, I wouldn't mind having a larger set of quarters, Sam."

Austin chuckled as he said, "I guess it's settled, Joe. Funny thing is that we've been talking about cabin assignments, and Sara is still aboard *KT-2*. She won't give it up while there's still some serious business outstanding."

"That doesn't matter," Joe said. "She has a right to that cabin with me once we're able to get back together."

CHAPTER THIRTY THREE

They'd been underway for a month, and Roetter was going stir crazy. The trip out on *KT-2* hadn't been a problem, since he'd been in charge and able to move around anywhere he pleased. This time, he could go nowhere and he was subject to the whims of a woman who made it clear that she wasn't wild about the arrangement. The close quarters reminded him every day that Powers was an attractive woman. While he had abided by her rules, he was sorely tempted to try to bend them a little.

Powers was off duty, sitting at her small desk and working on a report. She'd planned on getting together with some of her colleagues later to relax. She found herself spending as little time in her cabin as possible, since she, too, was aware of Roetter's issues.

Roetter was stretched out on the bed, listening to music through a pair of headphones.

There was a sound at the door. In an instant, there was a new tension in the room. Powers waved at Roetter to be sure he was listening. Without opening the door, Powers answered through the intercom, "What is it?"

A male voice replied. "It's me, Marty. I need to go over some stuff before our shift in the morning. Can I come in?"

Powers's eyes widened with alarm, although her answer was calm. "Can't it wait, Marty? I'm not up for anything right now."

Marty replied, "I happened to be coming this way, Mara. It'll save me plenty of time if we can talk now. I only need a couple of minutes, and then I'll be gone. How about it?"

Powers looked around in desperation. "OK, just a minute, Marty." With frantic haste she stripped off her jumpsuit and slipped out of her bra and panties, messed up her hair, and hissed at Roetter, "Get out of your jump-suit and shirt *now*! Get into bed and turn your head to face away from the hatch." His eyes widened as he under-stood. In an instant, his jumpsuit and shirt were on the floor, and he was in bed as instructed.

Powers moved over to the hatch and opened it. She leaned around it in a way to make it clear that she wasn't wearing anything. In fact, she made sure he caught sight of her breasts so he would take in a quick, shocked look at the cabin and see a pile of clothes on the deck and an uncertain image of a man in bed. Marty's face turned bright red as the scene explained why Powers had been reluctant to let him inside.

"Oh my God, Mara, I'm so sorry for disturbing you!"

Powers put an understanding look on her face. "It's OK, Marty. What was it you wanted to discuss?" She guessed that there was no way that Marty would be able to stay and have a polite conversation while she was standing there naked. She was right, and in an instant all she saw of Marty was his backside as he beat a hasty retreat. Even in the distance she could see streaks of bright red along his neck and ears. He mumbled over his shoulder that he'd let the others know that she wouldn't be joining them later that evening.

Powers shut the hatch, pissed over the fact that now she'd be stuck there for the rest of the evening. She wasn't looking forward to all of the prying from her friends about the identity of her "lover," either. While she clearly couldn't deny it, she'd have to stay coy about it for a lot of weeks ahead.

Without warning, she was grabbed by the arms and pinned onto the bed. She found herself staring into Roetter's eyes, which radiated extreme desire as they started at her chest and continued down her body. He'd moved so fast that she hadn't had any warning. All he was wearing was his shorts. She was flat against the bed and very much aware of how naked she was at the moment.

Her eyes widened. "What the hell are you doing? You know damned well that we just did that for show, to save our hides. I'm not interested in continuing with the show. You know the rules. If you don't like them, then find someplace else to hide."

A moment later, she was unsettled to hear a different tone in Roetter's voice as he said, "Rules can change, Powers. There's nothing you can do to me that won't bring attention right back onto you. Now that we've been underway for a month, you can't claim that I'm just a stowaway. You've been in and out of this cabin many times without telling anyone about me. Marty and everyone else will assume that we're an item. You can't turn me in now without people wondering why you were hiding me, even having sex with me. You now belong to *me*."

She gasped as she realized the trap she had created for herself. He heard the gasp, and an even more revolting look appeared. "I see you understand now. For some time, I've been wondering if the rest of your body would be as attractive as what I've seen thus far. I'm pleased to say that it is."

Powers stopped struggling. Roetter took it as a sign of surrender and whispered, "You can struggle a little if you want, Powers, so long as you behave. It makes it more interesting." As he reached down to kiss her, she saw her chance. A moment later, he was on the deck, writhing in agony over the fact that his shorts had in no way protected him from a well-placed knee. For good measure, she slapped him hard enough for his head to snap backward, and then followed up with a hard kick to his ribs. Roetter groaned, unable to defend himself.

Waves of disgust rippled across her face as she walked over to her clothes and pulled her jumpsuit back on. For the moment, she didn't bother with her underwear, as she just wanted to zip up as quickly as possible. She pulled out a spare pillow and blanket, and threw them at him with a contemptuous motion.

She leaned toward him and hissed, "I told you what would happen if you crossed the line and tried to get into my shorts! The only reason I'm not making you hurt even more is because someone might wonder about the screams. From now on, you're going to sleep on the deck." The tone in her voice was deadly as she continued. "If you ever try anything like that again, my next problem will be working out how to dispose of your corpse. If you think I'm bluffing, tell me now, because there won't be another chance if you try to test me later."

She straightened up and paused before walking away. "I'm going to the head to get changed. By the time I come out, you'd better be fully dressed. If you aren't, then I'll make sure it's even harder for you to walk than it already is."

As she walked toward the head, she scooped up her underwear in a fluid motion, and was out of sight. By the time she came out, Roetter was fully dressed, although he looked much paler than usual. Powers gave him one final look of disgust, then ignored him for the rest of the evening.

Six weeks later, matters had settled into a routine where they were back to dealing with each other strictly as professionals. Roetter seemed to have taken to heart Powers' threat, and had never again tried to make a move on her.

Her colleagues had been extremely curious about the identity of her mysterious lover. On a ship that large, it wasn't unusual for crew members to have temporary relationships or to keep those relationships private. It also wasn't unusual for those relationships to break up during the voyage. She'd decided that it was best to acknowledge the encounter but to declare that it had happened only that one night. They were disappointed to hear that she and her lover had broken up and decided to go back to being friends for the rest of the voyage. She told them that she wanted to avoid things becoming awkward with her former lover, which was why she wouldn't tell anyone his name.

Powers sighed as she thought about the reactions she'd received. Several of the women, not all of whom were single, wanted to get together with her former lover for some fun. They all promised not to tell anyone the man's name. She wasn't planning on taking that promise to the bank. Several of the men, some of whom were single, decided to ask her out, assuming that since she was open to having sex with one colleague, she would be open to having sex with other colleagues. Since Marty had revealed, reluctantly, that she'd been stark naked while standing in the hatchway, she'd had to work at resetting those expectations.

It had taken several weeks of persistent refusals on her part before the men and women stopped pestering her directly. She was aware that a couple of men continued to look at her when they thought she couldn't see them. Since the logical assumption among her colleagues was that one of the men had been in the cabin, everyone, especially the men, was wondering who had been the lucky one.

Powers and her cabin mate had had plenty of discussions about his plans and how he was going to get to Austin. Roetter's frustration about a key issue had been building ever since he'd boarded the ship. "In a sense, there isn't much to plan if Austin never sets foot off

Pathfinder," he said. "If each ship stays in its own quarantine, then Austin might as well be on the other side of the solar system for all the good it does us. Doesn't the captain have any more information?"

Powers shook her head. "There hasn't been any change. All we really know is that we'll stop near the beacon and see where we'll go from there. While the ultimate destination is Earth, we might stop first at Mars."

"I hope we do, because that might be the best time for me to get on board *Pathfinder*." His gaze drifted toward her chest. "You've demonstrated the distracting nature of your charms more than once, but it might be easier for one person to get aboard *Pathfinder* than two people."

Powers kept a neutral look on her face. "My 'charms', as you call them, might still work to get you aboard *Pathfinder*. Afterward, I can leave and they wouldn't know what happened."

"Maybe, maybe not," he replied noncommittally. "This brings us to the basic question, which is what happens when they learn from the beacon about my disappearance? It would be logical for me to try to get back to our solar system. They might figure out that the person who helped me escape brought me to a transport. They might be checking out everyone on board each ship." He gestured at his head with a sardonic look. "It's a good thing I don't look the same as I did weeks ago. It's been a while since my hair was this long. Come to think of it, I haven't had a beard since college."

Powers ran an appraising eye over his appearance. "We'll color your hair a few days before we arrive, to make it even harder for anyone to recognize you."

As Powers walked away, Roetter's thoughts turned to a subject that had been on his mind a lot lately. While he'd long considered himself to be someone who didn't let anyone intimidate him, he realized that things had changed.

For starters, he still couldn't get over how he'd been intimidated by Austin, especially after Austin had participated in Roetter's interrogation. The entire time he faced him, he could sense the man's intense energy waiting to unleash itself on him in a highly lethal manner. Austin's cold blue eyes seemed to burn right through him. He assumed the only thing that had kept him alive was the fact that he'd be needed at some point to confirm his orders regarding Citadel. The only consolation to discovering his fear of Austin was the knowledge that Austin wasn't intimidated by anyone and had, as claimed, faced down men who were a lot tougher than Roetter.

His thoughts shifted to Sara Albretti. At first, he hadn't believed her to be that tough. However, while he'd enjoyed humiliating her, she'd proven to be plenty tough. Not only had she not been broken by the brutality, but she'd kept her head and overpowered Roetter in what he had to admit was a fair fight. She'd also had the courage to turn back and try to face the aliens.

Things hadn't gotten any better when her husband had escorted Roetter to the head after Roetter's insolence toward Austin. Albretti had removed Roetter's restraints and Roetter tried to attack him. Albretti knocked Roetter on his ass without difficulty and pounded him in several places, most of which didn't leave visible marks, but made it hard for him to stand upright. Albretti made it clear that if he ever got the chance to deal with Roetter again, he'd kill him, or even better, let his wife do it. The last comment stung, as Albretti had known it would.

Mara Powers was the latest person to stand up to him without fear, and back it up in a brutal manner. Although the pain from Joe Albretti's beating had hurt a lot, Roetter had been humiliated by Powers. Not only had she sent him to the deck with a shot to his balls, she'd followed up with the kind of hard slap to the head that he liked to use to humiliate others. No woman had ever done that to him. He flinched slightly as he replayed that moment in his head. Not for a minute did he doubt her threat to kill him if he crossed the line again.

What bothered him the most about what had happened was that it made him wonder whether he'd lost his edge. He knew that doing what he did meant he had to be willing to take the offensive and push the boundaries, often with threats. He was worried that losing his edge, even a little, could mean the difference between success and failure. He was under no illusions about the penalty for failure.

CHAPTER THIRTY FOUR

Harrington's campaign had been effective in convincing plenty of people that an attack was imminent, and polls showed that she was within striking distance of being reelected. She scoffed at what she considered to be the weakness of some people in being willing to accept whatever the authorities said, especially if they thought their safety was at risk. She had ordered the Space Command placed on high alert. They knew generally where Austin would arrive but weren't sure just what form his attack would take. Knowing that Austin's people had managed to take out two more alien ships didn't make them feel any easier.

The day finally came when *Pathfinder* arrived, along with an escort of four transports that Curly Stephens had managed to provide. Harrington's office announced that all five ships were warships and ordered the Space Command to intercept them. In view of the tensions, she assumed that hostilities would begin shortly, validating her message.

At the same time that *Pathfinder* and her escorts arrived at the entrance to Earth's solar system, General Choi appeared before the press, with a special plea to the Space Command.

"To my comrades and colleagues in the US Space Command, I urge you to keep in mind that the mission of Sam Austin and Citadel is not war. The only person that wants war is President Harrington, to further her political agenda. Just as it is wrong for military personnel to concern themselves with political issues, it is equally wrong for them to be swayed by them. Only Congress has the power to declare war, and it has not done so with respect to Citadel. Likewise, Sam Austin has not attacked anyone in this solar system, so there is no need for any of you to engage any Citadel craft in a hostile manner. So long as you do not give in to the hysteria that President Harrington has sought to create, there will be no need for violence.

"While Sam Austin has made it clear that there will be a reckoning with Citadel, that reckoning will be between Citadel and President Harrington on account of the criminal acts that she has ordered to be committed.

"I have served under President Sam Austin, and I know this man in a way that few others do. He has assured me that he wants no hostilities against anyone. All he wants is justice for the people of Citadel, most of who are American citizens. I urge you to stand down and not be a party to any further unlawful acts ordered by this administration. There are many questions about the actions of the current administration that need to be answered. I am staking my reputation on the fact that we need to work with and not against Sam Austin to get those answers."

Although Choi was practically revered by the Space Command and the message was broadcast throughout the solar system, it wasn't clear whether it would make any difference to the outcome of the faceoff between the two nations.

CHAPTER THIRTY FIVE

Austin stood on *Pathfinder's* bridge with the main display featuring the Space Command vessels that were approaching their position. Although he had to consider how to deal with those vessels, he wasn't even watching them at the moment. He was equally concerned about the information that Yabuno had obtained from the now-functioning beacon. His face radiated a cold anger as he asked, "How the hell did Roetter escape?"

Yabuno replied, "Someone paid attention to some things that we should have noticed, like the fact that our values about things like long-term imprisonment influence what passes for prisons in our society."

"What does that mean?" Austin asked sourly.

"It means that we aren't keen on the notion of our society supporting people who sit in prisons instead of contributing productively toward our society. We also don't believe in having people do nothing but monitor the operations of a prison. Because of those values, when we set up a 'prison,' most of the operations are automated and don't even need direct human interaction.

Our prison is a modified holding facility, which means we didn't worry so much about external access. After capturing Roetter and his people, we never considered that anyone in our system might want to help them out. This left us vulnerable to someone who had the skills to circumvent the security features of the prison."

"What about the rest of his people?" Austin asked.

"They've all been accounted for by direct visual confirmation." Yabuno didn't hide the look of disgust on his face as he continued, "It doesn't say anything good about a man who would save his own hide and leave his people to their less-than-pleasant fates."

"Couldn't Roetter have escaped on his own?"

Yabuno gave an emphatic shake of his head. "While he's intelligent, there's no way that he could have gotten out by himself. The systems were disabled by someone *before* the asshole even left his cell. Since there's nothing in his cell that he could use to disable anything, we know he didn't break out and then wipe the records."

Austin paced for a moment before saying, "We've always worried whether we had another Brittel among us. Does this mean we can't trust anybody anymore?"

Yabuno was firm in his reply. "It means we're under attack by Harrington and her ilk. While we've been pretty damned careful in our screening of all people who want to be a part of Citadel, the most logical explanation is that they managed to get someone onto one of the transports."

"Why couldn't it have been one of our settlers?"

"Let's keep in mind some background and assumptions," Yabuno replied. "When we first set up the Citadel Group, we were just another outfit that was trying to get to another world. The assumption was that we'd fail, just like everyone else had failed. That means that no one gave a damn about us. Also, Harrington wasn't even in office when we departed. That rules out all of our original settlers and other personnel with our operations for mining, manufacturing, et cetera.

"Harrington only started becoming hostile toward us after we became a nation. That means that the only people we likely have to worry about are ones that joined us since that time." Yabuno gave Austin a wry look. "Brittel did us a favor in that regard, because we became even more thorough in vetting candidates. We sure as hell didn't want to bring on board any more snakes."

"That still leaves a fair number of people to check out back there, Bret."

"They were able to confirm the locations of all of the newer settlers," Yabuno said.

Austin did some thinking out loud. "The prison is in space, which means that all visitors would have to use shuttles to reach it. I take it that the planet-bound shuttles and their passengers were checked."

Yabuno nodded. "That's right. No shuttles from Citadel went anywhere near the prison."

"What about the other operations?"

"Same answer, which leaves only one other possibility."

A shrewd look appeared on Austin's face. "The transports. Someone from one of the transports paid a visit and sprung Roetter loose. What do we know about the shuttles from the transports?"

Yabuno sighed. "There was a lot of chaos as Curly was trying to get everything ready for the trip and people were moving around. You remember what it was like," he said with a shrug. "The transport crews needed to get away from where they'd been cooped up as virtual prisoners for the previous three months. They mingled with each other and with people elsewhere, and we didn't keep close tabs on them."

Austin nodded back to Yabuno. "Yeah, I remember. Who could blame them? No one would have noticed if a shuttle made an unannounced visit to the prison." Austin's expression darkened as he asked, "If it was someone from a transport, then it isn't likely that Roetter is holed up somewhere back in the Citadel system. He must be hiding on one of our transports. How do we figure out who's his accomplice and where he's hiding?"

Yabuno motioned toward the display. "We'll have other things to worry about soon."

Austin glanced at the display as well and said, "Yes, you're right. We need to reach Mars next. Nothing much matters if we're blasted to pieces. Let's worry about the Space Command; Roetter can wait. Open a link with the Space Command vessels."

"Go ahead."

Austin faced the display and began, "This is Sam Austin, the leader of Citadel and your former commander in chief. Just as importantly, I'm also an American citizen. I've learned that you have been fed a pack of lies claiming that Citadel has hostile intentions toward the United States. Shockingly, I've also learned that hostile actions have been taken against Citadel citizens, most of whom are also American citizens. I want to stress two important facts. The first is that while the current administration of the United States government has gone out of its way to initiate a war with Citadel, Citadel in no way wants to be at war with the United States. The other fact is that we have no intention of engaging in any hostile actions with your ships. While it appears that the current US administration hopes for a military confrontation that will provide a 'retroactive' justification for its acts of war against Citadel, the fact remains that we are on a peaceful trip to Mars.

"While our trip is a peaceful one, we will not accept any interference with our ships' operations. I hope that I can count on your good judgment in this matter. If you will avoid interfering in our activities, we will do likewise with yours. Thank you."

A small gesture from Austin ended the transmission. He turned to the others on the bridge and said, "I hope to God that there's enough wisdom on these ships to avoid doing something stupid. Set a course for Mars. Send a signal to our transports and tell them to follow us."

A voice called out, "We're ready, Sam."

Austin's face showed none of the stress that he had to be feeling as he said, "Let's go." Yabuno looked at the rail Sam was holding and noticed that the fingers were much whiter than usual. He admired Austin's control.

After they began to move, Austin called out, "Tell me what's happening with the Space Command. Do we have a response?"

Yabuno looked at a display and said, "No, Sam; they're quiet." His face lightened a bit as he said, "They're also not moving. I think they're letting us pass!"

As *Pathfinder* and her escorts continued on their journey to Mars, they encountered several more Space Command vessels. In each case, the vessels simply maintained a status marked by silence and allowed them to pass.

CHAPTER THIRTY SIX

Austin, Liz, Yabuno, and Joe Albretti met in Austin's stateroom to discuss the situation about Roetter. Albretti was quietly furious as he said, "When I took him to the head to teach him some manners, I should have drowned him when I had the chance, instead of just kicking his ass."

Austin's face showed a quiet moment of amusement as he said, "I'd guess his ass wasn't the only part of his that you kicked."

Albretti couldn't help but give an embarrassed grin. "OK, I kicked him in the balls, too, but he needed to learn not to mess with us."

"Agreed, Joe," Austin replied with a nod. "The question now is where the hell is he hiding? If he isn't in a rat hole back at Citadel, and I don't think he is, then he has to be on one of these ships. It could even be *Pathfinder* itself."

"No way could he be aboard *Pathfinder*, Sam!" Albretti declared flatly.

"Tell me why."

Albretti had an intense expression as he explained, "From what you've shared, Roetter's accomplice is probably someone who signed up since our encounter with the aliens in this system. That doesn't describe anyone on board *Pathfinder*."

Yabuno spoke up. "*Pathfinder* was built after that time, so everyone on your crew joined within the last year, Joe."

"Every one of them was already a member of the Citadel Group or even Citadel itself, Bret," Albretti countered. "Call it dumb luck or whatever you want, but we only wanted Citadel veterans, because they've already proven themselves as far as we're concerned. Besides, there's another reason why Roetter couldn't be hiding on *Pathfinder*."

This time it was Austin who asked, "What is it?"

Albretti waved his hand in an easy movement that took in all directions around the ship as he said, "While *Pathfinder* is bigger than her predecessor, we still can't carry anything remotely like the cargo that a transport can carry. What we would call 'cargo' would be a small set of supplies aboard a transport. Space is still at a premium around here; we don't waste it on areas that are large enough for someone to hide. I know this ship well enough to be able to figure out every single place where someone might hide. That still doesn't take into account the fact that a stowaway needs to eat and rest and make trips to the head, and probably get cleaned up now and then. Almost none of the potential hiding places would meet those needs."

"I can think of some places," Austin said.

"Yes, the crew cabins," Albretti agreed. "There aren't any other places on this ship that would work. The crew works on a staggered 24-7 schedule, which means there's no time where it wouldn't be insane for Roetter to try to sneak out. Our crew is small and tight enough that he'd be spotted immediately as an intruder. If he's on this ship, he has to be in a cabin."

Austin looked hard at Albretti. "I don't need to tell you how important it is to have someplace where we know we don't have to look over our shoulders, Joe. How do you propose to search this ship and make sure that Roetter isn't aboard?"

Albretti's look was equally hard as he replied, "Like I said, I know every place on this ship where there's even a remote possibility of someone stowing away. I'll take a team of people I trust and do a sweep of every one of those places. None of those places is shielded against infrared detectors, so that's one of the tools I'll use for the search. I'll make certain that multiple people cover each location, so that if for some reason the accomplice is one of the searchers, someone else will detect that asshole anyway. We'll do the same for each of the crew cabins. To be extra safe, no one will scan his own cabin."

"There'll be people in their cabins when they're off duty. How will you confirm identities of the people that show up on scans?"

Albretti grinned as he said, "The simplest way is to knock."

Austin stood up and said, "That sounds good, Joe."

Liz spoke up. "One other thing is the importance of making sure that your people don't neglect to confirm identities just because someone might be in the shower or because there might be a couple of people in the sack."

Her voice took on a wry tone as she continued. "Even in the twenty-second century, some things haven't changed. A naked woman can change the dynamics even of a thorough search. There's something about a woman's naked breasts that makes some men stay focused on them and makes other men forget what they're doing while they try to pretend to look somewhere else.

"That's just the kind of slip up that makes a search useless and lets the target off the hook. I'm sure that there will be women as well as men conducting the search. Make sure that there will be sufficient numbers of them to avoid any problems."

Austin agreed. "That's a good idea; we don't want to end up with a false sense of security, which we damned well can't afford right now. I also want it drilled into everyone that they are not to discuss any of this with anyone on the other ships. We don't want to tip off the accomplice to what we're doing."

A few hours later, the four of them gathered together in Austin's stateroom to go over the results of the search. They were reviewing an image of the ship's layout on the display as Albretti walked them through every place they'd searched. Yabuno whistled as he said, "Damn, Joe, I guess you have a more generous idea of where a man can hide than I do! Some of these places aren't much better than being in a coffin for three months."

Albretti grinned. "It's better to search too many places than too few. We also confirmed that there weren't any residual heat signatures from someone who might have been there but somehow got the word to go somewhere else during the search."

Austin nodded his approval. "Good work, Joe. How did the searches of the cabins go?"

Albretti grinned more broadly. "It looks like a few relationships are probably shot to hell, which can happen when people are found in the sack with people who aren't their partners."

Austin frowned. "I thought everyone had orders to stay quiet about this."

Albretti's grin turned a shade rueful as he explained, "There's not much you can do when it's some of the searchers themselves who discovered their respective partners in the sack with someone else."

Austin asked, "Why wasn't that considered when assigning the teams to specific locations?"

Liz explained, "That only helps when everyone is where you think they'll be. People aren't likely to talk about being where they aren't supposed to be, especially where sex is involved."

Austin gave up, grinning broadly in understanding as he asked, "Other than crew members, what did you find?"

Albretti's shoulders squared with pride as he said, "Not a thing. As I said before, there's no way Roetter could be on board this ship."

Austin let out a small sigh of relief. "Thank God. Now we have to think about which of the transports is his hiding place. We'll need to think this through before taking the chance of talking to the captains of the ships; the last thing we want to do is tip off the accomplice."

Yabuno had a wry look on his face as he asked, "You realize, Joe, that Roetter could be hiding on *KT-2*?"

Albretti snorted. "I doubt it. If Sara catches him, she'll probably cut off his balls or just turn him over to her crew and let them do it. He was pretty brutal, and she and her crew know him on sight, so he couldn't take even the slightest chance of being discovered. Besides, although I don't have the files on her crew pulled up, she may not have any recent additions to her crew either."

Austin said, "That brings us to the question of how the hell he would have gotten on board *any* of the transports. While it wouldn't be impossible to get a hold of a crew jumpsuit, he'd have to take a chance on being recognized. I agree that that means he wouldn't want to try boarding *KT-2*. He probably also had help from his accomplice in getting aboard a transport. The easiest way to make that happen is to get aboard your own transport, where everyone already knows you. The accomplice could vouch for Roetter and either claim that he was a new crew member or just visiting from one of the other transports. The latter would be the smarter option, since no one would be that interested in someone who wasn't going to be on your ship anyway."

Austin turned to Yabuno, who said, "No, you don't have to ask about whether all visitors were logged or recorded. We've already talked about the fact that we were all trying to get ready to head out. After we'd captured all of Roetter's people, no one worried about taking roll call."

"We'd damned well better worry about it when we get back," Austin said pointedly. "How hard would it be to hide someone aboard a transport?"

"It'd be a lot easier than hiding someone here," Yabuno replied. "There are multiple cargo holds, specialized compartments, recreation areas, et cetera. There are a hell of a lot more cabins too, considering that the crew is larger and the transports can carry a lot of settlers. It might even be possible for Roetter to have several hiding places lined up, in case of a search, especially with an accomplice to set things up."

"How effective would a search be?"

Yabuno frowned. "Not very, even if we eliminate *KT-2* from the search. Each ship has to be searched individually, and there are too many places to check out with a crew that hasn't been vetted the way this one has."

Liz said, "I wonder if one shortcut to the vetting might be to only use people who are committed couples to do the searches. Aren't the odds smaller that a couple would be likely to be accomplices?"

Yabuno shook his head as he said, "There's no way to know, Liz. Regardless, there's no possibility of keeping the search quiet, so we'd also have to assume that the accomplice would know what was happening, which means that Roetter would know as well."

"If I were Roetter, I'd make that assumption anyway," Liz replied. "He must know that we would have checked out any messages from Citadel on the beacon and that his escape would have been discovered long ago. If searches aren't the answer, how do we find him? For that matter, how the hell is he planning on getting off his ship? He can't be stupid enough to think we wouldn't check out everyone that leaves each transport?"

Albretti said, "There's a more basic question that may have an impact on the answers to the other questions, Sam. Why is he heading back to this solar system? Is he just trying to find some safe ground where he can hide, or is there something else for him to do as part of his mission?"

Yabuno looked nervous. "Roetter's mission was to capture and destroy the derelict, which he failed to do. He was also supposed to kill Sam if he had the chance." Yabuno looked straight at Austin as he continued, "If that's still his mission, then he'll try to get at you one way or another. Harrington could still end up with her war and get reelected."

Austin kept his expression neutral. "We didn't come all the way here to be outmaneuvered by a sorry excuse for a human being like that. I guess we'll need to be careful."

CHAPTER THIRTY SEVEN

The convoy from Citadel passed the last of the Space Command vessels without incident and approached Mars. Austin requested permission for their vessels to enter Mars space, which was granted immediately. As the ships maneuvered into their orbits, he opened up a secure link to the Mars government.

Almost immediately, a familiar face appeared on the screen, the warmth on her face overshadowed by the concern over recent events. President Amelia Gordon spoke. "Sam," she began, "while it is wonderful to see you and you are always welcome here, I am deeply troubled over the reasons for your visit."

Austin's face showed the same combination of warmth and concern as he replied, "Thank you, Amelia, for your kind words. If there is anyone who knows what it is like to be the leader of a people when you're beset by an external enemy through no fault of your own, it is you. As you know, it is much the same with me. In both cases, the enemy was willing to kill our people to get what it wanted."

For a moment, the concern on Gordon's face was replaced by gratitude as she said, "Sam, all of Mars knows that it owes you and Citadel a debt that can never be repaid. You, your people, and your ships are welcome to stay here for as long as you wish." A shrewd look appeared on her face as she continued. "Knowing you as I do, however, I assume that you have in mind something more than just staying on Mars. What can I do to help you?"

Austin grinned. "As it happens, I could use your help. I plan on continuing on to Earth aboard *Pathfinder*, without any escort of Citadel vessels."

The warmth on Gordon's face faded. "That isn't a good idea, Sam. Harrington wants to kill you. While I applaud the kind of statesman who sets an example for the rest of us by going to Earth unarmed as a gesture of peace, Harrington is too consumed by her greed and ambition to pull back now. If you do it, you will die, which would be a terrible loss for two solar systems."

Austin's expression became harder as he said, "That's where you can help me, Amelia." As he explained his plans, the warmth returned to Gordon's face.

Following his conversation with President Gordon, Austin faced the main display in *Pathfinder*'s bridge and began a message to all of the ships from Citadel. "Greetings, folks, this is Sam. The first part of our journey is complete. From the reactions of the Space Command ships to our presence, I can see that not everyone has bought into the lies that President Harrington has been spreading about Citadel and me personally. Some of you may be wondering what your purpose has been in this action and what it will be going forward. Put simply, in acting as escorts for *Pathfinder* on our trip to Mars, you have helped ensure our survival. It would have been much easier for the Space Command to attempt to take control of *Pathfinder* if she hadn't had your support.

"As far as next steps are concerned, this is the end of your journey for now. Now that we know what to expect from the Space Command, I intend to take *Pathfinder* the rest of the way to Earth. It is important to show that we have no hostile intentions toward Earth, and a single, unescorted vessel is a powerful reminder of our intentions. Mars has agreed to provide sanctuary for all of you, so there is no need to worry about anything for now. In fact, before you head down to the planet surface, you are all welcome to visit each other's transports and reestablish friendships."

Austin held up something before continuing, "In order to ensure your protection, the Mars authorities have requested that all of you wear an identifying wristband that will enable them to keep track of you." Austin held up his other hand to deflect any complaints. "Don't worry; these bands aren't intended to monitor your personal activities. They're really only beacons for you to use as needed, since your crew ID badges won't serve that purpose so far from your ships. This is necessary in order to ensure your safety in case of contact with any agents from the United States. Therefore, wearing the wristband is mandatory. You will receive them once you have boarded the shuttles to take you to the surface. Although my time here will be limited, I couldn't leave for Earth without passing through each of the transports to share with you my appreciation and good wishes. Once again, I offer my thanks to all of you for a job well done. Please wish me and everyone on *Pathfinder* good luck for our trip to Earth."

Powers and Roetter were wary about Austin's message.

"They know about me and are trying to track me down," Roetter said.

"Of course they are," Powers replied, nodding her head. "They're trying to make us believe we can get off the ship without a problem, by mixing up the crews. Once different crews are milling around, strange faces wouldn't be remarkable. They also believe that they've limited our options by insisting on everyone wearing something that has to be in plain sight. Otherwise, we'd just get rid of the one they gave you, assuming that they didn't spot you on the shuttle. They have to do something like this because it would be nearly impossible to search each of the transports thoroughly. The question is whether we can get around their plan."

Powers looked him over with a practiced eye. "You've changed radically in appearance in the last three months. The new hair color helps. Once people start to mingle from ship to ship, it would be pretty easy to pass you off as coming from one of the other ships. I doubt even the crew from *KT-2* would recognize you now."

"I hope we don't have to put that idea to the test," Roetter replied. "Can you disable the band?"

She pondered the idea for a moment and then nodded. "Yes, I can. You'll look just like another member of the crew, but they won't know that you're here."

"Won't they be counting the number of bands handed out?" Roetter asked.

Powers shook her head. "No, because they won't know in advance how many they'll need for each shuttle. All they'll care about is seeing that everyone is wearing a band and then activating them and counting the signals."

She sniffed. "Austin thought he was clever in telling us that the bands weren't intended to be used to monitor our personal activities. Of course they are! That's why they can just wait for everyone to exit and see which one doesn't pick up the information from his crew ID. That would be you."

"Why don't we just take the crew ID from someone else?" he suggested. "I could even wear the wristband and let it be activated."

Powers sniffed again. "They're probably hoping we'll do something like that. Once the band and crew ID are linked, it would be a lot harder for me to disable them so that you could remain anonymous. Silent alarms would probably be tripped if I tried. Besides, once the crew member is discovered, they'd know which ID to scan for, and they'd have you. The other problem is that we might not be able to get to someone alone to take his ID."

"That makes sense," he agreed. "Once we get away from the area, we can get me something else to wear and get rid of the band for good. I can then work on finding a shuttle that can take me out to a Space Command ship and back to Earth." A familiar look came back into his eyes as he continued, "We've talked about how I can get off this ship, but not in any more detail about my mission."

Powers kept her face neutral. "We've always assumed that that was your intent. We just haven't known how to go about making it happen."

A slightly avaricious look appeared on his face. "As you once pointed out, I failed in my primary mission. While I might be able to excuse my failure to capture the derelict on the grounds that it was captured by aliens, killing Austin would go a long ways toward rehabilitating me. It would also be a personal pleasure and would probably lead to the outbreak of the war that we want in the first place. My career would be assured."

Powers said, "We've gone over several possibilities in the past three months, but without knowing Austin's plans, we couldn't settle on any of them. Now that we know them, what did you have in mind?"

"Austin will be visiting each ship to pay his respects," he began. "I've never heard of him visiting a ship without stopping by the bridge and engineering. While it would be pretty risky to try to get onto the bridge, there will be plenty of people milling about in engineering. I just need to get close enough to him with this." He pulled out a wicked-looking knife he had fashioned from a piece of synthetic material. Powers didn't need to touch it to know that it was razor sharp. He continued, "I'll need you to arrange for a diversion so that we can get away to a shuttle in the confusion."

Powers nodded. "I can arrange for the fire suppression system to come online in engineering. The system will note that there are people nearby, so it won't be lethal, but there will be a huge mess, which will take a long time to clean up. Even better, the hatches to engineering will all self-seal within five seconds, so if we're fast, we'll be running for a shuttle without anyone chasing us. We won't look at all strange, either, as the fire alarm would be activated immediately and broadcast throughout the ship. Once that happens, protocols call for the ship to be evacuated in the event of a fire when in orbit. This will make it even harder for them to monitor the people in the shuttles the way they planned. We might not even have to worry about the wristbands, since there will be a lot of confusion on the shuttles as well."

Her cabin mate had a look of satisfaction as he said, "A nice bonus about this plan is that even if we fail to kill Austin, I can try again on Earth at a time of my choosing."

Powers gave her partner a direct look. "We should plan on *two* people getting onto a shuttle for a Space Command ship. Although people won't be focusing on me if Austin is dead, it's still possible that someone will see me activate the fire suppression system. If I'm going to take a chance on blowing my cover, I'll need an escape route too."

Although the look on Roetter's face showed what he wanted from Powers, he was smart enough not to press the issue. Powers ignored the look and reminded him. "Don't forget that I'm the one who will create the diversion that will get us out of there, and take care of that bracelet. Besides, if anything goes wrong, you may need my help."

Roetter knew she was right. "You're right, Powers. We're getting out of this together."

Powers pointed to some cleaning supplies in the bathroom. "It's time for us to scrub this place so that no one can tie us to it," she said.

Later, after they had finished and were ready to leave, Roetter reached over to pick up Powers's travel bag. He brushed up against her as he handed it over. Powers glared at him as she jerked the bag out of his hand, but didn't say anything. She couldn't wait for the assignment to be over so she could deal with him more permanently. He didn't see the feral look in her face suggesting that there might not be a career boost from killing Austin after all.

CHAPTER THIRTY EIGHT

As Austin moved among the transports, he was greeted like a returning hero. Although some people had expected that the crews would head straight for a shuttle to the surface of Mars, that wasn't the way it worked out. Even though most people had developed some level of cabin fever from the long trip, it helped just to get off of one's own ship, even if it meant going onto another ship just like it. Also, now that they knew they could head down to the surface shortly, they all wanted to spend a little more time as part of the Citadel family. So long as they stayed in orbit, they still felt like crew members of Citadel ships, which were the best in two solar systems. While having sanctuary was deeply appreciated, it made them feel somewhat helpless, which some of them had already experienced far too intensively.

True to form, although Austin tried to visit numerous areas on board each transport, there wasn't enough time to go everywhere. He did, in fact, visit the bridge for each ship, as well as each ship's engineering section.

Roetter was already there, although he'd been careful to not be the first one to enter. Although thoughts of Austin still troubled him, he decided that he still had his edge. He noticed that more people seemed to be visiting engineering. He saw jumpsuits that had to be from other ships and smiled to himself as it appeared that others had noted Austin's interests as well. *All the better to block people's views and for me to get lost in,* he thought. He knew he needed to get at Austin when he was far enough away from a hatch that he would be trapped there as he lay dying.

The man who would assassinate Austin made it a point to not look at Powers, even though he knew she was ready to do her part.

The crowd seemed to thin out just a bit, and he saw his chance. He edged himself over to within arm's length of his target. Austin's back was to him, which made it unlikely that he could save himself with a defensive move. The hunter eased his knife out while shielding it from view.

He struck at Austin like a cobra. He saw a hint of a flash as something intercepted his arm and twisted it back into his chest. He couldn't stop his forward momentum, so it took little effort on the part of his adversary to move Roetter's blade through his heart. The would-be assassin's last thoughts were of surprise as he looked at Joe Albretti, whose dark eyes showed neither remorse nor pity. Albretti had been a soldier before he'd been a pilot or settler, and he hadn't forgotten his training. The predator had become the prey. As Austin whirled at the commotion behind him, the prey was already sinking to the deck, his eyes glazing over.

Everyone else in the room froze in shock at the extreme violence they'd just witnessed. Roetter's knife could be heard clearly as it clattered onto the deck with a jarring sound. Austin looked down at the failed assassin, recognizing a death gaze when he saw it. He took note of Roetter's changed appearance, then dismissed the man mentally and looked back to Albretti with a small smile. "Thank you for saving my life, Joe."

Albretti nodded toward another figure and said, "Thank Sara. She spotted him before I did. She saw right through the hair and beard to the asshole underneath."

Austin turned toward Sara, who had been in a nondescript jumpsuit, blending in with the crowd. His eyes said everything as he spoke. "Thank you, Sara, for saving my life."

Sara moved toward the still figure on the deck and looked down at it without expression. A look of concentration appeared on her face as she leaned down and pulled something off the body. She held up a strand of hair for Austin to see. "This came from a woman. I'll bet his accomplice is in here with us." She began to look at the other people, turning slowly to make sure she didn't miss anyone.

At that moment, the fire suppression system went off. There was some movement near one of the exits, and then all the hatches sealed themselves shut. The room was flooded with a nonlethal cooling foam, which made it impossible to see much of anything or to move around without slipping. In moments they were soaked in the stuff. People were startled and stumbled into each other as they sought to remain standing. Someone fell against

Sara, sending her tumbling into the slimy mess. She tried to wipe the stuff out of her eyes, but without much success.

An alarm sounded throughout the ship, and everyone outside of engineering was jolted by the sound into a quick run for the shuttles. Powers joined in with the crowd and found herself on a shuttle heading toward the surface almost immediately. As she had predicted, no one was thinking about the wristbands, so she didn't have to worry about detection by the Mars authorities. She spent the ride down thinking about her next steps.

Austin cursed as he tried to contact the bridge to override the fire suppression system and open the hatches. Sara was cursing too, although for a different reason. As she wiped the foam away from her face, she saw that the hair strand she'd been holding was now lost in the mess somewhere. With Roetter's body covered in the foam and everyone slipping around, it would be nearly impossible to trace any strands they could find to his accomplice. Because they hadn't caught her in engineering, the woman could simply claim that the assassin must have brushed against her somewhere. Whoever she was, she had vanished with no way to track her.

The people surged out of the shuttle into the receiving area, doubly glad to be on solid ground at last. The fire alarm had revived their cabin fever and washed away any desire to stay aboard their ships. Powers could hardly believe her luck as she left the shuttle without being challenged by anyone. She saw the Mars authorities trying to collect the crew members, although they hadn't been prepared for such an influx of agitated humanity. She knew that on Earth, certain places such as entrances to restrooms might be monitored, so she was experienced enough not to go into one to change out of her jumpsuit. She saw some panels that had been erected for some kind of display. She was pleased to note that there was just enough room behind them where she could change out of her jumpsuit in a moment.

Like many of the crew members, she had taken a travel bag/backpack with her for the trip down to the surface. Unlike most of them, she'd planned ahead by wearing clothes under her jumpsuit that made her look like a local. That included a low-cut shirt that took full advantage of the fact that the gravity on Mars was only 38 percent of what Earth provided. She was out of her boots in a moment and stuffed the footwear and jumpsuit into her bag. A comfortable pair of shoes appeared on her feet. Her hair had been pulled back in a way that was common for female crew members. With a few quick movements of her hands, her hair looked very different and her transformation was complete. She didn't even need to get rid of the travel bag, since it looked like the packs that many people used when moving around the planet.

She walked right past the Mars authorities without receiving a second look. The next thing she needed to do was find a café and sit in plain sight where no one would see her as she planned her departure from Mars. She was pleased with herself as she considered that she probably had better contacts than her former partner. She also didn't have his mission, and didn't need to expose herself to capture by going up against Austin.

She had to decide whether to stay within her cover as a member of the *KT-7* crew. While she knew she'd been careful about not leaving a trail behind, she worried about the strand of hair that that bitch Albretti had found on the body.

She cursed to herself as she thought back on how a strand of her hair could have ended up on his body. Although they'd been careful to sanitize her quarters before they left, she thought back to their physical contact when he handed her travel gear to her. She had to face the possibility that there might be enough DNA evidence to tie them together, assuming that they could find her to get a matching sample. Also, while she had tried to be careful, she couldn't be certain about the extent of any visual surveillance and what it might show about her.

She decided that it would be too risky to try to stay in character as Mara Powers. She wasn't about to take a chance on whether her crew ID could be used to track her so far away from her ship, so she would wipe it clean and drop it into a recycling bin on the way out.

For now, it meant that she could afford to go back into hiding until she was needed again. Her sip of her coffee was slow and relaxed.

CHAPTER THIRTY NINE

Austin was still pissed about the fact that Roetter's accomplice had escaped, although he wasn't sorry that the asshole himself was finally out of the way permanently. He was back on board *Pathfinder*, preparing to depart for Earth. Joe Albretti, Liz, and Yabuno were with him, with Sara and the other transport captains appearing on the display in Austin's stateroom. Austin had asked the captains to fill him in on the status of tracking down Roetter's accomplice.

The *KT-7*'s captain's face showed that he was nearly as pissed as Austin as he said, "Our best guess at this point is that Roetter was staying with a woman named Mara Powers, who was a crew member aboard *KT-7*."

Austin frowned. "Why do we think so?"

"Powers is missing," the captain replied. "No one can remember seeing her after the announcement about arriving at Mars. Everyone else aboard the transports has been accounted for."

"Couldn't Roetter's accomplice have killed Powers to throw us off the scent?"

"It's possible," the captain admitted, "although when we searched her cabin, we found that it had been cleaned thoroughly, meaning we can't find a single trace of her DNA anywhere. For that matter, we can't find any trace of Roetter's DNA in there, but the fact that it was scrubbed is suspicious by itself. Powers was seen regularly during the trip, although she tended to keep to herself when she was off duty. If he was in her cabin during the trip, it must have been with her and not someone else."

Austin wasn't convinced. "The accomplice and Roetter could have killed Powers in her cabin and scrubbed it to make it look the way you have concluded. If they were able to dispose of her body, then we'd end up wasting our time looking for the wrong person."

The captain shook his head. A little color came into his face as he said, "I don't think so, Sam. While we were talking to people about any visitors or roommates, one of her colleagues reported that when he visited her at her cabin one time, she came to the door stark naked. He noticed that there was a man in the bed, although he couldn't see any of his features. He assumed that he had interrupted them having sex. It seems that he wasn't able to focus on the man very much."

With a wry expression, Austin looked over at Liz, who returned the look. Austin looked back at the captain and said, "That was her intent; clever of her."

"No one has any idea who the man was," the captain continued. "We've asked for the alleged partner to step forward, but there's only been silence."

"While it's possible that Powers really was interrupted having sex with another member of the crew and had nothing to do with Roetter, I don't buy that kind of coincidence, either. OK, it seems that Powers was a plant on the ship. What do we know about her?"

"Not much, as it turns out. Now that we know to check more deeply, it looks like her background is fake."

Austin wasn't happy about the news. "What do we know about any help she might have provided to Roetter's people during the trip out to Citadel?"

"There's no way to know. Maybe we can have our people do another round of interrogations of his people to see what they know. It's possible that she just stayed under cover in order to maintain her credibility with the rest of the crew."

"She clearly has some useful computer skills," Yabuno stated. "Could she have gotten access to any core technology before it was locked out?"

The captain shook his head emphatically as he answered. "I'm sure she couldn't. Powers simply didn't have the clearance needed, and the captain's permission would have been needed to get it. She didn't request it, and I sure as hell didn't grant it to anyone."

"What about during the trip here?" Austin asked.

"As you ordered, access was restricted before we started on our journey, so every possible point of access has been covered. Getting back to her identity, without any DNA, we might not be able to make a positive ID of her. We can't even be sure how much of her physical appearance is her own."

Austin hoped for some good news as he turned to Sara. "What about the hair you found in engineering, Sara?"

Sara's face turned darker as she replied, "It's gone, Sam. I couldn't hold onto anything once the foam got everywhere. I needed both hands free just to keep my balance, and then someone fell against me and I fell. It wasn't in my hands by the time I was wiping that mess out of my face. We looked for the strand while the place was being cleaned up, but there was no sign of it. Besides, from what I've been told, exposure to the foam may have compromised any DNA we might have had anyway."

"Are we sure it was from her?"

Sara gave him a look. "He didn't bother to hide his interest in the sight of women when we headed to Citadel; I saw the look directly. While we don't know the extent of his relationship with Powers, they were together for three months in close quarters. Regardless of whether they were sleeping together, there's no way he would have made contact with a woman other than his accomplice. Trust me; I'm a woman."

Joe gave a small chuckle. "She sure is."

Liz chimed in. "So am I, and Sara is right."

Austin chuckled as well and nodded toward *KT-7*'s captain before continuing. "Don't we have any images of her in engineering during the attack?"

The captain replied, "She must have been in there, ready to activate the fire suppression system once Roetter had killed you, but she doesn't show up on any of the images we have. She probably knew just where to position herself to avoid detection. She hasn't shown up on Mars, either. Mars society is opposed to being under permanent surveillance by the government, so all she had to do was get past the physical monitoring that takes place at the entry points. The emergency with the fire alarm helped her get there before they were fully ready for her."

He shrugged his shoulders as he continued, "There's no telling where she might be by now. While we have a photographic ID of her, there's a lot she can do to change her appearance. For all we know, she might have done some things to look like Mara Powers that are easily changed to take her back to her original appearance."

Austin summed things up: "In short, while we're pretty sure where Roetter has been hiding and with whom, we don't have much in the way of direct evidence to tie anything to Powers, if that's really her name. She could be anywhere on Mars by now, although she's probably planning on getting onto a ship back to Earth. If she's careful, and we know she is, she could do it. Mars isn't under quarantine and has too much traffic to be able to monitor everything, especially something that's outbound.

"While I sure as hell want to get our hands on her, we can't wait any longer. The primary mission is still getting to Earth to force the issue with Harrington. *She's* the one who's sought to wage war with us, not any individual operative."

Austin looked directly at the captains on the display. "While *Pathfinder* will be heading to Earth, each of you still has an important role to play, which I've already shared with you. Keep track of your people, because they may be needed sooner than you think. Good luck."

After the display went blank, Austin turned to Albretti. "Joe, has anyone other than *Pathfinder* personnel boarded this vessel since we arrived at Mars?"

Albretti shook his head. "Hell no, Sam."

"Have we taken on any new supplies of any kind since we arrived?"

"No. We made sure we had everything we needed before we left Citadel. Pathfinder's security has been maintained for every second we've been here."

Austin nodded his satisfaction. "Good to hear. It's time for us to do some sightseeing." Within the hour, *Pathfinder* was the sole Citadel vessel to continue on to Earth.

CHAPTER FORTY

Harrington was furious at Mars for effectively offering sanctuary to the Citadel vessels, although she wasn't completely surprised. Mars had long been grateful to Austin and Citadel for their help in saving many lives, and had been the first nation to recognize Citadel as a fellow nation. Mars had already offered sanctuary to other Citadel citizens and a safe harbor to other Citadel vessels.

However, it was one thing for various elements of Citadel to find refuge on Mars. It was quite another thing for Mars to offer sanctuary to a formal escort to the head of Citadel after he had threatened Harrington. She was determined not to let the harboring of hostile vessels go unchallenged. She ordered Space Command units to approach Mars and demand that the Citadel vessels be surrendered to US authority immediately. She made it clear that she expected them to take whatever action was needed to capture the vessels.

In the meantime, *Pathfinder* approached Earth. Harrington ordered that *Pathfinder* be attacked the moment it came within range of Earth's planetary defenses. To her shock, the head of the Space Command, who had been a good friend of Tim Buck, refused: "With respect, Madame President, I cannot obey what I believe to be an unlawful order. *Pathfinder* is a Citadel vessel. Since Citadel is a sovereign nation, attacking it would be an act of war. Congress has issued no declaration of war against Citadel, and there does not appear to be any emergency that would justify an attack."

"What's happening right now *is* the emergency!"

"That's just the point, Madame President. *Nothing* is happening right now except that a single space vessel is approaching Earth. The vessel has shown no signs of hostility, despite your assurances to the contrary. Plenty of vessels approach Earth every day, so that by itself cannot be the basis for declaring an emergency."

"What about all of the information that Citadel is withholding from Earth and therefore jeopardizing its security?"

"I know of no such information, Madame President. While I have read a great deal of commentary on the subject online, I have yet to receive any official reports in support of such a claim. For similar reasons, I will not follow your order to engage in an act of war with both Mars and Citadel by attempting to take action against the Citadel vessels that are under the protection of the Mars government."

"General, you are relieved of command."

"With respect, Madame President, my immediate successors are here with us and have indicated that they will follow the same course as I have." After the generals all nodded their agreement, the head of Space Command continued. "The authority cannot be delegated further without the consent of Congress, so if you plan on relieving each of us of command, there will be no one in command at all."

The senior general's posture seemed to become even straighter as he said, "On behalf of my colleagues, I state, respectfully, that you do not have the authority to relieve any of us solely for refusing to follow an unlawful order. Unless and until we are advised otherwise by the appropriate authority, we will disregard such an order." He gave the president a hard look as he added quietly, "We will not be a party to killing a former president of the United States."

"You will be court-martialed, General!" Harrington hissed.

"I welcome the opportunity at the appropriate time and place to discuss my refusal to follow an unlawful order, Madame President, but the refusal stands."

CHAPTER FORTY ONE

*P*athfinder entered into orbit around Earth without incident. Thanks to the efforts of Ambassador Preacher, Austin found two invitations waiting for him. The first was from the AN, inviting him to address the general assembly. The second was an invitation to make an address to a joint session of Congress. Austin accepted both invitations; the one before the AN would take place in a few hours, and the one before a joint session of Congress would take place later in the day.

Austin had a wry look on his face as he considered how to make his entrance. Although he didn't normally do it this way, he decided to take *Pathfinder* itself down, rather than wait for a shuttle. *Pathfinder* notified the authorities and was given diplomatic clearance to approach the AN complex. Because of the diplomatic clearance and Austin's status as a head of state, not even Harrington could prevent him from touching down in New York City to address the AN. She couldn't even use the power of a Security Council veto to object to the session.

Pathfinder touched down directly in front of the main AN building. Austin and Liz left the ship and were greeted warmly by Preacher, who escorted them directly to the huge chamber. In spite of the short notice, the hall was filled, and Austin was treated to a standing ovation as he made his way to the podium. Even after he reached his destination, the ovation continued for some time.

Austin's indictment of Harrington's actions was direct and short. From the reaction of the audience, it was clear that Austin was regarded as no threat to peace. After finishing his speech, Austin and Preacher returned to *Pathfinder* for a short trip to Washington.

Harrington was becoming frantic over her dwindling options. She sat with her campaign weasel and the rest of her collaborators.

Dormer was, increasingly, feeling his own stress as he was called upon to strategize on the fly. "You have to hold a press conference right away, Courtney, before Austin gets to Washington. You have to make the point that Austin is performing a stunt, but he's still here with transports that they've admitted also double as war ships. If they can take out alien ships, they can devastate our operations. Make the point that Austin is here with a not-very-subtle threat to use those weapons against the United States if he doesn't get what he wants."

The weasel's eyes shifted around nervously as he continued. "We need to try to blunt whatever he plans on saying to Congress. Most people don't watch addresses before the AN, but everyone will be watching the address to Congress online. If the public thinks we don't have an answer for Austin's charges, we've lost."

Harrington turned to Rainey and said, "Earlier today, I was informed by the head of the Space Command that he wouldn't accept my order to attack Austin's ship to prevent him from entering orbit around Earth. He also refused to order Space Command ships to take control of the ships that Austin brought with him to Mars." With undisguised fury, she continued, "He had the balls to declare my orders to be unlawful! The rest of the generals in the line of succession told me the same thing. They said they wouldn't be a part of killing a former president. What about protecting the *current* president?"

Walker broke in. "You can't just order an attack without a legitimate reason, Courtney, any more than they can carry out such an order. If they did, they would be subject to court-martial. They might even be charged with committing war crimes."

"Who the hell would charge them with war crimes when it's the president giving them the order?"

Walker replied, "That's the same argument that was made at Nuremberg, Courtney. It also brings to mind the Nixon defense, which is that an act isn't illegal if it is the president doing it. We know how those arguments turned out."

Rainey said, "The fact that they refused your direct order pretty much guarantees a court-martial, Madame President. At the court martial, the order would have to be reviewed to determine whether it was a lawful one. If Bering can't produce the support for these activities that he claimed he had, and there is no other evidence of a threat to the security of the planet from Austin's approach, then a court-martial would probably conclude that the order wasn't lawful. That means the case would be dismissed. While I could remove them from command, it would only make matters worse since my reason for removal would have to be based in the law as well. If my reason is simply to restate your order, then the same analysis would have to take place."

Rainey nodded at Chambers, who continued, "Keep in mind that Austin didn't do anything improper. He's still a head of state with diplomatic immunity that entitles him to address the AN even if we don't want him there. It has long been settled as far back as the old UN that the US has to hold its nose and live with it even when tyrants have been invited to address the UN. The law of nations hasn't changed for the AN, or for Citadel."

"There has to be a way to stop Austin from addressing Congress," Harrington said. "It's one thing to visit New York, but another to visit Washington. He'll be travelling awfully close to the White House. Can't we order that his craft be shot down on the grounds that he encroached into White House space and therefore endangered the personal security of the president? If that doesn't work, can't we ban him from approaching Congress on similar security issues?"

Chambers was becoming alarmed. "It's still an act of war to attack his vessel, Madame President. Besides, Congress has every right to invite whomever it wants to visit. We'd pretty much guarantee scrutiny that would be impossible to oppose if we acted against Austin during that flight. Also, the fact that Austin was allowed to land in New York without military intervention makes it easier for people to continue to refuse to take action against him."

Harrington turned away from her collaborators in disgust. She turned to an aide and told her to get the head of her security detail on the phone immediately. If she couldn't get Austin on the grounds of a threat to national security, she was going to get him on the grounds of a threat to her personal security.

Her collaborators increasingly wondered how much longer they would be able to control events. While they also wondered how much rational thinking was going on in her head, they were either too cynical or cowardly to do anything about it.

CHAPTER FORTY TWO

Austin, Liz, and Preacher chatted during the short trip. Liz sat next to Austin, holding his hand.

"Sam, Liz," Preacher began warmly, "we didn't get a chance to talk before, but I'm truly glad to see both of you!"

Austin returned the warmth. "J. W., it's been far too long since we've been face-to-face." The warmth left his face as he asked, "Tell me about what's been happening. Are things truly as insane as they seem?"

Preacher's face turned somber. "We've seen one of the worst examples of abuse of presidential power for personal ambitions that has happened in over a century. Harrington has allowed her desire for reelection to override all other considerations. One of the reasons why the international community has been willing to cooperate with us is her willingness to ignore the law of nations in her quest to stick it to Citadel and you. What can you say about someone who is willing to invade a formally recognized embassy, as she did?"

A look of disgust crept into Preacher's face as he continued. "It's becoming clearer practically every day that she's been hanging her hat on whatever bullshit her creature Bering is willing to claim to have dredged up about Citadel. Funny thing is, they never actually produce any of this stuff when called upon to do it. They overestimated the willingness of the courts to defer to bald claims of 'national security' as a means of justifying anything they want to do." He smiled with great satisfaction. "It certainly didn't prevent the Supreme Court from ordering *my* release."

Liz struggled to understand the weaknesses of men and institutions as she asked, "Why hasn't anyone stood up to her and demanded answers?"

Preacher's face was sad as he answered. "We still rely on the notion that the president has a fundamental respect for the Constitution and the rule of law in order for much of our government to function. We've been reminded just how far a person can go when the president respects neither of those things. The courts often don't want to become involved in so-called 'political questions,' and Congress is often ill-equipped to compel the president to carry out the laws faithfully."

The familiar fire returned to Austin's eyes as he said, "I hope to God almighty that we can help restore a proper insistence for that respect within the institutions that we have."

"So do I," Preacher said somberly. "That reminds me, while you pretty much had a straight shot to New York with *Pathfinder* because of your diplomatic status, it might not be as easy to approach Washington. It stands to reason that the White House would be likely to object to anyone encroaching on its airspace, even if the purpose is to address Congress."

Austin's expression hardened as he said, "One of the benefits of using *Pathfinder* is that I don't have to worry about whether my craft is licensed properly by the authorities. This is still a diplomatic vessel, and threats of sanctions against the craft, the pilot, or the owner aren't a concern."

"Threats of being shot down are, though," Preacher replied.

"That's true," Austin agreed, "which is why we're making a big detour so our path won't take us over the White House at all. We'll be approaching from the south, at the express invitation of Congress. Since Congress has already notified the White House of the invitation and approach path, it would be especially tricky for the White House to attempt to shoot us down." A wry tone crept into Austin's voice as he noted, "I understand that Congress made it *very* clear that anyone from the White House that screws with this flight can expect impeachment."

Preacher's face showed new understanding as he asked, "That's why the Citadel transports are still back at Mars, isn't it?"

"Yes, since it is just one ship, we emphasize our status as a diplomatic vessel instead of as a hostile fleet."

Joe sent a message to Austin. "We're approaching the Capitol, Sam."

"What does it look like, Joe?"

"We're being tracked all the way, but no one has locked any weapons on us."

"Good. Make sure to keep the nose facing the Capitol Building as we land on the east side plaza." Austin looked at Preacher with a darkly humorous expression. "If Harrington wants to use her sharpshooters from the White House, they'll have to shoot through the Capitol Building to get to us!" Austin turned back to Joe as he asked, "Are we ready with the images we discussed?"

"Yes, they've been recorded."

"Thanks, Joe," Austin said with a small smile. "Wish me luck."

"You have it, always." They shook hands as Austin prepared to leave.

The east side of the Capitol was the traditional side for welcoming visitors. As if to emphasize the fact that this was Congress's show, several representatives and senators stood before the ship to welcome Austin into their home. As they stood in front of the building, several members of the president's security team showed up and sought to prevent Austin from proceeding inside. The sergeant at arms directed his people to block access to the federal agents and told them, "This is *our* house. You don't belong here. Keep your weapons holstered and leave *now.*"

The agents had no choice but to comply. Austin, Liz, and Preacher didn't waste any time looking at them as they entered the building.

By tradition, a joint session of Congress was held in the House chamber. While the vice president, as the president of the Senate, often sat next to the Speaker of the House during a joint session, in this instance the vice president had been told in no uncertain terms that her presence was not welcome. Instead, the president pro tempore sat next to the speaker. Austin thought back upon a time, more than a century in the past, when he'd sat in that chair as the vice president.

As was the case at the AN, despite the short notice, the chamber was packed. All of the Supreme Court justices were sitting in their prominent traditional seats. Preacher and Liz had been escorted to the visitor's gallery and had front-row seats. As Austin's name was announced, the noise in the chamber became deafening as everyone rose to his or her feet and applauded. Austin saw men and women in the chamber that he knew personally and took a moment to greet several of them warmly before making his way to the podium.

It had been plenty of years since Austin had last addressed a joint session, and he was moved by the heartfelt outpouring of emotion welcoming him back. It took several attempts on his part to get the applause to die down enough for him to begin speaking.

With a twinkle in his eye, he began, "My fellow Americans, and we are *still* fellow Americans, no matter what some may have claimed, I would like to thank you for inviting me to speak before a joint session of this distinguished body. Although it has been many years since I was a similar guest of this body, my regard for it and the Constitution under which it was created remains high."

The twinkle faded as Austin continued. "The circumstances under which I am speaking before you are tragic, as they have involved the blind ambitions of a person who has been entrusted with an enormous responsibility as the president of the United States. Many people can claim in general terms to understand the nature of that responsibility. Having held that position for more than forty years, I understand that responsibility intimately.

"For many months President Courtney Harrington has been engaged in a campaign to convince you and the rest of the world and beyond that Citadel somehow represents a threat to the safety and security of this solar system. This claim is a cynical and morally bankrupt attempt to ensure that she is reelected as president, by first creating and then manipulating and exploiting fear.

"The fact is that there is not and never has been any threat to this solar system from Citadel. Make no mistake, there are threats to this solar system from outside, but those threats are from an alien race that has made its intentions perfectly clear. While there is a threat to the security of this solar system from humans, I am sad and outraged to note that the threat comes from President Harrington herself. I understand that during my trip here from the Allied Nations, she held a press conference in which she spread various lies in a desperate attempt to avoid facing justice for her actions.

"The facts are clear that President Harrington has engaged in acts of war against Citadel and its people, including imprisoning Citadel's ambassador and attacking Citadel's embassy." Austin nodded to Preacher in the visitors' gallery as he continued, "While I am deeply grateful that Ambassador Preacher is unharmed and no longer being detained by the United States government, everyone should be outraged at the violation of one of the most basic laws among nations, which is that ambassadors and embassies are not to be subject to attack by their host countries." Austin directed a warm look of gratitude toward the Supreme Court justices as he said, "I note that the United States Supreme Court has reaffirmed these principles in the strongest terms in rebuking the actions of this administration.

"President Harrington's other crimes include attacking Citadel's vessels and other operations, kidnapping and imprisoning Citadel's people under false claims of authority, and engaging in unlawful espionage against Citadel. She's even engaged in outright piracy through ordering the capture of Citadel's vessels in international space and forcing her crews at gunpoint to travel back to Citadel. Even worse, the crews were forced to try to capture a derelict spacecraft that was by that time already within Citadel's solar system and claimed by Citadel.

"President Harrington has sought to avoid the charges relating to the derelict by claiming that the derelict wasn't within the Citadel system at the time of the attempt to capture it under her orders." Austin paused for a moment to issue a stern look as he continued, "I remind everyone that regardless of the status of the derelict, piracy is not permitted to assert claims against it. Besides, Citadel's boundaries do not begin at the outer point of the radiation field that runs throughout much of Citadel's territory; Citadel's boundary extends well outside that field. Therefore, by the time that that act of piracy had resulted in eleven of Citadel's vessels reaching Citadel under force, the derelict was already within Citadel's solar system and rightfully claimed by Citadel. It has been many decades since any modern nation has committed piracy. It is shocking that the United States government would be the one to embrace it.

"President Harrington's forces committed multiple acts of murder during the voyage when they shot and killed unarmed prisoners to force the Citadel crews to cooperate with their demands. They committed further acts of murder after they reached Citadel, when they refused to release control of the ships to their crews to deal with an attack by a real threat. That threat was an alien vessel like the one that Citadel helped to destroy as it sought to obliterate human life on this planet and elsewhere in this solar system over a year ago."

Austin began weeping as he said, "Many members of the crews of nine of our ships were killed because they couldn't defend themselves while under the control of President Harrington's thugs. While we were finally able to capture these thugs, nothing will recover the lives that have been lost.

"What was the actual security threat that President Harrington claimed to have found?" Austin asked. "She has claimed to have intelligence to the effect that we have discovered new technology that will enable us to act aggressively against this solar system. She has also claimed to have intelligence that we have discovered technology that would help you to defend yourselves against another attack by aliens." Austin didn't bother to hide his cold fury as he said, "On behalf of Citadel and the lives that have been destroyed at her direction, I demand that President Harrington produce immediately any evidence supporting her claims."

The cold fury became disdain as he continued. "There are several problems with these claims. The first is that none of them is true. We still don't even know how to get inside the derelict or how it works. If we had any of the technology President Harrington has claimed we have, we would have used it to defend ourselves against the aliens when they invaded *our* space again and killed the crews of nine of our transports. We would have also used it to defend ourselves when we sought to recover the derelict they stole from us. Instead, we had to use our own technology to pursue the aliens and recover the derelict, at the loss of more of our lives.

"A more important problem with these claims is that they were never more than a pretext for an attack on Citadel. When I presented the officer in charge of President Harrington's thugs with the direct proof that the claims were false, he made it clear that his orders stood anyway. He knew all along that the basis for his orders was a pretext to commit hostile acts against Citadel.

"President Harrington realized that her efforts at demonizing Citadel in order to achieve her goal of being reelected were failing, so she decided to try to provoke an incident where hostilities would erupt between Citadel vessels and forces of the United States, once Citadel's vessels entered this solar system. Her orders to the Space Command to engage in hostilities even if we offered no provocation were clear. Fortunately, the collective leadership of the Space Command has finally understood that they had been lied to in order to gain earlier cooperation in attacking and commandeering Citadel vessels. Now that the Space Command leadership understands these lies for what they are, they understand their duty under the Constitution and the law and have refused to be a party to committing an unwarranted act of war and war crimes."

"I want to emphasize that while Citadel did not engage in hostilities against the forces of the United States, it had every right to do so in view of the multiple acts of war that United States forces have committed against it." A bit of pride crept into his voice. "I also want to emphasize that Citadel's forces have already demonstrated that they are perfectly capable of defending themselves. President Harrington tried to manufacture an enemy out of Citadel. I can assure you that you don't want the real thing.

"On the way here from my address before the AN, President Harrington made the claim in a press conference that the transports that escorted me from Citadel are warships looking for an opportunity to attack you. With the indulgence of the technical staff here, I invite you to take a look at the screen before us." A large video screen was displayed, showing an image of the inside of one of the Citadel transports in orbit around Mars.

Every set of eyes in the room took in the pictures as Austin continued. "As you can see, this is an image of the interior of one of the transports that escorted me all the way to Mars. You can also see that there are no weapons of any kind aboard her. You can see further that Amelia Gordon, the president of Mars, who has inspected all four of our transports, has confirmed that the only things aboard the transports are trade goods to replace the ones that President Harrington's forces confiscated. Numerous news agencies have been invited aboard all four ships to confirm this situation."

In a sarcastic tone Austin continued, "*These* are the terrible weapons that President Harrington has been telling you justified trying to kill me as I entered this solar system."

There were gasps in the chamber as a new image appeared on the screen. Austin allowed a look of quiet outrage to show itself as he said, "To give you even more insight into the criminal actions of President Harrington, the officer in charge of her thugs that we captured managed to escape captivity and stow away aboard one of our transports for the trip back here. While it would be tempting to conclude that he was simply trying to return to Earth, his actions were much more sinister. As you can see from the video, he tried to change his physical appearance so he could hide in a crowd of people aboard one of our transports and stab me in the back."

A look of revulsion appeared on Austin's face as he said, "In this case, his actions were very much in keeping with his master's actions and instructions. Fortunately, one of our people was able to intercept him. President Harrington's thug had already murdered two of our transport crew members and threatened the lives of many others while keeping them within a climate of terror for three months.

An image of a man who looked very different from the long-haired would-be assassin appeared as Austin continued. "We have confirmed his identity. His name was Major Marcus Roetter. His commission was issued to him through the National Security Authority, reporting to Director Bering. These are the same people who fabricated the claims against Citadel. We have confirmation that Major Roetter had express orders to kill me. Bering is President Harrington's creature, and he has tried to create a measure of deniability for himself and his master, but the facts are clear. Attempted murder is bad enough, but this was the attempted murder of a head of state of a nonbelligerent nation. We can add this crime to the already long list of President Harrington's crimes."

Austin had to hold his hands up for a while before the outraged cacophony quieted down. "While it is clear that President Harrington wants war, Citadel and I want peace. However, there is a price for this peace. Too many lives have been lost or otherwise ruined because of the actions of a person who has placed her personal ambitions above her duties as your president. While I have a high regard for this body, I must remind you what everyone must know by now, which is that Congress has failed to do its duty when it could have prevented President Harrington from venturing down this path. Notwithstanding that failure, this Congress has a clear duty under the Constitution to deal with the actions of President Harrington and the other members of her administration who have conspired to inflict war on a system that not long ago had to deal with it on a horrible scale."

Austin's gaze was unforgiving. "Once those actions have taken their course, I must remind you that Citadel, in turn, expects to deal with these people in accordance with *our* laws. *Citadel* is the one that was attacked without justification, after all. No one is above the law, not even the president of the United States!"

CHAPTER FORTY THREE

After Austin's departure, the moods in Congress and the White House were somber, although for different reasons. Many members of Congress were in shock over the extent of Harrington's crimes. The White House knew its lies had finally been exposed to the public.

The mood throughout the country was overwhelmingly one of outrage over the actions of Harrington against a former president, especially one as popular as Austin. No one had forgotten that Austin had risked his life against long odds to help them when they needed the help desperately.

Two weeks later, Austin was still feeling somewhat stunned by the unprecedented events that had taken place following his denunciation of Harrington. He tried to collect some of his thoughts in a message back to Citadel.

"Who would have believed," he mused, "that Congress would do the right thing so promptly? Over Harrington's veto, Congress appointed a special prosecutor with broad powers to investigate and if appropriate prosecute members of her administration who had committed any crimes in connection with her phony war. Congress also disbanded Bering's security forces and transferred their operations to other agencies. I'm pleased to note that career federal authorities, men and women J.W. knows and respects, are cooperating with the special prosecutor to pursue the people who had been the tools of Bering and Harrington's witch hunt. General Choi's warning to Major Wolfe has proved prophetic."

"That wasn't the only thing Congress did, however," Austin continued. "The day after my appearance before Congress, the House began an investigation to determine whether articles of impeachment should be drawn up against Harrington and the rest of her ilk.

"It's remarkable just how quickly things went downhill for Harrington after people like General Buck testified before Congress about what they knew. In the face of certain impeachment, Walker, Chambers, Rainey, and Bering resigned immediately, as did others who were part of her schemes.

"Harrington's poll numbers dropped into the cellar." Austin continued in a wry tone. "J.W. couldn't resist reminding me that her opponent, Pete Lee, ended up winning the election by a landslide that was almost as large as some of mine from back in the day, although he hastened to add that *anyone* would have been able to defeat Harrington by that point." His tone was more serious as he continued, "I hope Lee meant it when he said that once he takes office, he'll support fully the mission of the special prosecutor. He also promised to clean house if any of Harrington's people are still in place once he is sworn in."

"The House approved articles of impeachment against both Harrington and Molder in record time," Austin said without much enthusiasm. "While they deserved what happened, I always worry about the damage to the institution of the Presidency in these situations. There wasn't any choice, though. While they should have done the right thing and resigned, people that know them well weren't surprised that they were going to fight to the bitter end. The offices were too important a part of their egos for them to be willing to let them go voluntarily. Thanks to those egos being placed ahead of the interests of the country, for the first time in history, the Senate conducted a joint trial of an impeachment.

"Molder was a piece of work." he chuckled incredulously. "She actually had the nerve to claim that she would preside over her own trial in the Senate. She based her claim on what some people called a quirk in the Constitution. Some quirk!" Austin said sarcastically. "The Constitution provides that while the vice president normally presides over an impeachment trial in the Senate, the chief justice presides over an impeachment trial involving the president. Molder tried to claim that since the trial of a vice president isn't a trial of a president, she could preside over her trial.

"She didn't get very far with it," Austin said wryly. "The Senate declared Molder to be out of order. The chief justice agreed that it would be improper for Molder to preside over her own trial, especially since the trial was a joint one and the chief justice was already presiding with respect to Harrington. It didn't take the courts long to tell Molder that they weren't getting into a political dispute.

"The trial and verdict didn't take long, which wasn't a surprise," Austin reported. "The evidence against Harrington was damning, and there was little difficulty in proving that Molder had been part of the conspiracy. Molder's story was almost a farce," he said. "I guess she hoped to somehow weather the storm by claiming that she hadn't really known about what was happening." He shook his head and chuckled. "While lots of people can confirm her general cluelessness about things, there were plenty who testified about her active support for Harrington's actions."

"And in the end, both of them were convicted and barred by the Senate from holding any federal office," Austin said. "We're in uncharted territory now. The Speaker of the House is the new president until the president-elect can be sworn in a couple of months from now. Although there is still plenty of stuff for the prosecutors to handle, at least for now the reign of terror is over."

CHAPTER FORTY FOUR

The Citadel transports had arrived, and Sara had finally been able to rejoin Joe. After returning to their cabin on *Pathfinder* for several hours, they met with Austin and Liz at his request. Austin greeted them warmly. "How does it feel to be together again?"

The looks on both the Albretti faces were all that he needed for an answer.

Austin said, "I can't begin to tell you how proud I am of you. All of Citadel owes you both a debt of gratitude for everything you've done in helping to fight *two* wars!" With an amused look, he continued, "I could ask you about your plans, but that wouldn't be fair, since the last time we talked about them it was clear you wanted to make a life on Citadel. I mentioned the rules, and we haven't had time to talk about them since."

The look changed from amused to highly pleased as he continued, "I took the liberty of having Sara's medical history checked out by our staff, and it is well within the guidelines we have for settlers. In fact, Sara's own history, plus the fact that all of her grandparents are either still alive or lived to be at least a hundred years, in good health for virtually all of their lives, makes her a terrific candidate."

Austin looked over at Liz, who beamed. "We haven't asked anyone to look further into your background, Sara, because we don't think it's necessary. What's necessary is to remember that debts need to be honored. We can feel especially comfortable in honoring this debt, because the courage and resourcefulness that you've demonstrated are the things that would make you an outstanding settler. If the two of you are still interested in taking up together on Citadel as settlers, you will be welcomed by everyone with open arms."

Austin and Liz found themselves nearly knocked over by a joyful hug from Sara, followed almost immediately by Joe. After they'd disentangled themselves, Sara said solemnly, "Thank you both. Your words mean so much to us." She chuckled before adding, "Please don't take this the wrong way, but I hope we don't have to go back right away. I want to meet Joe's family, and I want him to meet mine. I think my grandfather will like him a lot."

"I think so too," Austin replied with a grin. "Don't worry about feeling rushed to get back to Citadel. There are some things I need to do here as Citadel's head of state that can't be done remotely. As usual, J. W. will be a huge help. We're going to have to put together a new relationship with the United States, for one thing. Despite our different sizes, it will need to be a relationship of equals, especially where space is concerned."

A mischievous look appeared on his face as he added, "*KT-2* will probably head back after finally getting the refitting she should have gotten months ago. *Pathfinder* won't go back until I do. Did you want to go back on separate ships?"

A special glow appeared in Sara's face as she took a hold of Joe's hand. "I've given up three months of sharing my husband's bed already, Sam. We needed to do it because of the emergency, so we understand. However, we have some time to make up. If *KT-2* needs to head back, she can go without me. I'm right where I want to be."

"That's fine. By the way, while you're here, you're welcome to stay at our home in California. Sara, you've been there before with the rest of your crew, but Joe hasn't. You'd have lots of privacy and beautiful scenery to enjoy. There's even a secluded lake up in the mountains. While Liz and I might stop by at some point, I'm sure we'll be here in Washington for at least a couple of weeks, probably longer."

There was a mischievous gleam in Liz's eyes as she took Sara aside for a moment to say something in private. Sara's eyes widened as she listened. She smiled and leaned over to Joe to say something about another kind of scenery they could enjoy and giggled. Joe looked back at Sam and chuckled. "Sara has persuaded me that we should take you up on your generous offer, after we've met each other's families."

CHAPTER FORTY FIVE

Austin sat in the Oval Office with the new president and the president-elect. After pleasantries had been exchanged, the new president explained why she'd asked them to meet with her.

"I want to start by assuring you, Sam, that until Pete takes office in January, I will extend the full cooperation of this office and of the United States government to Citadel in pursuing anyone who had anything to do with Harrington's scheme. I will not stand in the way of any prosecutions that have been or will be initiated against anyone, including against Harrington herself. I won't allow any claims of executive privilege to be asserted in order to avoid justice. I will not issue any pardons to anyone who has been a participant in Harrington's scheme, either. As you pointed out, no one is above the law."

President-Elect Pete Lee said, "I echo Carrie's sentiments as well. While it isn't right for me to make 'presidential' pronouncements while someone else holds the office, I haven't heard or seen anything at this point that would lead me to take any other action.

"One of our challenges, Sam, is that we'd like to know how you'd like this matter handled. I'm not suggesting that you tell the United States how to pursue justice. I *am* suggesting that we will have a major challenge when Harrington goes on trial for her actions. It's never happened before and, God willing, will never happen again. If Harrington is convicted, what is the appropriate punishment?"

Austin replied, "I'm very sensitive to the special issues around the presidency. I understand all too well the importance of not damaging the office so that it can't be effective going forward. As you know from history, I had to face that issue just a few months into my original tenure as president when former President Olsen's misdeeds came to light. I was still reeling from stepping into office as president due to the assassination of my immediate predecessor, Chuck Thomson, bless him. I've always wished I could have asked him for some guidance. Anyway, for the good of the country and the office, Olsen was allowed to avoid prison but had to live with something that hurt him dearly, which was the damage to his reputation. One thing I had to deal with that you won't is a Congress that still had plenty of Olsen's partisans in place who wanted to make things tough for me.

"This is a fundamentally different situation," Austin continued. "Harrington sought to wage an aggressive war against Citadel, with no justification at all. She also tried to have me assassinated when she failed to get the results she wanted from waging her phony war." Austin's gaze grew colder as he said, "Unfortunately, while the vast majority of the officers within the US military understand their duties under the Constitution, she still managed to find some that didn't."

"As you may recall from history, the Nuremburg proceedings established that waging an aggressive war is a crime, as well as defined certain actions as crimes against humanity. While you had to learn about it from the history books, I recall it because I was alive at the time. We also addressed the issue after the Bio War, because some people hadn't learned the lesson properly the first time." Austin's tone became deadly serious. "What was the punishment for those crimes?"

The new president's eyes grew larger at the implications of Austin's question. She was hugely glad that she wouldn't be the one to have to deal with the answer to that question. Lee actually gulped as the full impact of Austin's statement sank in. "Sam," he practically gasped, "it's hard enough for us to get our arms around the notion of a president being impeached and convicted for her crimes, since it's never happened before. It's even harder to deal with the notion of a former president being tried for crimes she committed while president. It would be even tougher to understand that she might be executed for those crimes. As much as the people are frankly appalled by and ashamed of what was done to Citadel in the name of the United States, the execution of a former president could be something that the people might not be able to embrace."

"I can understand the ramifications very well," Austin replied, "but I can't overlook what was done in the name of the United States government. What's the difference between what the aliens inflicted on Citadel and what

Harrington inflicted on us? In one case we were attacked by a race that might not have been able to relate to us at all. That's not an excuse, but it may provide some understanding. In the other, we were attacked by someone who knew us through the ties of friendship and gratitude. Which one is worse?"

Austin shook his head. "To this day, some people still cling to the notion that once a person becomes the head of a country, that person is somehow *ennobled* and can't be executed for his capital crimes. The attitude is curious, since for over a hundred years, that notion has been settled by nations as nonsense."

Austin began what seemed like a dispassionate analysis. "I suggest that there are at least four approaches to consider. Before I list them, we'll put aside a bit of bullshit. Harrington and her ilk are guilty of war crimes and crimes against humanity, and there is little point in having a discussion based on the notion that she is innocent. While that is the legal standard that applies, quite properly, in a criminal trial, the evidence of her guilt is overwhelming, and she's already been impeached and convicted. Therefore, all of these possibilities will assume that she will be found guilty and be subject to a real sentence.

"The first approach is to prosecute Harrington for her crimes and let her be sentenced, and let the sentence be carried out. The second is to prosecute Harrington and let her be sentenced, and then stay the proceedings so that you can turn her over to Citadel for trial and punishment. The third is that you prosecute her and turn her over to Citadel after conviction but before sentencing.

The fourth is that you simply turn her over to Citadel for trial and punishment.

"Each approach has merit. All but the last one ensures that Harrington is duly convicted on Earth for her crimes, so that there is a clear record and no question legally of her guilt. All but the first one ensures that Citadel is the one that does the hard work, and in a way lets you off the hook. The last one enables the party that has the strongest claim in the first place, which is Citadel, to deal with her before anyone else, but this approach may never get her guilt fully into the minds of Americans. In time, some people might even try to minimize the nature and scope of her crimes if we follow that step."

Lee asked, "Speaking purely from the perspective of what might be easier for the country and for me to do my job, simply turning Harrington over to Citadel might be the best approach. I'm not saying that I favor that approach; I could also be wrong over whether it is the easiest."

"I can see your point," Austin replied, "although I'm not sure if everyone will fully appreciate the scope of her crimes that way. There might not be a strong enough lesson to be learned if Harrington simply disappears to Citadel without having been declared criminally wrong here for her actions. I think the best approach is to try her on Earth for her crimes and sentence her so she can't claim the mantle of the innocent victim, and then deport her to Citadel for trial and punishment under Citadel's laws."

A measure of anxiety crept into Lee's voice. "That may be so. However, forget what I said about *any* approach being easy if she fights the charges. We'll have a nightmare for years if she takes that route. Hell, she wouldn't even resign instead of being impeached and convicted."

"It might be over much sooner than you think," Austin said, "but that's still *your* problem. Perhaps the presidents that are to come to this office over the next hundred years will think a lot more carefully before acting as if they've been given the right to screw with other nations. I might have that conversation with some of them," Austin said in a lighter tone. "By the way, in addition to working out a schedule of reparations, we will expect *all* of the conspirators to end up on Citadel for punishment as well."

Lee's shoulders slumped. "I guess we brought this on ourselves, and the legal nightmare that's coming is part of the price that we'll have to pay."

Austin continued, "Another price that will need to be paid is a complete reset on the relationship between the United States and Citadel. We should be the closest of friends and the strongest partners possible. We are none of those things currently because of the ambitions of one woman. The new relationship needs to be one between equals, without any more condescension coming from this office. Frankly, we've been reminded again that the stakes are too high for us to be at odds with each other."

Lee's face brightened as he replied, "I couldn't agree more, Sam. I never bought into the crap that Harrington was peddling; the fact is that Citadel can teach us some things about space. I want you to know that I'm not too proud to acknowledge it or to ask for help. With Carrie's support, I'd like for us to spend some time between now and when I become president talking through a lot of these issues so that both Citadel and the United States won't be wondering if there was a point to what's happened.

"I also want you to know that there's something that I hope I can do, notwithstanding everything that Harrington has caused the United States to do to Citadel. You're still a national treasure to the US, Sam, and I hope to be fortunate enough to be able to call upon you for some of that advice and counsel that you've been famous for offering to my predecessors. I have no illusions about whether I have all the answers for this job, because I sure as hell don't."

Austin was once again the former president of the United States as he replied, "I would be happy to discuss anything with you at any time, Pete. As I told Congress, I'm still an American as well as part of Citadel, and I always will be. My thoughts are yours for the asking, anytime."

The president-elect said, "There's one more thing that I've been meaning to ask, Sam."

"What's that?" A look on Austin's face showed he had expected the question.

"What would have happened if Harrington's plan had worked and you'd been attacked as you entered this solar system?"

A grim smile played across Austin's face. "Sheep don't last very long on a frontier, Pete, and we're not sheep. While I'm not afraid of death, I didn't come here to die, at least not like that. I would have blasted the hell out of any ship that opened fire on us. Please keep in mind that as a former US president, I would never take lightly any decision to order military action against the United States. However, I can't afford to take any options off the table. While I won't explain how we'd have done it, believe it when I say we would have been able to defend ourselves if needed. *Nobody* messes with Citadel, folks, not in deep space and not from here!"

The president-elect chuckled. "It was on Mars, wasn't it? Before the cameras were rolling, you worked out a deal with Amelia Gordon to hide your weapons nearby. If you'd needed them, you could have gotten them back on board in no time, and we wouldn't have had any idea until it was too late. I'll bet you even had sufficient weapons for transport *KT-5* hidden somewhere. It might have been tricky for you if someone had opened fire, but having backup from five armed transports available in short order would have balanced the odds in your favor. No wonder you were never worried about coming here!"

Austin didn't say anything, but Lee accepted Austin's cryptic expression as the answer to his question.

CHAPTER FORTY SIX

It was a cold, misty day on Citadel. In two solar systems, the phony war was already becoming known as Harrington's War. People weren't quite sure what to call the real one with the aliens, or to say if it was even over yet. With one major exception, all of the proceedings involving the war criminals had been completed, and they had been brought to Citadel. The final step had finished playing out, against the backdrop of multiple gallows that had been erected in the Square.

Among the families that were there to observe the proceedings were Joe and Sara Albretti. Sara was pregnant with their first child. They knew it would be a baby girl, whom they already planned on naming Gina in honor of the sacrifice made by Joe's late sister-in-law. Liz stood next to Austin.

Austin thought back on a private conversation he'd had with Harrington after her impeachment.

The disgraced former president waited for Austin to speak, but he was silent. Finally, she said, "Don't you want to gloat, Sam?"

With a melancholy face, Austin replied, "No, Courtney, I'd rather cry. I've spent many years being responsible for the welfare of people, on Citadel and on Earth; this is one of the saddest days for me. I wish to God that you'd backed off when it might have still made a difference as far as your punishment was concerned, as well as for the lives that were lost."

Harrington's face flushed slightly from her still-tender ego as she answered, "If things had worked out differently, *I* might have been the one deciding *your* punishment."

"I guess that's why we're here today," Austin replied with a shake of his head. "You still haven't grasped the notion that it isn't for you to decide the fates of others simply because you were elected president. I never did anything that warranted 'punishment,' yet that's still how you want to see things. So long as I insisted on fulfilling my role as the president of Citadel, instead of accepting some subservient role to you and your judgment, in your mind I had committed some type of crime for which punishment was appropriate. Never mind that to do it meant that you had to order the deaths of innocent people and violate both US and international law."

Harrington tried to brush away the comment. "Of all people, Sam, you should have understood the special role the US president plays domestically and internationally. You played the role for over forty years, and people deferred to you in a way that should have happened for me."

"I *earned* that deference, Courtney, if that's what you want to call it," Austin said with some heat. "In fact, it was more along the lines of *respect*, and it happened over the course of years of good decisions. One of the toughest things about my time as president was the constant need to make sure that I wasn't doing things on the basis of my ego as opposed to what was in the best interests of the people. If you ever bothered to check your ego, it didn't last for long. It's such a pity, since you had a great resource at your disposal."

"I suppose you're going to talk about *you* again." Harrington sniffed.

"I'm talking about my advice on how to make you successful, Courtney. It was there with no strings, but you never brought yourself to use it even once."

Harrington's face became defiant as she said, "Is this where you decide to pardon me if I show the right contrition, at least to spare me the death penalty? We're nowhere near that point, and probably never will be. Now that I've been impeached, I don't think any court on Earth will convict me of anything. Everyone will assume that nothing more is needed. Even if by some miracle I were convicted of something, I'll never face any significant punishment. I'll always be a US president."

"You're assuming that you won't have to face justice on Citadel," he reminded her.

"Am I? I guess that's true," she replied with a contemplative expression. "However, even if I were to end up on Citadel, you won't execute me. I think you have the same horror of executing a duly elected US president that most people have. You're worried about the long-term damage it would inflict on future presidents and the damage to their relationship with Citadel. There will always be some people that will hate Citadel for executing a US president, regardless of the circumstances. I think you're hoping to get me to say you were right and then you'll issue a pardon that will show that you're the enlightened leader."

Austin shook his head slowly. "Imagine what people would have said if you'd managed to kill *me*, especially by means that were clearly murder. At this point, we're *both* former US presidents. If you think you'd have been able to survive outright murder, on top of everything else you've done, then you're even more delusional than I thought."

The sadness in Austin's voice increased as he continued. "Besides, as much as I worry about the damage that you mentioned, I would worry even more about the damage from *not* taking that step against you. Citadel would suffer a terrible wound from which it might not recover, if people thought we wouldn't defend ourselves when attacked by our enemies. Bringing you to Citadel for the punishment you deserve will bring closure to the people there, and remind people elsewhere never to make the mistake of thinking they can make an enemy of Citadel without consequences."

Austin's look became more severe. "It might also persuade future presidents and future Congresses about the importance of insisting that presidents select a higher caliber of people for a presidential administration. While you might whine that the real failure was in your toadies not pushing back and keeping you honest, *you* were the one who selected them!"

Harrington flinched and turned deathly pale as she practically hissed, "Damn you, Sam Austin! The people will rise up against you."

"*What* people, Courtney? The ones you fed lies in a bid to be reelected? The people on Earth and Citadel who are dead because of you?" Austin had no more questions left as he walked out of the room.

"After watching these people, I couldn't help thinking about when Brittel was executed," Joe said. "While the circumstances were different, he would have fit right in with this crowd."

"These executions on Citadel were the first ones I've ever seen," Sara noted with unease.

"They weren't easy to watch, were they, Sara?" Liz asked with sympathy.

"No," she said, shaking her head, "but they *were* necessary. You'll have to fill me in on what happened prior to the actual executions, since I didn't want to listen to them try to justify their actions. I didn't want to hear their apologies, either, if they made any. The only part I wanted to watch was the executions themselves, for the closure."

Austin nodded. "I understand. These occasions are, thank God, rare and solemn events, where we're reminded that actions have consequences and sometimes the ultimate price has to be paid for certain actions. They also enable the families of the victims to have the closure you mentioned."

"Many of these people were at one time confident in their authority to order the destruction of people's lives," Liz observed. "It was almost pathetic to see how some of them chose to meet their end. Each was given a chance to say any last words. Some of them declined.

"Bering, who had always been willing to exploit the ambitions and weaknesses of others and make them pay for his actions, looked around in terror over his fate, as if not understanding why there wasn't someone there to pay his price for him."

"What a change for a man who was willing to give an order to have me murdered," Austin said with grim humor.

"At least he kept his mouth shut," Liz countered. "Molder was hip deep in everything, yet babbled that her only crime was that she wanted to be president herself someday and that she hadn't really understood what the others had been doing. Chambers stammered his way through a defense that was even more pathetic now than it had been the first time he'd tried it back on Earth."

"Did any of them actually accept responsibility for what they'd done?" Sara asked.

"Characteristically, none of them said anything about accepting responsibility for their crimes," Liz replied with disgust. "Walker came the closest to acknowledging his responsibility, but with his eyes rather than any words. His eyes gave away the fact that he knew that he had had a special responsibility as the attorney general to follow the law, and he'd failed to insist that others do likewise."

She shook her head. "He couldn't face any of the families whose loved ones had died as a result of the crimes that he and the others had committed. For a brief moment, his gaze locked on Bering, showing nothing but contempt for the man. The last thing his face seemed to show was contempt for himself."

"In some ways, it was hard to believe it was an execution—things seemed so ordinary," Joe said. "Within less than a minute, it was over for everyone." He looked at Austin. "What will happen to their remains?"

Austin glanced toward the sky. "Their remains will be cremated, with their ashes disbursed in deep space to avoid giving any enemy of Citadel a burial spot that needs to be respected and tended."

As they watched the gallows being disassembled and the components removed, Joe commented, "You'd almost believe there hadn't been any executions at all."

Sara disagreed. "There are plenty of families to serve as guardians of those memories for many years to come." She cradled her belly. "I'm so glad that little Gina will be able to start her life without having to worry about the monsters who thought they could get away with making up a war, like it was just another political ploy. I'm glad for the closure we have."

Joe said, "I'm almost sorry that Roetter didn't survive his wounds, so that he could have been up there when his people had to pay for their actions." Joe had a wry look on his face as he said to Austin, "Don't get me wrong, Sam, I'm damned glad I gutted that asshole when I had the chance."

Austin nodded in understanding. "It's OK, Joe, I get it. After we decided that some, but not all, of Roetter's soldiers should be executed, I'm glad Pete Lee agreed to take back the soldiers who we decided not to execute, and imprison them on Earth under terms we dictated. I hope it'll be a while before we have to worry about setting up a prison that is more than just a temporary holding area."

Sara turned to Austin and asked, "Where do you think we stand as far as Earth is concerned?"

Austin replied, "For starters, Pete's apologized numerous times on behalf of the United States. He's expressed remorse over the fact that others were willing to go along with Harrington's actions instead of doing what they should have been doing. I was glad to see that his attorney general went after the old guard with a vengeance to root out and punish anyone who was a part of Harrington's crimes. Likewise, the careers and reputations of people like General Buck have been restored. In fact, Buck is in line to head the Space Command when the slot opens up soon.

"Pete's agreed in principle to a reasonable schedule of reparations for the damage caused by the US, although that schedule hasn't yet been worked out. I've demanded that he order all US agencies to turn over to us all of the intelligence they developed relating to Citadel during Harrington's administration, with the requirement that no copies be retained for any reason. I've also demanded that all of their operatives of any kind in Harrington's War be identified and turned over to us while we determine whether their activities warrant further action on our part. That's a tough one for Pete, and he hasn't yet agreed to it."

Austin shrugged as he continued. "I'll give him a little more time to come around before I push the issue.

The last thing he wants is for Congress to make the decision for him, or for the people to do it directly through the states. I don't think it would be difficult to persuade the American people that the intelligence has blood on it and shouldn't be kept."

"As we've seen today, although it was a hard decision to make politically, Pete agreed to send the worst offenders to Citadel for punishment, even though it meant that former senior officials of the US government would face execution for the first time. Probably just as important is the fact that he recognizes that for many on Citadel or within the Citadel Group, it won't just be business as usual, at least not for some time. He knows he'll have to continue to take steps to demonstrate that the US can be trusted again."

Austin's expression darkened as he continued. "The problem is that he didn't make the political decision that he should have made, which would have done the most to help reset the relationship between the US and Citadel. The person central to the entire mess wasn't present on those gallows today. He refused to send Harrington here for justice and punishment, even though he knew that I expected him to do it."

"What happened?" Sara asked.

"He showed that he isn't yet tough enough for the job, Sara," Austin replied.

"I don't understand, Sam. Hasn't Harrington been found guilty of war crimes and crimes against humanity?"

"Yes," he agreed, "she's been found guilty, but she's been in some kind of legal limbo while they sort out some issues. One thing Pete got right was predicting that Harrington would try to drag out things as long as possible instead of accepting her culpability. The problem is that Pete hasn't shown enough leadership to cut through the bullshit and do what should be done. For now, Harrington seems to be under some kind of house arrest, instead of prison where she belongs."

"Does that mean they'll send her over here once those issues have been resolved?"

Austin sighed. "I'd like to think so, but I have a feeling they'd rather she stay in that limbo so they don't have to deal with what would happen to her if they sent her over here. She once made a prediction to me along those lines. I hope to God it turns out she was wrong."

"Doesn't that make them hypocrites?" Joe asked, his own face darkening. "The US has long been a voice for the notion that no one is above the law, even political leaders. This is especially true when it comes to war crimes. If they won't turn Harrington over to us, don't they really mean that every political leader *except* the US president will be held accountable?"

"That's the way it looks right now." Austin nodded. "I've had some blunt conversations with Pete about it. I've let him know that while reparations, an apology, and complete documentation of everything that the US did to Citadel and its people are the proper steps to take, it is just as important that there be full punishment for all of the guilty parties, including Harrington.

"He knows that until she's been turned over to us, there will be no resumption of any commercial relationships with the US. While diplomatic relations will remain in place, other cooperative arrangements will be placed on hold as well. While it's often the case that economic sanctions end up hurting the country imposing the sanctions at least as much as the country on the receiving end, that won't be the case here; we already have more commerce than we can handle. They can also forget about any cooperative work on the security of our solar systems for now; they need it more than we do, and I'm not about to reward Harrington's behavior."

Austin's face showed some distaste as he continued. "I've also made it clear that Citadel will not recognize the right of Space Command ships to issue orders to any vessels that are within open space. In addition, no other ships will be allowed to board our ships for any reason."

"That one will be messy," Sara said. "Aren't there some treaties on the subject?"

Austin gave a humorless chuckle. "Yes, but Citadel isn't a party to those treaties. If other nations want to agree that their ships can be ordered around in space, they can do so, but they don't control space itself. Someone who isn't a party to those treaties has every right to move about in space and tell the Space Command to stuff it. If some nations want to give up some of their sovereignty to an entity that just demonstrated how it can be abused, then they're welcome to do so. We'll pass on it.

"Pete's still fairly new in the office," Austin mused out loud, "and I hope he can grow enough as a leader to do what needs to be done, even if it is something difficult."

Joe said, "I hope everything gets sorted out soon, but for now, I'm just glad that, finally, the war is over."

"Harrington's War may be over," Sara replied, "but I'm not sure about the other one."

"Neither am I," Austin said. "I just hope that Gina doesn't have to worry about that one, either."

CHECKMATE CITADEL

The story continues in the next novel by Robert Adrian, *Checkmate Citadel*. Although Harrington's War, the phony war launched against Citadel by US President Courtney Harrington, is over, a new dispute is brewing over the failure by the United States to turn Harrington over to Citadel for justice following her impeachment and conviction for war crimes.

While Harrington remains on Earth in a legal limbo, her money buys people who work on a way to contact the aliens who waged a real war against humanity. If they succeed, she assumes that the aliens want the ancient derelict ship that wandered into the Citadel system. She also assumes that they will want revenge against Austin for fighting back against the aliens' attempts to exterminate them. She believes this will give her the leverage to make whatever deals she wants.

Harrington's desire for vengeance against Austin and Citadel leads her to play with fire. She doesn't care that the war she is willing to risk in order to destroy Austin and Citadel could end up engulfing everyone in two star systems.

Robert Adrian is the pen name of an attorney with more than two decades of experience working primarily with Silicon Valley technology companies. He grew up reading Robert Heinlein, Isaac Asimov, Ray Bradbury, Andre Norton, and other giants of the science fiction genre. Now, as the author of the Sam Austin Chronicles, he blends his passion for science fiction with other interests, such as historical and futuristic writing. Book two of the series, *Target Citadel,* is the sequel to *Destination Citadel.* Adrian enjoys completing projects in his workshop and participating in local music events, which is how he met his wife. They live in the San Francisco Bay Area with their three children.